JEFF NANIA

FIGURE EIGHT

A NORTHERN LAKES MYSTERY

LITTLE CREEK PRESS
AND BOOK DESIGN

Mineral Point, Wisconsin USA

Little Creek Press®
A Division of Kristin Mitchell Design, Inc.
5341 Sunny Ridge Road
Mineral Point, Wisconsin 53565

Copyright © 2018 Jeff Nania and Feet Wet, LLC

Book Design and Project Coordination: Little Creek Press

Cover Design: Chris Nania

First Published in 2019 by Little Creek Press
Printed in the United States of America

For more information or to contact the author visit www.feetwetwriting.com.
To order books from the publisher, visit www.littlecreekpress.com.

Library of Congress Control Number: 2018964361

ISBN-10: 1-942586-55-8
ISBN-13: 978-1-942586-55-5

This is dedicated to my family and friends
near and far, here and gone; you have made me
rich in every way that really matters.

John and Jay, I hope you enjoy the story.
If need be, I will read it to you
when I get there.

ACKNOWLEDGMENTS

This book could not have been completed without valuable contributions from many people in my life. My appreciation goes out to many who, in the interest of brevity, are not listed here.

There are a few individuals, though, who spent countless hours in the trenches with me.

First, I would like to thank three beautiful Nania women: Victoria, Rebecca, and Christina for their editorial help and relentless encouragement, and my sons, Christopher, who lent his considerable skill to creating the cover art, and Jimmy, who provided honest critique of the story. Thanks to Dr. Michael Chalifoux whose medical knowledge was invaluable in making John Cabrelli's treatment as accurate as possible; any mistakes made are mine, not his. And thanks to Jay John Nania for continually stealing the number two key while I was trying to complete this project; you are the light of our lives.

A special thanks to my early readers, the Huffaker Five, Tanya and the Bear, Mrs. Doc O'Malley, Marilyn, Dr. Jim L., Charlie, Peter E., Miller Law Office, and the whole Nania clan. I am thrilled that you enjoyed the story.

Finally, I would like to thank the professionals who provided their expertise to make this a better book. Kelly Dwyer, your unbiased, editorial assistance was much needed and greatly appreciated. I am indebted to the entire team at Little Creek Press for providing coordination and design, professional proofreading, and guiding me through the entire publication process to make this book a reality. ■

CHAPTER 1
Hospital

A faint, polite knock on John's door let him know someone was visiting. The nurses, doctors, and the maintenance guy never knocked; they just walked in. Most of the time he didn't care. They were pumping enough pain medication into him to seriously impact his ability to be concerned with his dignity, or reality for that matter. It also made it impossible to pee, which resulted in yet another personal assault.

Only visitors knocked. He didn't get many visitors. Doctor's orders, enforced by Nurse B. Holterman, a very tough old girl with the bedside manner of a night shift jailer. She was probably over a hundred and had clearly made her bones in a tent hospital in World War II cutting off limbs. People had tried to get in to see him several times, but she scared them off, never to return. They were feeling bad for old John, but not bad enough to run the B. Holterman gauntlet.

Today John was getting a visitor, and Nurse B. Holterman had attempted to intercede but finally relented. Probably based on everyone's unspoken assumption, John was on his way out, and even if he did survive, his probable future looked like something between bad and plain dismal.

The knocker now had a face and a voice. A young guy pushing 35 or so, good shape, healthy looking with tanned skin and probably wearing his best pair of jeans. He was carrying a notebook with a pen shoved into the spiral binding, tools of his trade, and didn't look like the kind of hard nose reporter from the crime beat John had come to know.

"John Cabrelli? My name is Bill Presser. I'm a reporter from the *Namekagon County News*, in Musky Falls, Wisconsin. My editor sent me to talk to you. Ah ... he said you requested me."

Cabrelli looked up from his hospital bed. He looked drawn and tired. Pain had taken its toll on the usual smiling face. His black, curly hair had begun to show threads of silver and was plastered to his forehead from the sweats. Tubes and wires were attached everywhere, and a monitor beeped quietly in the background. John Cabrelli truly looked like a man on his last legs, with one exception. If you looked close, you could still see his eyes were steeled in grim determination.

John answered, his strong voice shaky, but clear.

"Hey, thanks for coming. I know you're a busy guy. I'm glad you could make it. I think you'll find it worth your time. If not, oh well, it looks to me like you got a hell of a lot more time left than I do."

Presser was clearly uncomfortable. Even for the most detached, looking at someone who is struggling between life and death is tough. Where do you look? Their eyes? The tubes? The wires? The bandage? Presser picked the ceiling and the window. If John chose to die at that moment, it was clear Presser did not want to see it happen.

"Mr. Presser, it is my hope that we are going to spend a fair amount of time together. Time, again, is the operative word; I may not have much. You need to make eye contact, get over my current physical appearance, and listen to my words. Ask whatever you need to ask so we can get on with this. Try and make yourself as comfortable as you can."

Presser looked at John. "I understand. I'm sorry. Actually, you look pretty good for all you've been through."

"That's okay, Bill, I know I look like hell. Wounds like this tend to put you a little off your game."

"Can I ask what the extent of your injuries are?"

"Sure. I have one bullet still lodged near my spine. I took another one in the kidney, and that is the reason for all the machinery you see plugged into me. They removed one kidney and are hoping the other one will take up the slack. From the sounds of it, I was pretty torn up inside, and the surgeons had their hands full. Mainly though I just feel like shit; getting shot kind of does that to you. But I want you to know that I haven't had my usual doses of pain drugs today, so I can make some sense."

Sometimes identifying the elephant in the room is the best way to get something rolling. The straightforward answers from Cabrelli in an odd way made Presser feel more comfortable.

"Well, my big question is why would you request me? I'm just a jack-of-all-trades reporter for a small-town newspaper. You're a pretty famous guy now, a hero. There are a lot of folks that would kill for this exclusive. Why me?"

"First of all, I'm a little sick and tired of the whole 'let's try and kill John thing.' Secondly, you're honest, you're from Musky Falls, you write pretty well, and this story for you is a big deal. I need somebody to hear my story who thinks it's a big deal. Make no mistake though, I am no hero, and never refer to me that way. I have met real heroes, and I don't hold a candle to them."

"Sorry, I didn't mean to offend you. I appreciate you letting me know what's off limits. I will try to respect that. I need to say up front that we have no budget to pay you for this story. If your story is anything like it appears, I am sure one of the tabloids would compensate you very well."

"Yeah, Laura the Lawyer has had a few calls. Being a lawyer with a sharp eye for the bottom line, she's been pushing me to take the money. Right now money is not much of a concern to me. Don't think for a second this story is free, not a chance. You just aren't paying me with money. Here's my deal: I want you to hear the whole story start to finish. How I ended up here comes at the end. There is a lot in between. I need you to hear the in-between."

"You mean your life story, a biography?"

"No, just the last couple of years."

"Do you want me to write a newspaper story or a book? I'm not an author in the book sense. I can recommend a couple of guys from the cities that ..." John cut him off.

"Look, I am lying here full of bullets and not full of hydromorphone. According to this doctor who looks like he doesn't shave yet, the clock is ticking. I am sure he will be here to harass me as soon as his mother gives him a ride to work. If we are going to start, let's start. Otherwise, on your way out, tell the nurse to bring me drugs."

"I-I, I just don't know. I'd like to think this through. I just need some time."

"Again, let me restate the obvious; time is what you've got plenty of, not me. We start, or you go. I am not trying to be difficult, but like I said, getting shot makes me very cranky."

"John, to be honest with you I am not sure that I can do you and your story justice. I write about the winners of the Lion's Club fishing contest and the Musky Queen pageant for a small newspaper. There are going to be a lot of people reading this story, people from all over the country probably. I have never done anything like this before."

"Well, Bill, if you stick with that chickenshit attitude, it's likely you never will. Here is your chance, take it or leave it. Your choice, you make it. It's a hell of a story you'd be missing."

Bill Presser sat deep in thought, and Cabrelli didn't press him. He just waited. It was up to Bill now.

Presser finally found his voice, "My grandmother was a card player. When we were kids she used to tell us, 'Know when to hold, know when to be bold. If you're never bold, you'll always be playing someone else's cards for them.' I am guessing she was referring to situations just like this. I am honored that you want me to write your story John. I will give it my very best."

John was obviously relieved, "Thanks, Bill, I'm glad. I will try to make it as easy on you as I can."

"Can I record our conversations?"

"Please do. Let's get it right."

"My usual format is to ask questions and record the responses, using the information in the responses for more questions. Will that work for you, John?"

"No. Here is the format. I am going to tell you a true, but very hard to believe story. You can ask questions. I'll do the best I can to answer them. You are going to want to be able to corroborate my story. I will give you sources. I also have documents. They are hidden. When we are done, they are yours. My goal is simple: tell my story, expose the bad guys, and get justice for my uncle Nick."

"Fair enough. I guess we better get started."

"Thank God, *tempest* is *fugiting*."

John Cabrelli began, changing Bill Presser's life forever. ∎

CHAPTER 2
Cabrelli

"I've always been a pretty happy person. I'm lucky; I was born believing that life was the journey, not the destination. When I was a kid, I was plenty wild, but I never victimized anyone. I just raised a lot of hell: drinking, fighting, driving fast. Normal youthful behaviors in my neighborhood. Somewhere along the line I decided that I was going to become a policeman. Once I decided, I never really looked back. During my junior year in college, I was recruited. I finished school through the Law Enforcement Educational Assistance Program, better known as 'nobody wants dumb cops program,' and began my career as a full-fledged crime fighter for the Madison Police Department.

"I can remember the first day on the job. I had this overwhelming feeling that this was right; I was where I belonged. The whole thing was so exciting. But, not the shoot 'em up, badge heavy tough guy way…. I just felt like I belonged, maybe for the first time in my life.

"Some people, when they enter law enforcement, go through major life changes; some just can't do it. They're good people, but they can't make the adjustments necessary to survive working night and day in a very busy jurisdiction, most always seeing people at their worst, barging into their families, changing their lives, sometimes forever. I didn't have much of an adjustment period. I just wanted to get to work. Night shift patrol in a high-crime area was fine with me. I couldn't sleep very well mixing my days and nights up like that, but I never had a shift that dragged, and there was always plenty to do, things going on. First chance I got, I took the 3:00 p.m. to 11:00 p.m. shift. It was the busiest shift, but at least I lived my life in some semblance of normality.

"There I stayed 'til the end. I was decorated a couple of times and reprimanded a couple more. I liked the people in my beat. They didn't expect much. Most of them just wanted to be treated with a little respect and didn't like the dirtbags that bothered their lives any more than I did. I had some rules: don't bother kids, animals, or old folks. If you decide that you are going to victimize someone else, be aware that I will do all I can to victimize you. As years went by, people accepted my rules, and we got along just fine."

Bill Presser was now in full reporter mode, perched on the edge of his chair, recorder going, and taking notes in a spiral bound notebook. "What did you get reprimanded for?"

"Mostly kind of humorous stuff ... at least I thought it was funny."

"Like?"

"Like one night these gang bangers started shooting at each other in a residential neighborhood. Bullets were flying everywhere, going through walls, taking out a picture window, hitting parked cars. Well, in all the shooting, the little punks never even hit each other. The safest place to be was where they were aiming. So, we rounded them all up and took them into jail. I had an ad for private firearms training in my squad box. When I got to the jail, I made copies of the ad and handed it out to the gang bangers. I told them to do the community a favor and learn to shoot better. I said it would make the neighborhood safer and reduce crime by potential reduction in perpetrator numbers. A southside social worker complained to my boss."

"Funny, but I can see why some may have found it to be inappropriate."

"Yeah, well, whatever. I guess you had to be there.

"Anyway, I liked my job. I enjoyed the people I worked with and the challenges of not knowing what you would see day in and day out. Things were going along pretty good. In my beat, people were not blessed with an abundance of recreational opportunities, as a result, some folks when they got a little pocket money, their first stop was the liquor store. Then they would go home and start drinking. The result was family fight calls, officially referred to as 'domestic disturbances.' Sometimes we would respond to eight or nine in an eight-hour shift. Some were really bad. People beating the hell out of each other, people getting shot, stabbed, and everything else.

"One time there was this guy named Fritz. On a Friday night after work, he sat down to have a few beers with his crazy wife. The drinking led to a little preliminary bickering. Fritz, a diesel mechanic, got up and walked away, went in the bathroom to take a bath. So, he's peacefully sitting in the tub drinking a beer listening to this old radio. His wife walks in, says, 'Fritz, I'm leaving you.' Then she grabs the radio still plugged into the wall and drops it into the bathtub. Fritz survived, but both he and I found this display of aggression shocking."

"You have a very strange sense of humor, John. Is that what cops do, find humor in the tragedy of others?"

"Pretty much. It's the only way to survive. The more refined would call it a coping behavior. Look, I'm starting to feel pretty bad here, so how about I talk and you write down questions on your notepad, and we can come back to them later?"

"Fair enough."

• • •

Family fights are part of the job no one likes. It's usually the same people over and over again, and these disputes are dangerous for cops. Some people say they are the most dangerous. Emotions run high. Mix in drugs or alcohol and you can see how easily things can get out of hand. The best plan for a cop is to defuse the situation. Calm everybody down and then either take someone to jail or get them to leave. Whatever it takes. The story really starts with a call that came in as a domestic dispute.

It was about four o'clock in the afternoon, August 2. Hot as hell with the humidity near 90 percent. I was on a traffic stop when I heard, "579 can you break for a 1033 call?"

Ten-thirty-three is an emergency. I responded immediately.

Dispatch said, "579 we have a report of a disturbance, a possible family dispute, at Gonzalez Market, 215 Depot St. Subject is armed with a handgun and threatening." I was less than two blocks away.

I told the traffic offender it was his lucky day, let him go, and took off for the market. I knew this family and often stopped in the store for a bottle of pop and the like. They seemed like a good family, and I couldn't recall ever being called to the market for anything other than shoplifters and an armed robbery attempt about six months ago. I did recall that the armed robbery was only an attempt because Mr. Gonzalez had a Government Model Colt .45 he kept loaded under the counter, and the armed robber tried to scare him with a knife. Another rule broken; never take a knife to a gunfight. The perp took one look at the .45 and took off. I also remembered that Gonzalez was a military veteran and had the look of a guy that could handle himself pretty well.

Two minutes passed and I notified dispatch I was on the scene. I stopped a couple of doors down from the market and started to approach the store. I could hear yelling and screaming coming from the open front door. I heard a male shout, "I am going to kill you, you no good piece of shit." I got on my portable radio and called for backup. The dispatcher, ten miles away securely protected in the concrete and glass of the HQ tower, acknowledged and starting sending the troops.

I drew my gun, a Sig Sauer P226, nine millimeter. I kept my gun down along my right side as I approached the front door of the market. I couldn't see anything through the windows. They were covered with advertising, and on the inside shelves stacked with products were up against them. The fight was still raging inside but no shots, at least not yet. There was a small area next to the front door that I could use for concealment while I surveyed the situation. What

I saw was not good. Gonzalez had the gun pointed at a male in his early twenties—Damien Callahan, a bad actor I had seen around the neighborhood—a real punk with jailhouse tattoos up and down both arms bringing trouble wherever he went. The old man was in a rage and yelling at the guy in half Spanish, half English. The punk was giving as good as he was getting, and I got the gist of things. Gonzalez's daughter was pregnant, and this piece of shit was the father.

I knew his daughter was a good kid about fifteen or sixteen. She worked at the store and was always polite. Sometimes we talked about her plans once she graduated high school. She wanted to be a nurse or a teacher. I also knew that she was the only child and the pride of the hardworking Gonzalez family. I entered the store.

I called out, "Mr. Gonzalez, it's me, John Cabrelli. You need to slow down a little bit. I'm here. I can take care of this guy for you, but you have got to put down the gun. If you don't put down the gun, someone is going to get hurt here. Maybe him, maybe me, maybe you. Put the gun on the floor behind the counter and walk around the end over here to me."

I could hear the cars coming in the background, sirens yelping. Cops are a strange bunch, willingly driving a hundred miles an hour toward trouble. My radio was constant; chatter crackled as every patrol car anywhere close said they were responding, including the shift sergeant and precinct commander. It is amazing how a cop can be up to his ass in alligators and still hear the radio traffic.

I walked in a few feet further, and I could see that Mr. Gonzalez's eyes were wet with tears.

I could also see that he did not have the hammer cocked on his old Colt; the hammer has to be cocked for the first shot. From his military service Gonzalez surely knew this. Things were looking better.

The punk had a sneering smile on his pockmarked face. He looked high. "Mr. Gonzalez, please put the gun down. This is not so bad yet, but if you pull that trigger, things are going to get a lot worse. You've got a wife and daughter, and they need you. You've got a store here, and you have a life. Don't let this guy take that away from you. Just put the gun on the floor and walk away from it."

Gonzalez looked at me, gun still pointed at the punk. Pure sorrow in his eyes, the kind only a parent can feel when their child is in pain.

He said, "This vermin raped my daughter. She is going to have a baby. He is the father. He gave her a ride home from school and he raped her. He took my little girl. He took away her life. He came here to tell me to give him money, and if I did he would never bother us again. He has killed my daughter in her heart."

At that point the punk laughed. Some crazy kind of mean laugh. My brethren and sistren had arrived and stood outside the door, guns drawn. It seemed like the temperature in the room was 150 degrees. Mr. Gonzalez was trembling. He looked over at me and then started to put the gun down on the counter.

"On the floor, Mr. Gonzalez, not on the counter. On the floor." He put the gun down on the floor and sat down on his stool behind his counter and began to weep.

Callahan laughed again. I took my Sig and hit him as hard as I could in his smart-ass mouth, knocking him to the floor with blood running down his chin.

Backup burst in and cuffed the punk. They went for Mr. Gonzalez, but I stopped them. Rules are rules, but this guy was going to walk out the door and get in a squad with what was left of his dignity. They dragged out the punk, and Gonzalez and I walked out to the sidewalk. I put him in the back of my car, not knowing I had just made the biggest mistake of my life to date.

The now-handcuffed gang banger was standing on the sidewalk, putting on a show for the growing crowd. "You got no reason to arrest me, man. I didn't rape nobody. She was doing it with everybody. I ain't even the father! I was just trying to borrow some money. I want a blood test. You need to lock old man Gonzalez up and send him away for trying to kill me. I'm the victim, man. I got hit in my mouth. I want to make charges against that cop. Police brutality, man. It ain't right. He hit me for no reason."

Just then a woman screamed, and I looked up. I had momentarily forgotten about the gun, which I had left on the floor. Fifteen-year-old Angelina Gonzalez stood in the doorway of the store with her father's Colt. This time the hammer was back. She fired once; I drew and fired twice.

I think the technical term for it is akinetopsia, when time slows to a crawl during a crisis situation. That's what happened to me; the echo from the gunfire seemed to go on forever. I saw the ejected shell casings from my gun skip across the sidewalk. I could hear voices but couldn't make out words. My vision was clear, but everything seemed to be a blur. I saw Angelina rock back on her heels and fall against the doorframe of the store. Her big brown eyes just looked at me, and it looked like she was smiling. There were two crimson blossoms growing where my bullets had struck her chest.

I turned around to see Damien Callahan lying on the ground, holding his upper arm. Mr. Gonzalez had his face pressed against the glass of the squad car window, contorted as he screamed.

My fellow officers, guns drawn, were looking for another shooter. Others were staring at me.

I walked toward little Angelina Gonzalez with my gun drawn, training taking over. I needed to make certain that the threat had been neutralized. I saw her pretty face and realized what I had done. I decocked my Sig Sauer and secured it in my holster, and reentered the real world. All hell was breaking loose around me.

Julie Jones from the Northeast Precinct was screaming into her radio, "Shots fired, shots fired! We need an ambulance."

Dispatch was responding, clearing the air for all but emergency traffic and acknowledging that the paramedics were en-route.

People were rushing to the aid of the punk and to the aid of little Angelina Gonzalez.

Callahan was screaming in pain. Angelina said nothing.

I don't know how much time passed, but it seemed only seconds before the area got very crowded.

Ambulances and the shift commander arrived at the same time. The fire department paramedics were immediately busy with the punk and Angelina.

The shift commander was busy with me, "What the hell happened here, John? Jesus Christ. Did you shoot that girl or the guy? Who is the guy in custody in your squad?"

I started to respond, and then I stopped just to take a breath. Just when I was ready to start again, the shift commander told me to stand by. He walked over to talk to the precinct sergeant. During their discussion, the commander kept looking at me, then looking down. He came back, and told me not to say anymore until we got to headquarters. Then he called for a crime scene unit and directed other officers to secure my car, take my prisoner to headquarters, and wait for detectives to get a statement.

"Get in my car, John. We're going to head into HQ for your statement." Standard procedure in any police shooting.

We pulled into the parking area in the basement of the joint city-county building. As usual, it was all hustle and bustle: cops checking in, cops checking out, a couple of deputies leaning against a car trunk talking to a city cop. We pulled in and it all stopped. In a police department, general bad news travels fast. A possible bad shoot travels at warp speed. No one knows what to say. Everybody thanked God it was not them involved.

We walked to the basement elevators and, as the commander pushed the button, the doors opened. Standing there were two of the investigators from Internal Affairs, better known as the Rat Squad.

Police agencies need to have an internal investigation division. It is not a pleasant job to have, although I believe that most cops are exonerated in investigations. Most IA guys I have met have been fair. These two guys, Captain Herbert Kuehnin and Detective Martin Dumas, were not fair. They loved their job, and they were convinced that every cop was guilty of something, and they had no love for me.

"Captain, we will take it from here," Kuehnin said, and with no further explanation he grabbed me by the arm and took me over to the elevator, basically pushed me in, and then he and Dumas hit the button for the ground floor. That was where all the interview rooms were. When we got out, I saw the deputy chief standing there talking to the assistant district attorney on duty. They both turned and looked at me. The A.D.A., a friend of mine, looked down at his shoes.

"John, let's go into interview room two over there. Can I get you anything? Coffee, water?" asked Kuehnin.

"No, no I'm good," I responded.

I sat down across from the two internal affairs guys. Kuehnin looked iron clad serious; Dumas looked positively giddy. Another chance to take a cop down.

Kuehnin started, "John we have got to cover some bases here, so let's get that done. Just so you know, no one is accusing anyone of any wrongdoing. Everything that happens here will be recorded both in voice and visual. The recording is already on. We follow this procedure to make certain that events that transpire in this room are accurately recorded."

"Yeah, go ahead. I got it."

"First of all, I would like you to take your gun and put it in the evidence bag laying on the table. Handle the gun by its grip and make certain to keep your finger away from the trigger."

I looked across the table and could see that Dumas was drooling and ready for anything that may happen before the evidence bag was sealed.

"Do you want me to unload it, Captain?" I asked.

"No, just make sure it is decocked."

I put the gun in the bag and sealed it.

Dumas slid another bag toward me and said, "Now your other gun, Cabrelli."

I reached down toward my ankle and removed a short barreled Smith and Wesson Chief's Special .38 from an ankle holster. I put it in the next bag and sealed it up.

"Anything else, Cabrelli?"

"Nope, that's it."

"Mind if I check?"

"Yeah, as a matter of fact I do mind. I've got nothing else, Dumas."

He glared at me.

"Let it go, Martin," the captain said. He continued, "Okay then, let's get started. As I stated, we will be recording this interview. The recording will be maintained in the evidence vault until this matter is resolved and will be available to you and your counsel should the need arise. You are required by conditions of your employment to answer my questions as part of your report. Any information obtained during the course of this interview pursuant to department policy and rules cannot be used against you in a criminal proceeding. You are required to answer my questions, but you are protected under the U.S. Supreme Court decision *Garrity v. New Jersey*.

"You are being questioned as part of an internal and/or administrative investigation. You will be asked a number of questions concerning your official duties, and you must answer these questions to the best of your ability. Failure to answer completely and truthfully may result in disciplinary action including possible dismissal. Your answers and information derived from them may be used against you in administrative proceedings. However, neither your answers nor any information derived from them may be used in criminal proceedings, except if you knowingly and willfully make false statements. You retain the right to invoke your constitutional right against self-incrimination, at any time, without fear of employment repercussions. Do you understand what I am telling you, John?"

"Yes, Captain, I do."

"Are you ready to proceed?"

"I guess so. Yes, I am ready."

"John Cabrelli, I am Captain Herbert Kuehnin of the Internal Affairs Division. With me is Detective Martin Dumas, also of Internal Affairs. I am going to ask you to recount the situation that occurred at Gonzalez Market today to the best of your ability. I will ask questions of a clarifying nature as I need to. This is your opportunity to set the record straight and give an accurate account of the events that led to the shooting of Damien Callahan and Angelina Gonzalez, injuries sustained by Damien Callahan prior to the shooting, and the arrest of Roberto Gonzalez. The inquiry will proceed along these lines and may venture into other areas that I determine are germane to this inquiry. After this interview you will be required to write a formal report further detailing the situation. Are we ready to start, John?"

"Yeah, let's start, and we will see how this goes."

I knew I was guilty of something. Technically what, I didn't know. But I had killed Angelina Gonzalez, and no matter what the circumstances, it was a crime against God.

I answered the basic questions: name, rank, address, assignment, and that was about it.

Things started downhill right after that with Martin Dumbass asking, "John, it is clear that you violated department policy in not handcuffing Mr. Gonzalez, but we have more important issues on the table here than that, so how about we just agree that this policy was violated and come back to that later. We need to hear about the shooting. The press is already calling, and we need some answers to put them at ease."

"John, were you at the Gonzalez Market today?" asked Kuehnin.

I thought about the seemingly harmless question and then took the fifth and asked for a lawyer. I knew this was going to be bad. I didn't need my big mouth to make it any worse.

I was put on administrative leave with pay pending the outcome of the investigation.

• • •

I doubted a lawyer could do much. The facts of the case were crystal clear. I had taken a suspect into custody and led him from the scene unhandcuffed. In the process of violating this department policy, I forgot about the loaded gun on the floor behind the counter, where I explicitly told the suspect to place it. I walked the suspect outside and left the scene unsecured. Angelina Gonzalez, a probable rape victim, had come out of the back room where she was hiding, picked up the gun, walked to the door of the store, and fired one round at Damien Callahan, the man who allegedly raped her. I, in turn, drew my weapon and fired two rounds striking Angelina Gonzalez in the chest. Callahan was in surgery at a local hospital for his arm and broken teeth. Angelina was dead, and I was the one who killed her, in a split second stealing all her life's possibilities.

It was almost six in the morning before I caught a ride back to the precinct from one of the central cars. My chauffeur was a buddy of mine, Eddy Gilmore.

"Bad break, John. Sounds like the shoot was good, but a bad deal how it went down. That Callahan is a real piece of work. He's got a sheet a mile long. Done some time. I'm sure this will get worked out."

I got in my car at the precinct and started the ten-minute drive home. On the way, I tried to listen to some music, but quiet seemed like the only thing I could stand. As I pulled into the driveway, my cell phone rang. It was a reporter from one of the newspapers. He asked if I wanted to comment on the events and the "tragic death of the Gonzalez girl." I threw my cell phone against the garage wall.

My house seemed like a refuge. I closed the door and locked it. For the thousandth time, I wished I had a dog. Someone to come home to that was always happy to see me. No place for a dog in the city. Maybe one of these days I'd buy a place in the country then get a dog or two.

I am not much of a drinker, but that day seemed like a good time to start. The only thing in the house was a bottle of whiskey I had gotten for a Christmas gift a few years before. Whiskey it was. I looked out the window and drank until I passed out on the couch. ■

CHAPTER 3
Cabrelli

I woke up about 11:00 a.m. to someone pounding on my door.

My head was fuzzy from the whiskey, and I made the mistake of answering. Another reporter—a slick haired, capped teeth, talking head I recognized from a local TV channel accompanied by a camera crew. "Officer Cabrelli, I am Edwin Bailey with Channel Three. We'd like to talk with you."

He was in his mid-forties with dark brown hair and glasses. He wore a short-sleeved dress shirt with a red power tie. The heat was making him sweat through his carefully applied on-screen makeup. In his hand he held a small recorder. One of his feet was close to my door as if he was about to make sure I wasn't going to close it. I lived in a small three bedroom house then with two concrete front steps. His other foot was on the step below kind of bracing himself. His camera crew guy stood just beside him filming and recording everything. I was immediately aware of my unbrushed teeth, whiskey mouth, messed up hair, the fact that I was wearing the clothes I had slept in.

"I don't have anything to say right now. The department is still looking into things, and I'm kind of tired," I said.

"Officer Cabrelli, are you aware that there have been statements made to us and others that say you acted inappropriately, and, as a result, Angelina Gonzalez is dead, and Damien Callahan is severely wounded? People are blaming you for what happened. We are here to give you a chance to respond."

"I don't want to ... I'm not going to," I said.

The reporter kept pushing, telling me that there was talk of bringing charges against me for reckless homicide. I tried to close the door, but he put his foot in the way. I asked him to leave me alone, but he just kept pushing.

So in my smooth Cabrelli way, I told him and his camera boy that if they didn't get off my porch, I would shove the camera and microphone up their asses. I pushed the reporter backward and closed the door. It became prime time news footage.

I turned on the TV to see what they were saying. I caught the end of an interview with a local radical community leader. He was talking about yet another outrage perpetrated against his hard-working community. They would not be satisfied until John Cabrelli was brought to justice. Cabrelli deserved the most severe punishment allowed by law: the death penalty (which the state doesn't have). In twenty-four hours, I went from just doing my job to people calling for a needle in my arm. Little did they know, I was already dead. I had died the minute I shot Angelina Gonzalez.

The next few weeks went from bad to very bad to much worse to absolutely horrible.

Damien Callahan, with priors for sexual assault, burglary, and possession with intent to deliver a controlled substance, became the press's new hero of the year. The autopsy showed that Angelina was three months pregnant. DNA positively identified Callahan as the father. His lawyer cleaned him up, dressed him up, and paraded him in front of every news camera he could find.

Damien, the punk, told the story of how he and Angelina had been boyfriend and girlfriend. They'd had a falling out when she discovered she was pregnant. He went to the store to try and talk to her father and borrow some money to take care of her until he could get a job. Her father became angry and pulled a gun threatening to kill him, all while he was trying to explain to Mr. Gonzalez that his intentions were honorable. He wanted to care for Angelina and the baby. His only hope was that they could work things out. Then this cop, John Cabrelli, showed up. After he convinced Mr. Gonzalez to put down the gun, he hit poor Damien in the mouth for no reason and then said to him, "You deserve to die." (For what it's worth, I didn't say that although the possibility exists that he is a mind reader.) His lawyer went into how we would never know if Damien and Angelina could have had a happy life. A gun left by a cop in reach of a distraught woman had ended his dreams. The bullet fired by little Angelina Gonzalez had left Damien permanently disabled, and now he would never be able to work. The brutal blow from Cabrelli disfigured his face. Callahan was due compensation, and the lawyer would file suit for damages, but no amount of money could ever bring back Damien's Angelina.

The community as a whole was outraged. The department was keeping a pretty tight lid on things but, as always, there were leaks. They demanded a statement from the department or me. The question was no longer if I'd be charged with a crime, but what crime I would be charged with. My lawyer, Laura Davis, was doing a pretty good job. She arranged for cops to be stationed at my house to convince the now daily press visitors to leave me alone, but they still kept a 24/7 vigil across the street from my house. It was no longer just Channel Three; it was CBS, NBC, and ABC. All wanted a piece of old John. The day of reckoning was coming. I only left the house to go to HQ for interviews with investigators or to buy booze and groceries. When I did that I tried to go late at night, cut through the backyard, and disguised myself with sunglasses and the now several week old growth of beard. People still looked at me.

At 5:30 one afternoon, Laura the lawyer came over. "John, we need to talk. First let's turn on the six o'clock news."

I did. It was bad. The department had released my personnel file to the press. My commendations were never mentioned, but my reprimand for comments and actions involved with a certain gang gun battle years before were relived time and time again. Here was a police officer that condoned urban gang violence as a way to control crime. An obvious bigot and a dangerously violent man. A threat to society. The reporter from Channel Three was now being interviewed, having witnessed John Cabrelli's violence firsthand. The reporter had inside information from reliable sources that Cabrelli was to be charged tomorrow with various crimes, possibly even being criminally responsible for the death of Angelina Gonzalez. Mr. and Mrs. Gonzalez were also interviewed; they did not know how they could go on. The death of their only child had destroyed them. They wanted to sell their store and leave the state and stay with relatives. They did not call for my head, even though they of all people certainly deserved to do so most.

"John, tomorrow the department wants us in at 8:00 a.m. They have completed the investigation, and they want to tell what they are going to do. I don't have to tell you that things don't look very good. But this is interesting. Under normal circumstances, Internal Affairs would hold a press conference with the D.A.'s office and announce criminal indictments, grabbing the spotlight, as the champions of justice they are. For some reason they want to talk to us first. It could be a good thing. Just in case, I've brought a property bond for you to sign. You'll have to put up your house as surety, but at least you should be able to make bail."

• • •

Laura picked me up and just about ran down two reporters that stood in front of the car trying to get pictures.

I could tell she was ready for war, dressed in a knife-sharp creased black suit with a red shirt. Her dark hair tied up on her head. She was built sturdy and compact and walked with a determined confident step as we entered the very same building that a few years before had been where I started my career in law enforcement and had filled me with a sense of belonging, of having my place, having a purpose. Today the feeling was different; I was filled with dread, and it was all I could do to walk up the steps. One foot after the other. I tried to fill my head with positive thoughts, but all I could think of was, "They can't shoot ya, and they can't eat ya, so it could be worse."

Laura kept trying to keep my spirits up, telling me that if I was to be charged they would have a hell of a time getting a conviction. She would pull out all the stops. This wasn't negligent homicide—it was a mistake made in the heat of a very tough situation. The gun was left there only for a few minutes, not a week. Failure to secure my prisoner was at worst a three-day suspension. I was a decorated officer, not some stumble bum. She would call character witnesses to refute the allegations of racism. I was a good cop caught in a bad situation. Unfortunately, the more she talked, the more I became convinced that she thought I was going to fry.

On the way to the conference room, we ran into lots of the troops. They patted me on the back and said words of encouragement, but it all seemed hollow and useless. My life and its future was waiting for me behind the door of conference room GR17. I just wanted to go in and get it over with. The punishment could not be near as bad as the waiting. Whatever they gave me I deserved, and I would take it without a whimper. I had earned this, all of my own accord.

They could never do anything that came close to the pain I felt every day, seeing the face of Angelina Gonzalez every time I closed my eyes. Her little smile, her big brown eyes. The look on her father's face when he saw his daughter fall to the ground. Sometimes I felt like the needle would be a preferred alternative. Sometimes the pain got so bad I thought about ending it all and blowing my brains out.

We walked up to the door and were met by the inscrutable ace detective, Martin Dumbass.

"Attorney Davis, you and your client may have a seat over there on the bench. We aren't quite ready for you yet."

Laura jumped all over him. Her face was hard, her jaw set, green eyes as hard as stone, "You said eight. It's eight, and we are here. If you guys think we are going to wait around for you to get your act together, then you are mistaken. This travesty starts in five minutes, or we are gone."

"Well, how about we just arrest him right now Ms. Davis and save us all a bunch of time?" Dumbass sneered.

That took the wind out of Laura the lawyer's sails. They were going to charge me. Dumbass had said as much. I was going to trial. I was screwed.

We waited for almost half an hour before the door of GR17 opened. My precinct commander, Bill Freise, stepped out. He couldn't look me in the eye, a very bad sign.

"John, you and your attorney can come in now."

We walked into the room and it looked like a convention, with no fewer than ten people seated around the table: Jim Boyle, the D.A. and his assistant, Chief Jerry Nolan and his assistant, two captains, two detectives from homicide, and last but not least, Captain Herbert Kuehnin and Detective Martin Dumas. No one was smiling except Dumas, and I have often attributed his smile to simple-mindedness.

The chief directed us to two chairs opposite the crowd. It was clear he was going to run the meeting. He always did. I liked the chief; he was a straight shooter. He had a little bit of a John Wayne complex, but a little bit of that is good. I also knew he liked me. He had often called on me in the past for special assignments in my area. I never let him down, mostly because I found special assignments to be fun.

I was working overtime one night in a nice part of town and responded to a complaint of a loud party. It was a party with high school kids at different stages of intoxication spilling out across the lawn of a very nice house. As we were putting a stop to things, I heard a young woman giving one of the rookie officers a hard time. I turned to look and saw that the young lady in question was none other than Marisa Nolan, the youngest daughter of Chief Nolan. I interceded and tried to take Ms. Nolan away from the crowd. She would have none of it, and, as I tried to lead her away, she sunk her pretty white, brace-straightened teeth right into my arm. I hogtied her with plasticuffs, threw her in the back seat of my car, and took her home to one very grateful, but pissed off papa.

It wouldn't get me very far, but at least I knew that he didn't have a grudge to settle.

The proceedings were called to order by the chief.

"John, I have decided to call this meeting because I feel that there are some issues we need to resolve. I have asked all the principals in the investigation to be present. Some of us share the same opinion of how this incident should be handled, while others differ. I am sure you find this format extremely unorthodox Attorney Davis, and I would not blame you for taking your client and walking out. As a matter of fact, I am not so sure that I wouldn't recommend it. I want to assure you of one thing. I am not here to hang John Cabrelli. Regardless of what brought us here today, he has been a fine officer and a credit to this department. In my book, that means a great deal. Others," the chief continued as he stared at Dumbass and Kuehnin, "feel that it has no bearing, but until somebody replaces me, I am the boss. I make that call. District Attorney Boyle has some additional comments."

Boyle looked up over reading glasses, his time worn, "seen too much eyes," focused on John and Laura. "Attorney Davis and Officer Cabrelli, thank you for coming in. I too share the chief's feeling about this meeting. At best it is unorthodox, at worst it is detrimental to our criminal justice system. I want to make it clear that the district attorney's office has reviewed the very thorough investigation of this tragic incident. It is my opinion that you have some culpability here. Your actions regarding the striking of Damien Callahan and failing to secure the scene that resulted in Angelina Gonzalez retrieving a loaded firearm is inexcusable, possibly criminal. The failure to secure a prisoner is a department issue."

I had just heard some music: the words "possibly criminal." Not definitely criminal, not we are going to charge you criminally, just "possibly criminal."

This was definitely not lost on my able counsel who kicked me under the table and immediately piped up, "Mr. District Attorney, do I understand this to mean that you have not yet decided to criminally charge my client?"

"Don't jump to conclusions, counselor. All it means is that we are still fact finding, and some questions need to be answered," Boyle said.

"That's why you're here, John, to answer some questions," said the chief.

"I have advised my client, who has been completely cooperative with this investigation, to answer no further questions. Continuing to question him over and over is just an attempt to confuse him and cast doubt on his version of the events. On behalf of my client, we respectfully refuse any further questions."

"I see," said the chief. "And I understand. This meeting has come to an end."

As everyone got up to start to leave, I knew that this had to be over today, win, lose, or draw. So I said, "Chief what is it that you want to know? Ask me."

Laura looked as if she was going to deliver a calf right on the spot. "John be quiet. Don't do this. This is a bad idea. I am telling you, as your lawyer, to shut your mouth right now."

"Sorry, Laura, this has got to be done. I'm ready for whatever comes. Chief, let's all sit back down and you ask me your questions. I'll see what I can do to help you out."

"Counselor, do you have anything further to say?" District Attorney Boyle asked.

"My client does this against my advice. If he chooses to answer these questions, he proceeds at his own peril. However, I will remain present to protect him from himself in the best way I can."

I looked the chief right in the eye and said, "What is it that you want to know so badly that you have filled this room with every principal from the investigation so they could hear the answer? Ask me."

"Again, John, let me caution you. This is against my advice," Laura jumped in.

"Counselor, I know you're a good lawyer and a good friend, but this has got to be over. I need to know when I walk out of here where I stand. Good or bad, I just need to know."

"Okay, John, but please let me determine the rules before you say anything. We don't know what the rules are. If you say something it can be used against you. We need to know what the parameters of this interview are going to be."

"Okay, Laura, that sounds reasonable. Go ahead," I responded.

"Mr. District Attorney, in what context are these questions being asked? Are they part of a criminal investigation, a disciplinary review, or just for the entertainment of all present? Does my client have any assurances of your intentions? Do you intend to Mirandize my client?"

"Yes, Attorney Davis, we do. This is an official part of an inquiry into the death of Angelina Gonzalez and the wounding of Damien Callahan. Anything your client tells us can be used against him. All information we obtain may or may not become part of our case should we decide to prosecute. Our focus is not on the disciplinary process. We are only interested in the case regarding the death of Gonzalez and the wounding of Callahan. We will advise Officer Cabrelli of his constitutional rights."

"John, this is definitely not smart. We need to leave this room now. We need to talk," Laura said.

The room was dead quiet. Everybody was looking at me. I was looking at the ground. I knew in my heart that this was it. The facts of the case were the facts of the case. The truth will set you free or lock you up, depending. I had baited suspects in many situations like this before. "Tell me the truth, get it off your chest. You'll feel better and I will get a conviction." Being on the other side of the table gave me a new appreciation for that situation.

Everybody was waiting for me.

"Okay, here is the deal. I don't want to hear my rights again. That will almost certainly make me puke. With my lawyer present, I waive the reading of my rights. Chief, ask me whatever you want. I will answer if I can. Let's get it over with."

The room turned silent.

The chief leaned forward on his elbows and started. "Okay, John. When you were in the store after Gonzalez had put down the gun and after you had hit Callahan in the mouth, did you ask Gonzalez any questions?"

"What kind of questions?"

"Any questions you recall."

"Give me a hint. I was pretty busy at the moment, you know just having talked down a gun and all."

"John, did you request information from Mr. Gonzalez about anyone else that might be in the store?"

"I don't really, don't...."

"The answer is either you did, you didn't, or you don't recall," said the chief, clearly agitated.

Just for the record, the only answer to that question, if you don't know how it's going to go for you, is always, "I don't recall."

I replayed the events in my mind, trying to fill in the conversation. I didn't say anything to Gonzalez but "Come with me." I didn't say anything else. I definitely did not ask Gonzalez whether or not anyone else was in the store. I wish I had asked him because it might have made a difference. If I'd have known his daughter was there, I would have sent someone to get her or asked her to come out.

"John you need to think here. It's important, important to you."

"Chief, you are obviously looking for something specific. If you clarify what you are looking for, maybe we can be of more help," said Laura.

Chief Nolan looked at D.A. Boyle, who looked at Captain Kuehnin. No one looked at Dumbass.

Seconds became eons.

The D.A. broke the silence, "Officer Cabrelli, in the statement of Roberto Gonzalez, he said that before you led him from the store, you asked whether or not anyone else was in there. I quote, 'When I started to come out, after John Cabrelli stopped them from locking me in handcuffs, he asked me if there was anyone else in the store. He asked me if Angelina was there. I told him no, no one else was in the store.' Do you recall this conversation Officer Cabrelli?"

That was it. Mr. Gonzalez had got me off the hook. I killed his daughter, but he got me off the hook. In his version of the story I had exercised reasonable efforts to make certain that the scene was secure while taking my prisoner into custody. He told me no one else was in the store, and I believed him. I still should have secured the gun, but now it was different. Laura could and would argue that I'd thought the scene was secure and that I'd made a decision to remove the participants before I went back to process. Not the best decision, but a defendable one. A set of circumstances that no one could have predicted. I had operated on the best information available at the time.

Again everyone was staring at me. I knew what I said next could determine whether or not I was charged. Everyone was waiting for me. I gave the only appropriate answer given the situation.

"I don't recall. Like I said, I had just talked down a gun, and the adrenaline was really flowing."

"This meeting is now concluded. We will present our findings of fact in writing within the next seven days. They will be made immediately available to you and your client, Attorney Davis. Although the press is pushing us for details, you have our promise that the results of our investigation will be withheld until you have time to review them," stated the D.A. matter-of-factly. ■

FIGURE EIGHT. A NORTHERN LAKES MYSTERY

CHAPTER 4
Cabrelli

Seven days, seven months, seven years all seemed the same.

Laura said that if they charged me, we would beat it in court. The great unknown was the influence that public pressure was going to have on this case. The daily news conferences and demonstrations had slowed down to weekly, but the fuse on the powder keg was still smoldering. While waiting, I hid out and continued to refine and appreciate my relationship with demon whiskey. Friends from the department called but not near as many or as often as before. Who could blame them? I was not exactly a fun guy to talk to or be around. I only answered the phone when I was drunk and let it ring unanswered when I was sober. I never answered the door and kept the curtains drawn.

The call came: report at 0800 November 22, a few days before Thanksgiving. The same day that, decades before, a punk with an army surplus Carcano rifle delivered a hammer blow to our country.

Everyone wanted to finish this before the holidays. A noose hanging in the background tends to dampen the Thanksgiving appetite and the Christmas spirit.

Laura was kind enough to pick me up in her brand new spectacular jet black Japanese sports car. She said it was the least she could do seeing how I had paid for it. I told her to step on it, that we were late.

We weren't late, but I hoped she would get a ticket. She made the trip unscathed.

It was good old conference room GR17 again. Painted a depressing light gray with fifty or so World War II surplus chairs for the audience facing four long metal tables pushed together, behind which were chairs occupied by the chief, the D.A., and company. One thing was noticeably different. This time there was a court reporter to take down everything for the record, the official record of what could only be the demise of a once promising officer. We walked right in where everyone was already waiting. The air was oppressive. I even thought for a second I was having a heart attack. *That'll fix 'em. I'll die on the spot.* No such luck.

The chief was again presiding. It looked like he had aged in the past months. His hair looked grayer, the lines on his face deeper. He hunched his big-shouldered boxer's frame over the table and snapped everyone to order and began without wasting any time.

"Is the court reporter ready?"

"Yes, Chief Nolan, I am."

"Let's begin then and get this over with," said the chief. "Officer John Cabrelli, you are present in person and represented by your lawyer, Laura Davis. We have reviewed your case and considered all the evidence. We regret that this has taken so long, but there were many issues to consider. First, the district attorney had to consider whether criminal charges were warranted. He will present his findings as soon as I have concluded my opening remarks. Then the department needed to determine whether or not you were in violation of department policies and procedures. Lastly, we had to answer claims that you violated the civil rights of Damien Callahan, requiring us to refer this to the Federal Bureau of Investigation. The district attorney and the Department Board of Inquiry have completed their investigations. All leads have been exhausted, and I am convinced that the investigation has been fair and impartial. The results of the investigation by both the district attorney and this department shall be made available to you and your counsel as soon as this hearing concludes. Mr. District Attorney, please go ahead."

Boyle stayed seated but assumed a ramrod straight lawyerly posture. His face reflected the gravity of the situation. "Officer Cabrelli, I have thoroughly reviewed the facts of this case. Regarding the death of Angelina Gonzalez, we have found no probable cause to file criminal charges against you. Your actions may or may not have been consistent with acceptable police procedures, but that is not our concern. Regarding the battery of Damien Callahan, we have determined that your actions were inappropriate and likely constituted criminal battery. It was my intent to file charges. However, there are extenuating circumstances. The victim, Damien Callahan, was arrested four days ago for the delivery of crack cocaine. He was arrested as part of a sting operation conducted by Metro Narcotics. The lead officer on that sting was one Lieutenant J. J. Malone. I believe you are familiar with him as you were once partners and academy classmates. Callahan says that he was set up. Be that as it may, he is currently working with narcotics folks, rolling over on anyone he can to keep from going back to prison for a long, long stay. He has no interest in pursuing charges against you or proceeding with his lawsuit against the city. Lastly, there is no evidence to support that you violated the civil rights of anyone involved in this incident. The matter will not be referred to the FBI. I have nothing further."

"Thank you, District Attorney Boyle. Any questions, Attorney Davis?"

Laura was afraid to breathe, much less ask questions. I had already gone into respiratory arrest. "No, Chief. We are ready to continue," she whispered.

"Very well then. With regard to disciplinary issues. Officer John Cabrelli, we have found that you violated sections 101.7, 205.1, and 335 of the Policies and Procedures Manual. These sections deal with excessive physical force, arrest and restraint of prisoners, and evidence seizure and protection, respectively. You received and signed for the official department manual. Thirty days after you received this manual, you signed an affidavit stating that you had read and understood this manual. You were offered the opportunity for a more detailed explanation if you felt it necessary and you declined in writing."

Like almost every other cop, I had never read the manual. Signing the paperwork was just to make it go away so I could get to the business of being a cop.

"Based on the result of our investigation and previous disciplinary actions, you are terminated, effective immediately. We thank you for your years of service, and I am truly sorry that your career has ended this way. You have the right to appeal this decision, and you must file your appeal within 60 days of this date. This hearing is concluded."

At that, everybody got up and left. On his way out, Martin Dumas smiled at me. I didn't even want to smack him, I was in such shock. No trial, no jail, no job, no life. A cop was all I had ever been. There was nothing past that. I should have been glad not to be facing criminal charges, but all that mattered was the job. It was my family, my life, my purpose. I had gone to work one day, like so many days before. Started my patrol shift just like always. Then things changed, a series of events I could have never scripted came crashing down around me. As a result, Angelina Gonzalez lay in a cold grave, and her parents would mourn forever. I had not been charged with a crime, but in my mind I had murdered little Angelina. The emotional pain I felt seemed inexcusably selfish and a just reward for my actions.

I had never understood the term "lost soul" until that day. Laura offered to buy me a drink on the way home. I wasn't interested. I wanted to be alone. I didn't want to talk to anyone. I didn't want anyone looking at me. To hell with everybody. I sat in a chair by the closed window drapes and drank myself into unconsciousness. To hell with Laura, the chief, Callahan, Dumas, and Kuehnin ... and to hell with myself.

• • •

The next morning, the morning after that, and the mornings (afternoons and evenings for that matter) for what I thought were the next two weeks were hard to recall, blurred by despair and alcohol.

Laura had called and stopped by. I just couldn't answer the phone or the door. My former co-workers did the same. My response to them was the same. It became clear that people were now avoiding me. I can't say for sure, but it appears as though my surly, angry attitude and the fact that I was always drunk might have had something to do with it.

My mail had begun to pile up, and there were several letters from the department. I had never felt more alone in my life. I was just marking time. I had found a store that offered grocery and liquor shopping by phone, with free delivery service. I never had to leave the house. Actually, I had convinced myself that I was pretty content. I watched a lot of TV, slept a lot, and pretty much wallowed in my own self-pity. Everyone should be allowed to wallow at least once; wallowing was good. I would probably still be there, permanently preserved by 100 proof, if not for Laura and the chief.

It was a glorious day, about 10:00 a.m. I had just gotten out of bed and moved to the couch, now dining on my recent favorite breakfast of a cheese and salami sandwich and a little brandy mixed with orange juice. It appeared as though the sun was shining outside, and I had just turned on the TV for my daily dose of adventure with Magnum P.I. What would Magnum get himself into today? What a crime rate Hawaii had!

All of a sudden, someone was pounding the crap out of my front door. Not knocking, pounding. I was trying to ignore the noise, but it was seriously impacting my ability to concentrate on the conversation that Magnum and Rick were having about Higgins and the details of security at the Island Flower Show. That Higgins, what a guy.

The knocking stopped, and for about 20 seconds, I thought the invaders had retreated. Then the door came flying open aided by the chief's size 13 shoe. I looked up from the couch and saw Laura and Chief Nolan in my living room. I tried to leap up in outrage, but I caught my foot in my blanket and fell back down on the couch.

Looking to rescue the moment and a little of the minuscule amount of dignity I had left, I said, "Hey, Chief. Hey, Laura. How nice to see you guys. Chief, you must be a welcome visitor, knock twice then kick in the door. I am sure kicking in your friend's doors makes you a popular guy, you know, adding a little excitement and criminal damage to property to your visits."

"John, shut up! Open your mouth again, and I am going to come over there and shut it for you," growled the chief.

"Might not be all that easy, Chief, so if you feel froggy, jump," I responded, again searching for dignity scraps.

"John, what are you doing to yourself?" Laura said. "You look horrible. This place smells, you smell. When was the last time you took a shower? My God, John."

In the two minutes since they had interrupted Magnum and company, they had already worn out their welcome. I was not about to put up with any crap from the chief or Laura in my own house. I didn't invite them, and I wanted them to leave.

"What's the big deal? I think I deserve a couple of weeks off after all I've been through. I realize that I've let the place go a little, but I have a cleaning service coming in starting next week," I lied.

"John, listen to me. Look me in the eye. Sit up, look me in the eye. Focus for one minute. Just listen for one minute," the chief commanded.

"You have got one minute before I throw you out of here. By the way, I will be sending a bill for the door. Where do you get off kicking in—"

"Shut up, John. Stop it and listen to me. Listen for one damn minute," the chief bellowed.

It was then he decided to hit me with two sledgehammers, and it was difficult to determine which in fact was more painful.

"It hasn't been two weeks, it's been two months. You've been holed up in this toxic waste dump for two months. Eight weeks."

They said I looked at them like they were from Mars. After a minute or two, I started screaming, calling them liars. Laura picked something out of the bushel of mail and showed me the date. It was seven weeks going on eight. Sledgehammer one: delivered.

According to those present, myself excluded, it was at that point that I lost it. Laura says I was screaming so loudly that they couldn't make out the words, but they could see my intentions as I charged across the room. Blood was in my eye.

The chief stood his ground and dropped into a low crouch. Forty years ago, he had been a Golden Gloves boxer, some even said a contender. A tough guy during his days as a street cop, but he had been off the street for twenty years and had gone soft. The punch he hit me with was anything but soft. I went down and stayed there.

Sledgehammer two: delivered.

They left me where I fell. I tried to open my eyes many times, but I kept closing them waiting for the dream to end. I can't say how long I lay there, but when I eventually got up, the room had become very crowded. The chief and Laura had been joined by my old partner J.J. Malone and his wife, Tanya.

They had begun the process of shoveling out my house. Laura was at my kitchen table going through the mail. J and Tanya were filling trash bags and pitching them out the back door. Someone had a batch of laundry going. Fresh coffee was brewing. Even though it was January, the windows were open, and I smelled this odd scent that I soon figured out must be fresh air.

I made it back to the couch, and Tanya brought me a cup of coffee. I reached for the brandy bottle, but it was gone. The chief, J, and Tanya pulled kitchen chairs around me.

Tanya looked at me with sympathetic eyes wearing an old WPPA t-shirt. Her face was smudged by dirt from the mess I'd left. When she spoke, it was from the collective heart of those assembled.

"John, we're your friends and we're here to help you. You need to know that. You can count on us. We'll help you get through this. You have to help us help you," Tanya pleaded.

It was all too much for my booze-soaked brain to take in. Who was this guy they were talking to? It could not possibly be John Cabrelli, decorated police veteran. It must be someone else.

I can't tell you what happened, how they got through to me, but they did. I knew I was in trouble. I knew I needed someone. I needed help. As long as I live, I will never be able to thank those people—they saved my life. They treated me with respect. They never left me alone.

They listened. They helped. They held me. I went from a complete menace to crying like a baby. Each day I got better.

Laura deposited checks that had come in the mail for unused vacation time and my final paycheck. She paid my past due mortgage, phone bill, and other bills.

She met with the pension folks and told me that I had enough years of service to qualify for a small but decent pension. She filled out the paperwork, and all I had to do was sign.

I started taking a walk every morning, then every evening. Always someone with me and always someone there for me. It took two days to compensate for every one day I had spent holed up. I slept a lot less for two reasons: I felt better when I was awake, and sleep brought me the face of Angelina Gonzalez, smiling, dying.

I got stronger. Laura signed me up at a health club, and I started to spend each morning there, pushing myself, purging the pain. Tanya got me going on the basics of weightlifting, and I began to feel strong again. J.J. and I just sat and visited. We never seemed to run out of things to talk about. It seemed like forever, but one morning I woke up and it was spring. I was looking forward to the day ahead, something I can't explain to someone who hasn't been there. I walked out to my car and found myself whistling "Sunshine, Lollipops and Rainbows." What an idiot. ■

CHAPTER 5
Cabrelli

Life was getting better, the house was back in order, and my dear friendship with booze and the "shop by phone" grocery service had been terminated. I did laundry, worked out, and even started reading. I was ready to move to the next level in my life. I knew I had to find a job. My pension checks were covering the basics, but I needed to supplement my income.

Laura the lawyer had become Laura, my perky, pretty, very sexy companion. I am not suggesting that our relationship was anything other than platonic; it wasn't. It doesn't mean that I wasn't thinking along those lines; I was. She and I went out to dinner at least once a week and sometimes worked out together. We got along great.

One night I was grilling steaks for us, and I told her I was going to start looking for a job. We talked about what I might be interested in, and I showed her an ad for an insurance investigator. Laura to the rescue. She had been thinking about putting on a full-time investigator, someone to do fact checking on cases and looking into various matters she was working on. She would love it if I would consider taking the job. I didn't even ask the pay before I said yes. I couldn't wait to get back to work.

My days were great, and my nights were getting better. Weekly, I attended a group therapy session that Cops Helping Cops put on.

Cops all working on things, all trying to fight demons. I found myself saying things that I didn't even know I thought. It was cleansing. Mostly it helped me realize that while John Cabrelli wasn't perfect, he had some redeeming features.

Laura and I made a great team. We worked very hard and won most of our cases, mostly because before we really jumped in with both feet, I would launch our own investigation. I knew we needed to know everything we could before some opposing lawyer pointed it out to us in front of a judge. Good cases got our best efforts, while bad cases got sent down the road.

We spent a lot of time together mostly as good friends, but we were consummate professionals when necessary. I enjoyed her company, and I could tell she enjoyed mine. Occasionally, I began to struggle with not fixating on how attractive she was.

Business at the firm picked up. We had a very difficult case against an insurance company that claimed that the insured's policy had expired before the aforementioned insured spent an afternoon at the bar and on the way home crossed over the center line and hit our client head on. The insurance company pushed very hard for an early court date, which means one of two things. Either it was going to be a slam dunk for them, or there was something out there they didn't want us to find. We went with the second assumption. We subpoenaed the financial records of their client.

To make a long story short, we found a check that had been written and sent to the insurance company. The insurance company was in the process of dropping this guy because of his driving record. There was a 30-day grace period attached to the policy. The check had been received and cashed by the insurance company on the second to last day before the expiration of the grace period. That was exactly 24 hours before the guy had crashed into our client and three days before the company notified him by registered mail of the termination of his policy. We called them, they settled, case closed. My lovely Laura cut me a bonus check for my stellar investigative work.

She announced her intentions to trade in her snappy little car for a new model. I bought it from her. On my days off I took to driving fast on the back roads of Wisconsin. I had scored a retirement ID that served me well with those conscientious souls that chose to interrupt my forays with radar units and speed laws.

My road trips were fun, but I thought they would be perfect if this beautiful lawyer I knew was sitting beside me.

My social life, my life actually, all centered around Laura and work. We spent many evenings together, mostly business but lots of laughs too. I didn't know much about her personal life. It was actually something we hadn't discussed. I had tried to bring it up casually but hadn't made any progress. I knew there were a couple of other professional women that she hung out with, and they played tennis once a week in warm weather. Mostly, I figured that since she was my social life, I was kind of hers. I was also convinced that she was growing more and more interested in me, which is understandable because I had turned on the old Cabrelli charm. I knew she was single. She was very pretty, smart, and we got along well. She had on numerous occasions suggested that I start dating. Her words, "You need to get a social life, John."

An opportunity then presented itself. A case we were working was hitting full speed. We needed to travel up to Green Bay, set up camp, and get to work. I started devising a plan.

I got on the Internet and located a very nice resort hotel on the shores of Green Bay. I told Laura that it was the perfect place to stay, centrally located, with in-house restaurants and gym. She never gave it a second thought, and we booked two rooms. The fix was in. It would be the perfect opportunity for me to broach the subject of Laura and John on weekend road trips.

I picked her up in my new car. I have never been known as a *GQ* dresser, but I had gone to a local clothing store and the salesgirl had successfully matched some new duds. I was dressed in the style known as business casual and had treated myself to a pair of handmade Italian loafers, deep brown and as soft as could be. I was in good shape and thought I was looking pretty good. Laura looked beautiful. Her brunette hair was down on her shoulders. Her typical business wear had been replaced by a pair of not too tight fitting jeans and a lightweight fleece. I was certain that I saw a new spark of interest in her green eyes.

She put her case and luggage in the trunk and got in. "John, you look very nice. New clothes?"

"No, I bought these a while ago and forgot about them. I just decided to break them out."

"Well, you look very handsome." My plan was working.

As we pulled away, I popped in a CD of Sinatra love songs. The plot thickened.

The trip up was fun; we talked and laughed. She told me that she had sold me this car too cheap. I told her that she was lucky to find a sucker willing to take it off her hands. It was a nice day. On the way, I bought her lunch at a cute little place.

It was going well. Cabrelli was pulling out all the stops.

We drove into Green Bay and went right to the courthouse for a meeting. About two hours later we headed to our hotel. There were things we needed to prepare for the morning, so we agreed to get room service and have a working supper. I offered to host the event in my room, and she agreed.

I was like a schoolboy. I called room service and tried to communicate my special dinner requests. I left nothing to chance and went down and talked to the hostess myself. A hefty tip ensured my every wish would be honored.

Two hours later, Laura called to say she would be over in twenty minutes. I told her that I needed a little more time. I alerted the kitchen of my guest's imminent arrival.

Room service could not have cut it any closer. They wheeled in the dinner, set the table, and arranged the grossly overpriced bouquet of flowers. Five minutes later, Laura knocked on the door. I let her in, and I could see by the look on her face that you could have knocked her over with a feather.

"Oh my God, John. This is beautiful! What is the occasion?"

"No occasion. I just thought we should have a nice dinner to thank you for all you've done for me."

I had safely returned to the status of occasional light drinker, enjoying a glass of wine now and again. For the occasion, I had ordered a bottle of her favorite: a cabernet from Washington State. God, I was smooth.

She sat down. I poured her a glass and one for myself. It was perfect; we smiled and talked, and I could feel something in the air. The dinner was excellent, but I have got to admit that I didn't have much of an appetite. After dinner, I poured the rest of the wine. It was time. Decorated former police officer and now ace investigator John Cabrelli was ready.

"Laura, I have something to tell you, and I am plenty nervous, so please just hear me out."

At that moment, she got it. Her mouth opened slightly, and she stared at me.

I took her hand and looked into her eyes. Nothing could stop me now.

"Laura, you've been such a big part of my life. I don't think I would be here today if not for you. Not just your skills as a lawyer but as my friend, my shoulder, the one thing I could count on no matter what. What I'm trying to say is...."

"No, John, stop," she said in a soft voice.

"I'm not stopping. Hear me out, then we'll talk. I want nothing more in the world than for you and I to become something more than business associates and friends."

I was moving forward, and I thought it was going well. As I said the words, I realized that she had become more to me than even I recognized. I looked at her and said something I never intended.

"I am hopelessly in love with you. Please give us a chance."

I waited and saw a tear roll down her pretty cheek. I knew it was a tear of joy, a tear of love. I had just told her what she had wanted to say herself.

She held my hand tightly.

"Oh John, you sweet man. I have never met anyone like you. You are truly a wonderful person. I care for you very deeply, but there is something I have to tell you."

"But" is not good. There should be no buts. She was to fall into my arms, and we were going to make love for hours and hold each other all night.

"John, I really don't know how to say this other than to say it. You are a great guy, and some woman will be lucky to have you. That woman will not be me. You are not my type. I am not interested in having a personal relationship, with a man."

What did that mean? Had she been hurt badly? Had some guy dumped her? The bastard. I would kick his ass. Here he was raining on my parade.

"I promise I will never hurt you. I will treat you like you deserve. Please give me a chance," I pleaded.

"You don't understand, I am already in a relationship. I have started seeing someone. John, her name is Elizabeth."

Elizabeth! I was stunned, for a second, then it hit me. There is a danger that all good investigators must avoid.

It involves the obvious suspect, the one you pursue because everything points to them. You spend all your time and energy trying to button up the case and put the guy away. Then you sit down to catch up on some calls and paperwork, there are five phone messages from the same person.

You return the call and a nun from a local church says that the guy you are looking at so hard cannot be guilty because he was volunteering at the church when the crime occurred, just like he did every week. She also mentions that she saw a person similar in appearance walk past the parish office a duck down an alley at about the same time. Then you look over everything again the information you should have been paying attention to sprouts like mushrooms.

With lovely Laura I had a severe case of tunnel vision. I charged forward, ignoring all cues. Combine that with a healthy dose of male density when it comes to women, and well, John Cabrelli strikes out. ∎

CHAPTER 6
Hospital

One may have thought that Attila the Hun was assaulting John Cabrelli's hospital room. It wasn't Attila himself, but it was certainly one of his descendants in the person of Nurse B. Holterman.

"What is going on here?" she demanded.

"Mr. Cabrelli is in no condition for this type of taxing behavior. It is after visiting hours, and you (pointing her finger like a pistol at Presser) will leave immediately."

"I'm sorry. I've been listening to John at his request. I wasn't trying to cause a problem. He called ME! I'm just trying—"

Nurse Holterman cut him off at the knees. "You will leave right now, this minute. Out!"

Nurse Holterman didn't threaten to call security; she didn't need to. Unless they sent up a complete tactical unit, no one in security was more formidable.

Bill Presser could not gather his papers and recorder fast enough. As he was leaving, the nurse stuck a syringe into John's IV and filled him full of pain meds. The teen doctor walked in a few minutes later, and John tried to protest, however, his ability to form sentences was rapidly diminishing.

"Doc, I need to talk to this guy. Please let him talk to me. He needs to finish. I need him to ..." were John's last words as he drifted off to the land of LaLa.

···

The doctor and nurse examined John's wounds and dressings. They poked and prodded and measured and made notes on his chart. The doctor told the nurse that he wanted an x-ray first thing in the morning to determine the current position of the remaining bullet and any fragments. Something would have to be done soon, although everyone knew a successful surgery would require not only the most skilled hands, but also some divine intervention. John wasn't certain whether he deserved that type of intervention but hoped maybe his good points outweighed the bad.

When the doctor and nurse left the room, Bill Presser met them in the hallway.

"Doctor, could I have a moment please?" he asked.

"Yes, but just a moment. I have many other patients to see," replied the doctor curtly.

"I want you to know that it is not my intention to cause John any further complications. He requested me, and I'm trying to respond to that request. I am not an unsympathetic person, and it's clear he's in a fair amount of pain. However, after spending this time with him, it's also clear that this is what he desperately wants to do. This is his story, and he needs to tell it. From what he has told me, this may be the last request of a dying man. I have committed to honoring that request. Whether he thinks so or not, he's a real hero and has earned this right," Presser pleaded.

"Mr. Presser, my responsibility is to keep John Cabrelli alive. That includes making certain that he does nothing to jeopardize his care. I don't care about his hero status. I don't care about his story. I care about keeping him alive and healing him. That's it. To that end, I will allow no visitation from anyone, period."

End of discussion. The doctor walked away. Nurse Holterman fixed Bill with a chilling look, but ended with an almost imperceptible nod of her head before she walked off.

···

That night was a bad night for John. His temperature increased, reaching a point that a night nurse was covering him with cool packs trying to bring it down. At three in the morning the doctor on call was dispatched to his room. The increased temperature along with significant abdominal tenderness was a clear sign of some type of infection, possibly bullet damage missed during the initial emergency surgery. Doses of IV antibiotics were increased. For what seemed like the millionth time in his life, John Cabrelli was in big trouble.

Due to the heavy doses of pain drugs, John was only somewhat aware of what was going on. He dreamed not of Angelina Gonzalez but of a cabin on a small lake. He was sitting on the porch sorting out his fishing tackle box. Sunset was approaching and the air had turned cool, then cold, and John began to shiver. He couldn't get warm no matter how hard he tried. He just couldn't get warm.

Morning for John came at around 2:00 p.m. A new doctor had now joined the team. They were gently trying to wake him, and he was coming to, fuzzy, but awake. There was a lot going on.

"Mr. Cabrelli, my name is Dr. Árnason. I am a surgeon from U.W. Hospital in Madison. I would like to talk about your condition. Do you feel up to that now?"

"Go ahead, Doc. I think this is about as good as I get right now."

"We feel that you are suffering from a severe internal infection. At this point your body has not yet begun to launch its own immune response to fight this infection. Your weakened state will further compromise that. We are administering heavy doses of antibiotics with little result. In my opinion, and it is shared by my colleagues here, we need to go back in and try to determine the source of the infection, and we will remove the remaining bullet in the same procedure."

"Doc, I thought that you were going to wait to remove that slug. I thought it was too dangerous until the, the uh ... rest of the damage was healed," croaked John. His mouth felt like he was sucking on cotton balls.

"Nothing has changed, John. There are certain risks involved. Our choices are limited, but we must do something. The risks are far greater if we don't," the doctor explained. "John, I want you to be aware of the risks. Do you have any next of kin that we can talk with about this surgery? A wife, son, daughter?"

"I really have no one. No one at all."

It was then John realized exactly how this was playing out. The hospital chaplain had entered the room and came to sit by John's bed.

"Mr. Cabrelli, I am Pastor Steve Martin. Is there anything I can do to make you feel more comfortable? Is there anything you want to talk about? Anyone you want me to contact?"

"Steve Martin? Like the comedian? I could definitely use a comedian right now."

With that, John went to sleep. The pre-surgical anesthetic had been administered, and he was on his way to surgery. The last thing John remembered was Nurse Holterman holding his hand. His last thoughts were of her sawing it off at the wrist.

• • •

John came to, maybe hours, maybe days later. The first face that greeted him was a vision of loveliness: Nurse Holterman had been replaced, and another nurse that was infinitely more pleasing to the eye was there, and she even smiled.

"Mr. Cabrelli, welcome back."

"I am glad to be back. How did I do?"

"You did very well considering the circumstances. The doctor wanted to be notified as soon as you were awake, and he will fill you in."

A few minutes later Dr. Árnason came in. "Mr. Cabrelli, how are you feeling?"

"I have definitely had better days. How did I do?"

"Things went very well considering the extent of the damage. We successfully repaired an area of the intestine that had been damaged by one of the bullets. This was the source of the infection. When the bullets entered your body, they fragmented, and we were able to locate several small pieces and remove them. I am sorry to say we were not able to remove the second bullet lodged next to your spine at this time. With the current complications, we determined that the risk factors were too great. Once your immune system and the antibiotics do their work, you should start feeling much better, and we can make plans to remove that bullet. For now, just take it easy and concentrate on getting well."

"Doc, how long do you think it will be?" John fell back asleep before the doctor answered.

It was a full three days before John was back to a recognizable form of himself. The narcotics were reduced, and he was able to self-administer the pain medication by pushing a button. He was anxious to see Bill Presser again, but visitation was restricted to immediate family, of which he had none. So no visitors. He broached the subject with Nurse Holterman, asking if Presser could visit. She responded as expected.

"Absolutely not."

Not one to waste a chance to dish out a tongue lashing, she continued, "We at the hospital are trying very hard to give you the best care possible. You must be part of your care and do as instructed. Much of the staff is feeling pressured by your presence here. The press calls to the nurse's station are to the point that they are taking time away from the care of other patients. It seems that the news is out: John Cabrelli is at our hospital, and there is a rather disturbing rumor circulating that you have died."

"I don't think I'm dead. What are they saying?"

"Clearly Mr. Cabrelli, you are very much alive. I do not choose to participate in gossip about you and your situation. I do not care what brought you here. My only responsibility is caring for you while you are here."

"Nurse Holterman, please listen to me, just for one second. Just listen."

"Very well, go ahead."

"I have got to see Bill Presser. It is important to me. I need to see him. You make the rules. I'll handle it however you want it handled. Just let me see him."

She said nothing and just fixed him with that loving look of hers, kind of like an ice cube down your shirt.

"We'll see, Mr. Cabrelli. We'll see."

• • •

A day later, Bill Presser was ushered into the room by Nurse Holterman. He looked like a schoolboy being sent to the principal's office. He rolled his eyes, just as the nurse looked at him.

"Do you have an issue, Mr. Presser?" Nurse Holterman demanded.

"No ma'am, no issue at all."

"I thought not," she said.

"You may spend as much time with Mr. Cabrelli as I determine is consistent with best healthcare practices. If you choose to attempt to thwart my authority or ignore my orders, I will make absolutely certain that you will never enter this hospital again, unless it is for emergency surgery. Are we clear?"

Both Cabrelli and Presser nodded their heads at the same time.

Nurse Holterman did a crisp about-face and left the room.

"Jeez, John, sounds like you're in for a long haul. I heard them say they're going to have to operate on you again to get that second bullet out. You do look a little better though, I mean compared to the last time I saw you. Is there anything I can do?"

"Yeah. Sit down and get ready. We have a lot of ground to cover." ∎

CHAPTER 7
Cabrelli

I went to the mailbox. It was a warm sunny day. I got a letter from Derek Anderson, Attorney at Law, 115 Main St., Musky Falls, Wisconsin. The letter stunned me.

Dear Mr. Cabrelli,

I am the legal counsel for Nicholas John Cabrelli, now deceased. I have been charged with the execution of his will. Mr. Cabrelli has named you as his sole heir. Please contact me at your earliest convenience.

Sincerely,

Derek Anderson, Attorney at Law

Uncle Nick was not really my uncle. He was like my father's cousin or something. He had lived on a lake in Musky Falls for as long as I could remember. We had often gone there in the summer when I was a kid, swimming, fishing, running around in his boat. He was a good guy. He had been married to Aunt Rose since they were kids. They didn't have any children. Uncle Nick was some sort of engineer and had moved to Musky Falls to work for a forest products company.

I used to love it up there. The air smelled so good. Aunt Rose would make these cinnamon rolls that would melt in your mouth. I can still smell them. After my father died, we had lost contact. A few years ago, I was in the area and stopped by his place. No one was around, so I left a note but never heard anything back. I figured that if I was his sole heir, then Aunt Rose must have also passed away.

I've got to be honest. After I got the letter I was kind of excited. I felt guilty about feeling that way, but it was how I felt. I had always enjoyed my time with Uncle Nick and Aunt Rose, but they hadn't been part of my current life for many years. They had had a good run living, I was sure, well into their eighties, although I didn't know how long ago Rose had died.

They had a small but very nice house, kind of like a log cabin but with squared timbers for the walls. The thing I remembered best about the house was the fireplace. The kitchen and living room were all one area. The centerpiece was a huge fireplace that Uncle Nick had built himself with smooth round stones he had collected in the area. Even on our summer trips up to Musky Falls it sometimes got pretty cool at night, so we took full vocal advantage of our discomfort to get Uncle Nick to build a fire. As soon as the fire was going, Aunt Rose would bring out a covered pan with a long handle filled with popcorn, which we'd shake as we held it over the fire. Boy, I loved sitting in front of that fire munching popcorn with Uncle Nick telling me stories about the Northwoods, his and my favorite being those that involved close encounters with bears. I even saw a bear right in his yard one morning. I had gotten up early to go fishing when I heard a loud noise back by the trash cans. I went and took a look, to be met head on by a huge black bear. I was sure he weighed at least 1,000 pounds. Uncle Nick was on my heels as I went out, and he yelled at the bear. It sauntered off into the woods. He told me that I needed to be careful.

"Black bears will leave you alone most of the time. They are as afraid of you as you are of them. That is unless they feel like they are cornered. When they feel cornered even a yearling cub like that one can do some real damage."

I took exception to the description of this behemoth as a yearling cub; clearly Uncle Nick's vision was failing.

Now that I was thinking about it, some of my best childhood memories centered around a visit to Musky Falls.

●●●

I called Laura and told her what I had received from Counselor Anderson. She was excited for me.

"John, some of these northern lake properties in Wisconsin are worth a fortune. The market is driven by buyers from the Twin Cities, Milwaukee, and Madison. I have a friend who's been trying to buy a place up north for a least a year. Nice places on good lakes are hard to come by."

"Well, I'm going to take a few days and go up to see this guy, check the place out, and see what he has to say."

"Do that. It would be good for you to take some time off. We don't really have anything pressing until the Crather case comes up in two weeks. Take all the time you need."

I started packing my zippy little sports car five minutes later. I looked high and low through my clothes, and other than blue pressed jeans, one flannel shirt, and a Swiss Army knife, I didn't have much in the way of backwoods gear. And if I do say so myself, I had become a little more in tune with fashion. So even though I put on the jeans, I also slipped on my custom Italian loafers and headed out the door. I figured what the hell, it's not like I am going bushwhacking. I am going to meet with a lawyer; my loafers would do just fine.

So on a sunny day in mid-June, I headed off on the interstate toward Eau Claire. The trip was uneventful. I watched my speed pretty closely. Troopers don't have the same sense of humor regarding speeding that city and county cops do.

I had not taken this trip in a long time, and as I traveled along, fond memories of days long past flooded back. Days of pure innocence and happiness. Swimming in the lake, fishing for muskies, sitting by the fire at night. In everybody's life there are those places and memories that bring comfort. This was certainly mine. At Eau Claire, I jumped on Highway 53 North toward Superior. What I remembered as a narrow meandering Northwoods road had been widened to four lanes and a 65 mile-per-hour speed limit. Had it all changed? In my absence, had the north country succumbed to the urban pressure, turning quiet roads into super highways? Unfamiliar businesses lined up as box containers filled strip mall after strip mall. What I recall as small white signs with pointing arrows had become big green signs: "Exit 89 Jim Falls."

About an hour later, I turned east onto the old St. Croix River Highway. The road narrowed and slowed. Within five miles, I had been transported from the rush of super travel to the scenic beauty of Northern Wisconsin. A road sign read "Musky Falls 22 miles." I crossed the fast flowing Namekagon River, a river in which I had fished for trout as a boy with my uncle. I used to love wading into the current in my shorts and tennis shoes, feeling the press of the water against my legs. Walking along the river seemed like a trip through the uncharted wilderness. No one for miles, the river all my own, fish waiting to be caught.

The Northwoods of Wisconsin, while changed, remained largely intact. The integrity of the landscape had been protected by acts of Congress creating the Chequamegon-Nicolet National Forest. In addition, thousands of acres had been protected in perpetuity by state land purchase. Northern Wisconsin, a place so special, people from across the country had seen fit to protect it. I always thought it was pretty cool that Minnesota had the "Land of 10,000 Lakes" on their license plate, yet Wisconsin is home to 15,000 lakes. Maybe more importantly, Wisconsin had the Packers, and Minnesota was stuck with the lowly Vikings.

I pulled into Musky Falls at about 1:30, just in time to meet Counselor Anderson on Main Street at the Fisherman Bar and Grill for lunch, just as we'd arranged. Parking a couple of blocks away, I walked past the shops to the restaurant. As I passed the fudge shop, I couldn't help but stop in front and watch what appeared to be the same old gal I remembered, still stirring fudge in two big copper bowls both at the same time. I am not much for sweets, but, God, I love that homemade fudge. I could eat it by the pound. Many of the stores had changed; Main Street Bait and Tackle was now the Irish store. However, the flavor of the town remained the same.

• • •

Musky Falls was a community of 2,500 people, a population which, during the summer months, grew to 25,000. They came from Madison, Minneapolis, Chicago, and Milwaukee to escape their self-imposed prisons of constant movement. Never enough, never fast enough, never enough time to stop and smell the roses, people wishing their lives away, looking forward to retirement only to find they no longer had the will to slow down.

I was definitely that guy. I loved the fast-paced life—something happening, danger, challenge—first as a cop, then as an investigator for a lawyer. High speed, intense, make it happen. Carry a gun, be ready for anything, be tough, be the man, be ready.

For whatever reason, for the first time in many years, I felt the weight of my chosen life bear down on me as I walked down Main Street in Musky Falls, Wisconsin. I knew then and there I could walk away, should walk away, from leading the life I no longer needed or wanted. It was time for a change, time to regroup, time to make decisions about the next half of my life. No bullshit. I decided this all in two blocks. John Cabrelli was moving on. ∎

FIGURE EIGHT. A NORTHERN LAKES MYSTERY

CHAPTER 8
Cabrelli

I walked into the Fisherman Bar and Grill. This was the perfect Northwoods restaurant with mounted wildlife covering the walls interspersed with hunting and fishing artifacts. Several people were sitting at the long wooden bar, and most had tap beers sitting in front of them. I found Attorney Anderson at a back table. I pegged him immediately as a lawyer, kind of slick looking, big fish in a small pond sort of guy. He looked forty or fifty—hard to tell, every hair in place and exactly the same color, wearing high-end golf casual clothes. I walked up to his table.

"John?" he inquired.

"Yeah, John Cabrelli, at your service."

"Glad to meet you. I hope you had a pleasant trip. I know the traffic from Madison to Eau Claire can be a beast."

"The traffic wasn't bad," I responded. "As a matter of fact, it was a very pleasant drive. Lots of things have changed since my last trip up. Lots of things have remained the same."

"This remains a unique paradise. People from big cities have moved in and driven lakefront property values through the ceiling. Once they're here, they fight like crazy to prevent the next guy from building. Time and again, they come here and try to close the door behind them. The tougher they make it for the next guy, the higher values become on existing properties, like your uncle's Spider Lake property, for example. Your uncle expressed to me many times that he couldn't believe how much his property is worth. Yes, indeed, you have inherited a real gold mine."

The lawyer had a look on his face kinda like a fisherman who had just put out a baited hook and leaned back in his chair, waiting to see what John would say.

"I guess I never really thought about it being valuable until a friend of mine mentioned that lake properties had become scarce."

"Not only is your property valuable, but I also have very, very good news. I have with me an offer to purchase the property. An out-of-state buyer has offered the appraised value for the property with no contingencies. As a matter of fact, he can close on it within thirty days after you accept the offer," the lawyer said.

With that, the good counselor pulled out the offer and dropped it in front of me. He pointed to the top line, and I almost gasped. When people said the property was valuable, I hadn't even considered the possibility that it meant seven figures. But there they were, right in front of me.

Cops, like myself, are very clever at remaining in control in the face of the unforeseen. Basically whirling on the inside while remaining cool on the outside. I have got to say though, it was hard. Here in front of me was a million and a half bucks. I would be set for life, see the world, no worries. It was dazzling. It was also clear that Attorney Anderson fully expected to dazzle me with the flourish with which he delivered the offer. Another lesson in the book of lessons I will someday write: Never make the deal in the room the first time you see it. If it is a straight deal, it will be there tomorrow. Take your time.

"That is impressive, Counselor. I'll take it and look it over and let you know," I said.

"I wouldn't let this offer linger too long. I know this buyer is looking at a number of properties in the area. If you don't act quickly enough, this opportunity may be lost."

He handed me a menu and said he was going to have the Fisherman burger, a Leinenkugel's on tap, and a side of deep-fried cheese curds.

The waitress walked up, and we just had her double the order. "You know, John, that property is really something. However, if you choose not to sell it to this buyer, I think you might have a hard time finding someone else willing to pay top dollar, even though lake properties are hard to find on any lake much less one of this quality, a Class A musky lake to boot. I would be more than willing to handle the details of the sale. We could finish up the legal paperwork today, and tomorrow you could return home, get on with your normal life, and just leave all the details to me."

"Again, let me thank you for looking out for my interests. I am not in any hurry to return home. After lunch, I want to take the keys and go out to the place and take a stroll down memory lane," I said.

"Well, I wouldn't want you to be disappointed. I'm afraid the place is in a state of disrepair. Your uncle was in an area nursing home for some time before he died. Your aunt Rose had died a couple of years before this, and there was no one to take care of the place."

"Attorney Anderson," I started.

"Please call me Derek."

"Okay, Derek. What exactly happened to my aunt and uncle?"

"Your aunt died, I think, two years ago in February. She was a wonderful gal. Everybody in town just loved her. She was the first one to volunteer to help when help was needed. She ran the hospital charity event every year for as long as I can remember. She even wrote a little column, *News from Spider Lake*, every once in a while for the local newspaper. She reported on the happenings of the area: who was visiting family; who was sick; elk, wolf, and bear sightings. Everyone got a kick out of that column. As I remember, she had been feeling poorly for several months and finally decided to go to the doctor. It was cancer, advanced. She was gone within a few months. I think your aunt was 82, but she didn't look a day over 60. I believe she's buried over at the Town of Spider Lake Cemetery. I can find out for you."

"Thanks. I would appreciate that. What about my uncle Nick?"

"Now your uncle. There was a different sort. He was a brilliant engineer. As a matter of fact, he held over a dozen patents for innovations in the timber industry. One, which by the way was sold on a royalty basis, produces income each month. In fact, that process and the machines that make it happen are used in over half of all the papermaking companies in the world. I'll explain all this later. Like I said, your uncle was a different sort. Even after he retired, he was always working on something. Out at their place he built a huge shop area, heated and wired and the like. When he wasn't out hunting or fishing, he was in his shop working on something. He was friendly enough, but Rose was the social one. It must have worked because, as a couple, they got on great.

"As far as what happened to your uncle, he would take a walk every morning between 5:00 and 6:30 a.m., just like clockwork. He hiked along a trail that led through the woods along Spider Lake and ended up at the highway. He would walk across the highway and have a cup of coffee at the Spider Cafe, chew the fat for a while, and then head back home down the trail. He was crossing the road one morning just like always when a truck came out of nowhere and ran him down. Everyone was pretty sure it was an accident. Some tourist driving too fast, but the driver didn't stay around. The sheriff investigated and ..."

"Two Fishermen burgers, two Leinies, and two orders of deep-fried cheese curds. Can I get you gentlemen anything else?"

"Nope, that will be fine, Amanda," answered Derek for both of us. "Dig in, John. This is the best burger in Wisconsin."

I couldn't believe what I was hearing.

"Wait a minute, Derek. Are you telling me that my uncle Nick died from vehicular homicide, a hit and run?"

"Not right away. He survived the accident but was badly injured. After they let him out of the hospital, he was transferred to an after-care center, kind of like a nursing home. I am afraid he didn't last long after that. One night his heart failed, and that was it."

"So, you said the sheriff investigated. What did he find?"

"I'll tell you what, John, let's eat these burgers and curds before they get cold and drink these Leinies before they get warm. Then we'll go to my office, and I'll answer any questions I can. If you want, we can call the sheriff up and get a copy of the accident report."

So we dined on what turned out to be a great burger, and Derek filled me in on how people had been doing fishing and on general news of the area. He talked to me like a local would talk to a tourist, general chit-chat, not much substance. The fishing was good; people were getting some nice walleyes. Muskies had been spotty, but people have been catching them. He hadn't heard of anyone getting any really big fish. He told me that the Musky Falls area was a great place to visit, but a tough area to live in year round.

"It's a great place, but winter brings three things that send a fair number of would-be residents back to where they came: snow, cold and no winter jobs. That's why I am so excited about the offer to purchase your property. Not many folks around here can come up with that kind of money. It is a real opportunity for you."

After lunch, Derek suggested we adjourn to his office and go over the details of Uncle Nick's will.

I responded, "Actually, Counselor, I would really rather go see the place, if you don't mind."

"No, no that's fine. I just don't want you to expect too much. I was not hired to be a caretaker, and you know how quickly a place runs down after it sits empty. I've got the keys with me, and I'd be glad to drive you out."

"Tell you what. Why don't I follow you out in my car? That way you can head back when you need to."

• • •

We drove east out of Musky Falls past, of all things, a gigantic Walmart store. They truly are taking over the world. A mile past that joint and the beauty of the area again unfolded before me. It was a beautiful Northwoods day. I couldn't help but put the window down. The air was fresh and clean, full of piney scents that triggered wonderful memories of times past. The two-lane highway was full of curves and hills bordered on each side by the dense woods and wetlands of Northern Wisconsin. It looked the same as it had in my youth, pretty and unspoiled. I remember as a kid looking off into those woods, thinking they probably never ended. As a matter of fact, Uncle Nick told me you could walk straight north to Lake Superior and never cross anything more than a fire lane cut into the forest.

We passed the Spider Lake church and took a left on the next road. It was a narrow stretch that meandered through the woods and crossed Spider Creek. The driveway was marked by two stone pillars about four feet high built by Uncle Nick. A sign hanging from a wrought iron frame read "Nirvana" and underneath it "Cabrelli." As I drove down the long driveway toward the house, I was a kid all over again, with the same excited feelings. I wanted to jump in the lake, take the boat out and cast for muskies, pop popcorn over the fire, listen to the sounds of the night through the screen of the window by the bed where I slept.

We pulled up in front of the house. Based on what Derek Anderson had told me about no caretaker, I had expected the place to be overgrown. That was not the case—the yard was neat, and there was no evidence of any disrepair. In fact, except for a few zillion pine cones and needles, the place was immaculate. Off to the side was a big steel sided building with colors that matched the house down to the shutters. It looked to be at least 40' x 60', and I guessed right that it was my uncle's shop.

We got out, and I took off around the house to the lake side. There it was, the sparkling expanse of Little Spider Lake, one end of a chain of lakes. It was even prettier than I remembered. Out on the water a guy was drifting along in his boat, casting the shoreline for hidden behemoths. It was like a scene from a painting. I walked down to the shore and out onto the dock. Blue flag iris in the height of bloom grew from the shore, while white and yellow lilies covered the water. The air was permeated with the smell of sweet fern, the perfume of the north.

I was just staring, taking it all in, just wanting to saturate myself with all before me, when the lawyer piped up, "It is a beautiful spot, John. Like I told you before, there are not many properties around like this anymore. The offer you have is very good, and I don't think we'll have any problem turning this into cash. You can sell this and head back to your life in the city with a solid nest egg. Yes you could."

At that point, Anderson had begun to become a significant irritation. I just wanted him to go. I needed to be alone and share this moment with myself and my memories.

"Counselor, I appreciate you coming out here with me and all your help, but I just want to look through the place by myself. I'll let you know what I decide about selling when I decide about selling. Right now I just want to be here."

"I have a very light schedule today. I'd be glad to stay with you and help you go through the place. I can show you what all the keys are for. You know, just give you a hand."

"Counselor, that won't be necessary. I will figure this out myself. Thanks anyway."

"Your uncle would have wanted me to stay and help. I wouldn't want to let him down."

"Were you a good friend of my uncle?"

"Well, everybody knew him. Like I said, he kind of kept to himself. He was a man who valued his privacy."

"That didn't answer my question. Was he a friend of yours? You know, a guy you went out of your way to say hello to?"

"Your aunt was a sweetheart. Everybody loved her, that's for sure, but your uncle was kind of a difficult man. Friendly enough, but not the easiest guy to get along with. He was very demanding, wanted things his way. I remember the dog he had, a big old Chesapeake. Every time I stopped out here that dog just glared at me like it was waiting for me to move wrong. It was friendly to most everybody else. He and the dog were kind of alike."

"Derek, do you have any kids?"

"What, kids? Er ... no I don't. The truth is, I don't like kids all that much."

Uncle Nick had taught me a lesson long ago: kids and dogs are one of the best indicators of character. If kids or dogs don't like someone or if someone doesn't like kids or dogs, watch out. I got the keys and sent Attorney Anderson on his way, promising to catch up with him later.

As the noise of his car disappeared, I stood silently. The silence was beautiful, broken not by the honking of horns or cars vibrating with rap as their owners speed on the way to joining the ranks of the hearing impaired. Bird songs and the distant putter of an outboard motor were the only sounds, blending into the landscape.

I knew I was putting off the inevitable and walked up to the back door of the house. I looked through the bail of keys Anderson had given me, and I found one marked back door. The trained investigator I am deduced that this would likely fit in the lock and grant me entry to a place so special. I was a little apprehensive. I did not want to burst the bubble. You know how sometimes those things that are most special to you turn out to be not what they seem. I remember one time when I was young, there was this kid's TV show that was on Saturday morning. I thought the guy was the coolest thing since sliced bread, and then I found out he was arrested in an adult theater. Definitely an image dimmer.

• • •

As I opened the door and walked in, I saw that little had changed. The truth was that although my buddy Derek had told me the place was not kept up, it was as neat as a pin. Windows clean, floors swept, no dust anywhere, and it smelled like flowers, gently sweet but not overbearing. It was as I remembered. The stone fireplace dominated the main room. I had helped Uncle Nick collect many of the stones along Lake Superior the summer he had rebuilt it. Each stone was like a piece of a puzzle; each stone fit into a special place. The wood rack that sat next to the fireplace was filled with white birch, neatly split and stacked, ready to take the edge off the first hint of winter blasts.

In front of the hearth was a big old stuffed chair with a footstool covered with fabric that depicted bears, deer, and wolves. Next to that chair was a rocker made of cherry, the arms worn shiny. I could see my aunt as she rocked back and forth, always busy, mending something, cleaning wild blueberries, or reading. I could see her and Uncle Nick by the fire on a cold winter night. Partners forever, content with life, watching the fire dance as the winter wind howled outside the large picture window.

I remember once I went fishing with Uncle Nick in the late fall. I had reached over to pull my lure where it had stuck in a tree along the shore. I fell over the side up to my neck in fresh, freezing lake water. Uncle Nick pulled me out and gave me his coat, but we still had a long boat ride home. By the time I got out on the dock my teeth were chattering. We went inside and Aunt Rose was quick to get me some dry clothes and throw another log on the fire. "Johnny," my uncle said, "you can never understand the value of a warm fire until you have been really cold." I will never forget how good that fire felt.

The kitchen was off in one corner divided from the living room by a big table whose top was made of pine planks pinned together and finished to a satin sheen. Eight chairs surrounded the table, two at the end showing a little more wear than the others. How many stories told and dinners eaten by people sitting around this table, I could only guess.

It had been a long day, and I decided to sit in Uncle Nick's chair just for a minute. The chair welcomed me with its softness, and the footstool beckoned me to take off my fancy shoes and put my feet up. I could hear a light breeze stirring outside and only gave passing thought to why the window would be open before I fell asleep. ■

CHAPTER 9
Cabrelli

I slept the sleep of those at peace, something I rarely enjoyed. I was dreaming of swimming through the lily pads, dive mask on my face, trying to catch a glimpse of the ever-elusive giant musky that lived off the dock.

I was brought back to reality by a kick that knocked my feet from the footstool and brought me instantly awake. Old habits die hard as I leaped up, ready for whatever. I stopped cold when I saw the two huge holes at the end of a double barrel shotgun pointed directly at my head.

A voice yelled with menace, "If you don't sit back down right now, I am going to blow your head off."

So I sat.

"What are you doing in my house? Who are you? What do you want?" the voice asked.

As the sleep left my eyes, I began to focus and saw that I was faced by a woman who was holding a shotgun rock solid, her finger on one of the triggers. There was absolutely no doubt in my mind that she would shoot me if I didn't comply.

Again she demanded, "Who are you? What do you want?"

"Give me a chance to answer, and I will, but I'm afraid that if I even breathe you're going to shoot me."

"Start talking. Just don't move anything but your lips."

"First of all, I think this is actually my house, not yours. Second, what I was doing here was sleeping in this chair. My name is John Cabrelli. This used to be my Uncle Nick and Aunt Rose's place."

"John Cabrelli? Your name is John Cabrelli? Let me see your driver's license."

"It's in my wallet in my back pocket. I'll be glad to get it out, but I don't want to do anything that's going to make that shotgun go off."

"Shut up and get it out. Just don't try anything."

As I moved my hand toward my back pocket, I could see her tense. She was intent on her purpose, but I sensed she was also scared, a bad combination. All she had to do was jerk that trigger and my head would cease to exist. I got my wallet out and handed it toward her.

"Throw it on the table."

Again, I was glad to comply.

She wasn't taking any chances and walked around to the other side of the table before reaching for the wallet, keeping the table between me and her. I sat as still as I could. If her goal was to shoot me, I would have already been dead. There was something else going on. I hoped if I could bide my time and let things tone down a little, I could try to use my innate charm to try and defuse the situation.

She looked down at my wallet and up at me. Then down again, up again. Then she just stood there staring at my face.

I took a chance, "Look, I don't think you want to shoot me, and I know for sure I don't want to be shot. Why don't you put the gun down and you and I have a conversation? Try to sort this thing out. You can always decide to shoot me later after you've heard me out."

"I am not putting the gun down, so if you have something to say, start talking."

I told her my story, and I could see that she believed me; her shoulders relaxed a little, and her finger moved off the trigger. When I finished, she looked at me with what appeared to be disgust and said, "John Cabrelli, the prodigal son returns."

"Actually, kind of a nephew, but yes, I have returned."

"Yeah, to pick the bones of Nick and Rose. I should just shoot you anyway, probably do the world a favor."

"Maybe it would be a plus for the world, but I would appreciate it if you didn't." I continued, "You know my name now. Any chance you would share yours?'

"Julie, Julie Carlson."

With that, she put the gun down on the table and headed toward the kitchen. She reached into a cabinet and took out some tea, filled a pot with water, and put it on the stove to boil, moving around like she owned the place.

"Would you like some tea?"

"I would, if you don't mind. Is it okay for me to get up now?"

"Get up, do whatever. After all, like you said, it's your house."

It was my first meeting with the indomitable Ms. Carlson. A woman unlike any other I have ever met. Beautiful blue eyes that could spit fire. Slim, fit, durable. Pretty but in a way that would not land her on the cover of Vogue. She was a better kind of pretty. Healthy with just a sprinkle of freckles across the bridge of her nose, with blonde hair pulled back in a ponytail. Her jeans and flannel shirt attire the perfect match.

We sat facing each other. She added milk and some honey to her tea, stirring it slowly. The tea tasted like it was brewed from lawn grass, but I decided to drink it anyway. We didn't say anything. At one point she got up and grabbed the shotgun, only to place it in a corner by the back door, the same resting place used by Uncle Nick. Now that the potential prowler had been neutralized, the steam seemed to be leaving her, and by looking at her face, I could see that she definitely had something on her mind.

"Julie, right? Can I call you Julie?

"That is my name. Most people I know are called by their name."

"I meant Ms. or Mrs. Just forget it."

"What are you doing here so soon, Mr. Cabrelli? No one told me you were coming."

"John, call me John. First, I want to apologize. I had no idea that anyone would be here. In fact, the lawyer told me the place was deserted and kind of run down."

That got her fired up again. "Deserted?! I have been living here for over three years. Run down! Does this place look run down!? I take care of this house and property like I would if it were mine. Maybe it just doesn't meet your pavement and city slick standards, but we work hard at it. Derek Anderson absolutely knew I was living here. Otherwise, why would he give me notice to move out by next Friday? He said that you had sold the property to some big shot rich guy from the cities, and they were moving in heavy equipment to demolish the place. You were taking the money and running back to the city."

It took me some time to digest this, and I stared out the front window at the lake for a minute or two before I said anything. "I see, but let me set the record straight. I have never heard of you or met this lawyer before today. First, I don't even know what I have inherited, and second, I don't think I have sold anything to anyone. I don't know anything about a rich guy from the cities, heavy equipment demolition, or anything else."

Her ire began rising. "I am just telling you what I was told, and by the looks of that fancy little car and those ... ugh shoes, you probably are itching to sell the place and get out of here before you step in a puddle. I mean that's what you're going to do, isn't it? Well, isn't it?" Steam was rolling again. "And for the record, I am living here until next Friday when I will gladly get off your land, but not until then. So, I would appreciate it if you would get out of my house, get back in your car, and go. I have grading and work to do."

She was getting so worked up I couldn't help but keep glancing over at the shotgun, ready to make a dive for it before she did.

"Please, Julie, just take a breath. There's no need to get all wound up again. Here is what I'm going to do. I will get in my car and head back to town. I am going to check into the hotel and take a breather. Tomorrow I'm going to meet with the lawyer and get this thing figured out. Clearly there are some questions I need answered. After I meet with him, is there any chance you and I could get together to discuss what I find out?"

"No, well yes, no. What do I care? I have to get my work done and keep packing and get moved out of here before I get crushed along with this place by a gigantic bulldozer. Do whatever you want, just leave me alone. Your aunt and uncle would be ashamed of you if they knew you were tearing this place down. I hope they haunt you. They loved this place so much. They were such good people, and you show up with your fancy car and shoes and walk around like you're something special, making yourself at home in his chair. Who the hell do you think you are anyway?"

I could be wrong, but I was pretty sure I now saw steam coming out of her ears.

"Look, I'm leaving. Give me a phone number, and I'll call you when I find out what's going on. If you want to talk, answer. If not, don't."

She just stared, too mad or upset to hear anything.

"Julie, before I go, could I ask you one thing?"

"Whatever."

"Is that shotgun loaded?"

She looked at me like I was an idiot.

"Of course. What good is a shotgun that's not loaded?"

I went out the door and off the porch and walked toward my car. About halfway there I stepped in a puddle that went over the top of my beautiful Italian loafer. Crap. What a day. For some reason, as I drove out the driveway, I couldn't help but smile and wonder. John Cabrelli, what awaits you now?

With that, I drove back to Musky Falls, and I will admit that even though she had pointed a loaded shotgun at me, I was pretty intrigued by Julie Carlson.

I needed to find a place to stay and pulled into a motel that was in the shadow of a giant fiberglass musky and booked a room with no predicted checkout date. They offered continental breakfast, hot tub pool, exercise room, and a bar. The large lobby had comfy stuffed leather chairs set around a fireplace. I couldn't wait to lay back and close my eyes for a minute. Days like this were a little much. I headed up to my room and stretched out on the bed. As I was taking my shoes off, I noticed the puddle planted loafer had water stains. It was probably ruined. Sleep came quickly, and I slept through the night. I hadn't set an alarm or asked for a wake up call. I woke without either at 5:30 a.m.

I decided to go down to the pool and hot tub area, but then realized I didn't have a swimming suit along.

"Put that on the list," I muttered to myself.

I did, however, head down to take advantage of the breakfast bar. Even though it was early, the room was already half full. There were three older couples, and the rest of the occupants were rough and ready looking guys wearing boots, work shirts, jeans, and reflective vests that had Northern Mining Company emblazoned across the front and back.

The breakfast bar had regular, decaf, and gourmet coffee, scrambled eggs, sausage, bacon, and everything else on the list of foods not to eat as part of a healthy diet. I hesitated for only a moment before diving in and bellying up with the miners and eating my fill.

I had a third cup of coffee while sitting in one of those big leather chairs and picked up a copy of the *Namekagon County News*, the local newspaper. The headline read: "Locals Speak Out at Mining Hearing," and underneath it were the words: "Northern Wisconsin residents express concern about potential environmental impacts of a proposed mine. Do the risks outweigh the need for jobs?"

The article that followed briefly described the proposal. Northern Mining wanted to open an iron ore mine in Namekagon County. The mine was a huge operation and would impact thousands of acres of natural landscape. It would bring hundreds of good paying long-term jobs to an area that had about the highest unemployment rate in Northern Wisconsin. The mayor of Musky Falls called it a boon to the local economy. A local science teacher said it would be an environmental disaster. On and on. On the second page there was a map of the proposed mine area. I looked at it with little interest until I noted that it included the southwest corner of Spider Lake and all the property around it. If I was not mistaken, it included Uncle Nick and Aunt Rose's place—all of it plus some. Interesting.

I tried Attorney Anderson's cell, no answer. So I decided I would just stop by his office and see when we could meet. I drove up Main Street looking for an open parking spot. It is a one-way street, and all the stalls are angled to allow for maximum parking. The disadvantage of this arrangement is that when you are backing out, cars or trucks on either side of you tend to obstruct your view. Such was the case with a lifted crew cab, four-wheel drive truck that backed out into oncoming traffic, namely me. I stopped; he stopped, but not before we made minor contact. I got out of my car and walked up to the front to look at the damage. As I did, the truck driver met me. He was well over six feet tall and dressed in brown duck overalls and an old flannel shirt that did little to hide his massive upper body.

Not a man to tangle with unless all other forms of negotiation failed.

Instead of an attitude befitting his size, he blurted out, "Jeez, I'm sorry. I didn't see that little car. I've got insurance so don't worry. I'll take care of everything. I am really sorry, mister."

The American-made full-size 4x4 off-road crew cab pickup truck was a marvel of toughness and durability. This was further clearly evidenced today by the fact that while no damage was visible on the truck, my entire Japanese right front fender was smashed, and pieces of plastic littered the ground.

Cars had already begun to get jammed up behind us, so we moved the cars around the corner and out of the way. The truck driver showed me his driver's license, and I showed him mine. We agreed that a police report was not necessary and that I could call his insurance agent, who actually had an office in this block. As a matter of fact, he suggested, "Why don't we just walk down there and get this squared away right now?"

We did. The agent's office was in a small storefront between a rock shop and a jewelry store. The walls of the office were adorned with two huge whitetail deer buck mounts, with a mounted musky in between. A plaque beneath the fish read, "49 ½ inches Tiger Cat Flowage." There were also a number of plaques noting top sales years, donations supporting local causes, and a lifetime membership to Safari Club International, the Northern Wisconsin Chapter.

The receptionist greeted the truck driver, and he relayed the story to her. She got up, walked 10 feet to the inner office, and repeated the story to a hidden person inside. A minute later, she said, "Come on in. Dennis is ready for you."

Agent Dennis Targett reached his hand out to the truck driver now known to be Arvid "Bud" Treetall, and said, "Bud, what brings you in here?"

"Well, Dennis, I was backing out of a stall by the hardware store, and I didn't see his little car, and I backed into it. I am afraid I smashed in the fender pretty bad."

"Anyone hurt?"

"No, everybody is just fine," I replied.

"Any damage to your truck, Bud?'

"Nope, Dennis. Nothing I can see anyway."

"Well, let's go out and take a look."

We followed the insurance man out to the street. He walked around and looked at the car and truck from every possible angle. He squatted down and pulled at the pieces of my fender, causing more to drop to the ground. Then he took a few pictures. He turned around and asked us to follow him back into the office, and we did.

We sat down in his office, and he looked at me and asked for my driver's license. I gave it to him.

He looked down at the license, looked up at me, then repeated the same exercise.

"You're John Cabrelli. You must be Nick and Rose's son."

"More like their nephew," I replied.

"Jeez, Bud, not a very nice way to welcome your new boss to town. You see, John, Bud here is the caretaker and maintenance man for Nick and Rose," Dennis explained.

Bud gave me a big grin and reached out a huge paw to shake my hand. "I'm real glad to meet you, John. I knew you would be working your way this way one of these days. Nick and Rose were good people. I'm sorry about them passing on. It must make you feel pretty sad. My cousin Julie and I will miss them both," Bud said.

Dennis chimed in, "I heard they named you as their heir. They have a life insurance policy with me that names you as the beneficiary. I had planned on getting together with you when you came up. So we'll have to get to that, but you know, first things first. Let's take care of the matter at hand. Mr. Cabrelli, do you want to get your car fixed around here or get it done when you get back to Madison?"

"I'm not sure. When we drove the car and truck around the corner I could hear something rubbing on the tire. I should get that checked out before I drive anywhere."

"Okay then. I am going to give a call over to Musky Falls Autobody and see if they can take a look at it right now and give us a diagnosis. If it can't be driven home, we will be glad to get you a rental car to use in the meantime."

I took the car over to the shop, and the body man looked it over thoroughly before telling me that he didn't think I should drive the car. The front suspension had been damaged, and it could cause a serious problem if it let go. He sent me two blocks down the street to another garage where they could help me out with a rental.

"Just down the street is Bill and Jack's Garage and Guide Service. Talk to Doc O'Malley. He owns the place. He'll fix you up. I'll give him a call and tell him you're coming."

When I got there, I saw they had a ten- or so year-old Jeep Cherokee running in the lot. I walked up to a guy bent over the hood of a pickup truck.

"Hey there. The body shop guy sent me over."

He turned to face me with a big smile. The name tag on his shirt said "Bill."

"You must be the guy who just got his fancy sports car crunched," he said.

I put my hand out, "Hi, Bill. I'm John Cabrelli."

"Good to meet you, John, but my name is Steve. Most people just call me Doc. Guys down at the body shop said you needed a rental. This is the best we have. It's a little older, but it's clean and runs great."

The jeep did look all right, but I thought of the long drive back to Madison and all the running around I had to do and asked, "Is there a Hertz or Budget or something like that around where I could get something a little newer?"

"Sure there is," he replied, "about seventy miles northwest of here in Superior."

"I'll take the jeep."

"Keys are in it, and it's full of gas. Dennis said he would take care of the bill and paperwork, so you are good to go."

I got in the jeep and started to drive out when a squad car pulled across the driveway, blocking my exit.

The officer driving the car got out and started to walk toward me, while the guy I had rented the car from was also walking toward me. Then I saw him look up at the cop. He did an about-face and headed back into the garage. The cop was one of those hard-ass looking guys: buzz cut hair, attitude busting out at the seams, a swaggering walk.

"Can I help you, Officer?" I asked.

He came to a stop right in front of me and just looked. "Are you John Cabrelli?"

"I am."

"You the one that inherited your uncle's place out on Spider Lake?"

Normally when I am faced with a line of inquiry similar to this I tend to shut up and go on my way. But pissing off the local cops the second day in town is probably not the best idea, so I went along, and answered.

"Yes."

"I heard you were in town." Small towns. Bless them.

"Yeah, I came up to meet with my uncle and aunt's lawyer at his request. I'm still trying to understand the whole thing."

"Are you planning on staying around long?"

"I can't really tell you that. Like I said, this is my second day here, and I'm just trying to get my feet under me. As a matter of fact, I was just on my way to talk to my lawyer and set something up for tomorrow when I got in a fender bender."

"Heard about the accident, you and Bud Treetall. Sounds like there wasn't enough damage to be reportable, but I'm curious, based on your background and all, why didn't you call it in and get an officer to take a report?"

"It didn't seem necessary with Bud's insurance man being so close and Bud's ready admission of fault. I thought about it but decided against it. Just didn't want to add complications."

"Are you sure it wasn't because you didn't want the local cops to know you were in town?"

So now this guy has said "based on my background," so he knew something about me, and was suggesting that I had reason to avoid local cops. He definitely had something going on.

"To be honest with you, local cops never crossed my mind."

"Really? I heard you were looking for a copy of the report about the hit and run on your uncle. Sounds like you are interested in local law enforcement efforts to me."

The guy definitely had something going on, and now was not the time or place to pursue it.

"I was just curious. This is the first I heard about the accident, and that it was a contributory cause of his death. Thought I would just do some reading. It is public record, right? Look, Officer," I looked at his name badge, "Officer Lawler, if you got nothing more for me, I would like to get going."

"You can go. Just stay out of trouble while you're here, or you will be seeing me again."

"Wouldn't want that," I replied. He got back in his car and drove out, giving me a cute little wave as he passed.

I had, to that point, only one conversation with one person about the death of Uncle Nick and the police report. Kids and dogs are rarely wrong.

I drove back over to my lawyer's office and caught Anderson just as he was walking out the door.

"Mr. Cabrelli, how did your time go at your uncle and aunt's house?"

"It was very interesting. I was sitting in my uncle's chair and was accosted by an attractive woman that took exception to me being in the house and made it clear that she wanted me to be gone. Her name is—"

"Oh my God, Julie Carlson, good Lord. I thought she had already moved out. She is nothing but trouble," he continued. "She is just a temporary tenant. Julie Carlson is a local teacher of sorts, who teaches ne'er-do-wells and hoodlums in a special school just this side of the reservation. Your aunt and uncle used to volunteer at the school, and somewhere along the way, she convinced them to rent her the small cabin out back of the main house. I'm sure she didn't pay them much, if anything. The next I knew it, she had moved into the main house and was doing chores and other menial tasks for the Cabrellis. Nick wanted her to stay on after he went to the nursing home and keep the place up. She's really not much better than a squatter, and if she is not out of there by tomorrow, I will take legal action and have the sheriff throw her out. I am sorry you had to deal with her. I'm sure it was difficult."

"Derek, forget the sheriff for now. I need to talk to her first."

"You'll get nowhere talking to that one. She is nothing but trouble and has a real temper to boot. Anyone dares take exception to the behavior of one of her little juvenile delinquents, and look out. My advice to you is to steer clear of her."

Clearly Attorney Anderson was no fan of Julie Carlson. "Derek, how about we set a time to get together and go over all the paperwork you have, spend some time bringing me up to speed on what I inherited, what my obligations are, and so forth."

"I am free all morning. How about now?"

"Works for me."

"Well come on in and have a seat in my office. My receptionist is out today, but I would be glad to make an attempt at brewing up some coffee, if you would like."

"No thanks, Counselor. I am coffeed out for the moment."

• • •

I have always thought you could learn a lot about somebody by what they hang on the wall of their home or office. Dennis Targett was a fisherman and hunter and a successful insurance man, all evidenced by the décor. His office furniture was not fancy, but he had a desk and comfortable chairs. Derek Anderson's office was a different deal altogether. His desk was huge and looked like some kind of antique. The chairs were leather adorned with brass studs. The walls had framed diplomas and pictures of Anderson with several different groups of, I assumed, dignitaries. One I recognized as the Wisconsin governor. There were also two plaques placed conspicuously, both acclaiming in polished wood and brass what an all-around good guy he was.

"Nice desk," I said.

"It should be; it cost a small fortune. There is a company in Superior that makes furniture from logs they retrieve off the bottom of Lake Superior. I ordered it as a reward to myself after a successful deal I put together. You have to take those rewards when you can along the way."

He sat in his desk chair and I in one of the fancy leather ones facing him.

As he looked for my file he said, "I heard about the accident. I hope they can get your car fixed soon so you can go about your business and be on your way. I know the fellas at the body shop, and I will phone them and tell them to give your car top priority."

"Thanks, Counselor, I appreciate that, but I think I will be fine with the jeep for a while."

"Well then, let's get down to business. There are three major parts of your uncle and aunt's estate. First, there is combined cash and securities of just over $219,000. There are also royalties from his patented invention that come in at about $5,000 per month in a structured buyout agreement that has several more years to run. That has a value of $300,000. There is a buyout clause as part of the agreement should your uncle Nick or his heirs decide to cash out. It would be 75% of the value and is payable in 30 days after the notice is filed.

"The biggest asset is the property. Here is a map of the holdings. There are several parcels of land involved, all contiguous. Over the course of his life, when a next-door property would come available, your uncle was a ready buyer. The total is 240 acres. It is kind of an odd-shaped parcel, much longer than it is wide. Much of that is wasteland, you know wetlands and such, not much value there. Some is forest land and contains marketable timber but has not been managed in years. The most valuable parcel is the water frontage along Spider Creek and Spider Lake. As you know, it is a beautiful secluded spot, the kind of property people will pay for. If you were to use comparable sales to determine a value, it would become difficult in that not many properties like this are sold. However, $1.5 million is at the top end of value, so the offer you received is very generous, and you can see why I'm anxious for you to seize this opportunity. If we cashed this all out, you could walk away with about two million dollars after fees and such. A man like you could do a lot with that kind of money."

"Who is the buyer?"

"Well, that is the hard part here. I actually don't know. He, or I guess it could be she for that matter, is represented by a law firm from Minneapolis. It's a very prestigious small firm that has the reputation of serving high-end clients. People like that often want to remain out of the spotlight. I assume that is probably the case here. The Community Bank here in town has, however, been able to confirm that what they say is true, that they have funds on deposit to draw from to pay for the property. They have the money, and they are ready to go forward."

"What are their plans for the property? Are they going to keep the buildings?"

"I don't know, and I don't think you should worry about it. Those buildings are old, and although they look very quaint, they are a maintenance headache. No one wants to spend all their time fixing up old buildings. Once you sell the property, you don't have to worry about it again. You can head back home a millionaire and resume your life."

At some point, even the most casual observer would note that almost everyone I had met so far in Musky Falls was anxious to see me return home as soon as possible. I was getting the feeling that this was not the friendly town that I'd remembered. Then again, maybe it was just me they didn't like.

"Derek, I need to ask you something else. Julie Carlson said—" Anderson cut me off.

"Oh my, not her again. Anything she says has little credibility in my book. She is the last person I would waste time listening to."

"Just humor me. She said that this was all a done deal. They were moving heavy equipment in next week to bulldoze the place. Where would she get that impression?"

Attorney Anderson started to look a little ruffled.

"Mr. Cabrelli, I don't know what she is talking about. This is a small town and rumors run rampant. If you are smart, you will take this offer and run. In my opinion, it would be very foolish to turn this down."

"Let me ask you another question about the property. I saw a map in the newspaper of the proposed mine area. It included Uncle Nick and Aunt Rose's property. You know anything about that?"

His ruffled look worsened, and he began to sweat.

"Those maps are on such a large scale when they are printed in the newspapers that the boundaries often cover areas that are not in the planned acquisition zone. It is impossible to judge by the newspaper what lands are in or out of the proposed mine area."

"Could you get a copy of the real map? An accurate one, big enough that we can tell whether or not this property is part of the mine?"

At this point his face took on a strained look, and his voice changed to almost a snarl. The normally cool and friendly lawyer lost his cool and friendly attitude.

"Sell the damned property, Mr. Cabrelli! Let's get this over with! I don't have time for this. Just sell and be done with it. If you don't, you will wish you had."

The last part came out more like a threat than good advice from my lawyer.

A second later he was back to his old self. Every hair in place and a 100-watt capped-tooth smile.

"John, I am sorry. That was uncalled for. I didn't get much sleep last night. Really, I am just trying to do the best for you, that's all. Your welfare and future are my only concern."

"Well, thanks for that, Derek. I'm going to head out now for a while."

"What about the property sale?" he asked, clearly exasperated.

"I'll get back to you."

"When, John? When can I expect to hear from you?"

"Soon," I responded. "Very soon."

I walked out and, unknown to me at the time, stepped off the cliff into the abyss. ■

CHAPTER 10
Cabrelli

It was a beautiful day, and I decided to head out to the house.

However, before going, it was clear that a wardrobe change might be in order. I stopped by the Fleet store where they had everything I needed. I found a comfy pair of boots, some work jeans, t-shirts, and a sweatshirt. I asked the clerk if I could change clothes in the changing room at the store and take the tags up to the checkout. She acted like she got this request all the time. Who knows? Maybe she did.

"Sure, no problem," she said.

At the register, they gave me a bag to put my other stuff in and then checked me out. The total for everything was slightly less than half of what I had paid for my Italian loafers. I left the store feeling pretty good, especially about my puddle-proof footwear. Truth be told, I couldn't wait to find a puddle in which to try them out.

I drove a couple more blocks, stopped at Crossroads Coffee, and got one for the road. I was set and took off down the highway. The jeep handled a lot differently than my little sports car did, but it had a substantial feel, sitting higher up, and a little whine from the mud and snow off-road tires went up and down with my speed. I kind of liked it. Trading Italian loafers for boots and a sports car for a jeep kind of made me feel a little more ... *manly*, I guess would be the word.

I pulled into my uncle's property and there, parked down by the lake, was a familiar crew cab pickup. The tailgate was open and *someone* was pounding on *something* with great exuberance. I walked over and was greeted by the smiling face of Bud Treetall. He was bent over a piece of boat dock and was trying to straighten out a bent leg.

"Hi, Mr. Cabrelli. I didn't think you would be up and out so soon. I knew this boat dock needed to be fixed and thought I would come out and get it done before you walked on it and had it tip over. I did the handyman work around here for your uncle whenever he needed help. Well, when he had the accident and went to the nursing home I just kinda kept things up. I had forgotten about the dock though and figured I better get it done. Even though I know you're going to bulldoze the place."

"That's very nice of you, Bud. How about if I hold that leg so you can get a better whack at it."

"That would help for sure."

So I held the leg while Bud wailed away at it, and eventually it was pretty straight. I helped him slip it back into the dock section, and we prepared to level it.

• • •

At that point Bud said, "Mr. Cabrelli, if you'll stand on the dock with this wrench, I'll get my waders on and get in the water. I'll lay this level on the deck. When it's level, just take the wrench and tighten the two hold bolts."

"You're going to lift me and the dock to level?"

"That's what I was thinkin' anyway."

"Wouldn't it be easier if I wasn't standing on the dock?"

"I suppose, but I don't think it'll matter much, and I only have one pair of waders, and I wouldn't want you to get all wet."

With that, I positioned myself on the dock, wrench at ready. He lifted me and the whole works up with no problem. Once we got it to level, I set the bolts and he climbed out.

"Bud, you are one helluva strong man. I couldn't have lifted me and that dock section together on my best day."

"Yeah, I guess I am. It sure comes in handy sometimes," he replied.

We headed back to the house, and I went to unlock the door. I knocked as loudly as I could to see if Julie Carlson was lurking inside waiting to give a blast of buckshot. No answer.

"If you're worried about Julie being home, forget it. She teaches during the day and doesn't get home usually until 4 or 4:30."

I reached to unlock the door and it swung open. It was already unlocked.

"Bud, you got keys to this place?"

"Yup, got keys for all the buildings."

"Did you unlock the house?"

"No, I didn't need to go up to the house. I had my tools with me and just went right to the dock. I wouldn't worry too much about it though. A lot of people around here don't lock their doors."

"Does Julie usually lock up?"

"I think she does pretty much all the time. Not that she has to worry. Anyone dumb enough to bother Julie would be making a big mistake."

We pushed the door open, and it was instantly clear we'd had a visitor. My uncle's desk drawers had all been emptied on the floor, and the desk was tipped over. Someone had then hacked away at the bottom and the frame leaving a pile of wood fragments.

"Jeez," said Bud, "someone smashed the shit out of your uncle's desk. Why would they do that?"

"They were looking for something, Bud. They thought it was in the desk. By the looks of it, they must have thought the desk had a hidden compartment. Wonder what they were looking for."

"Probably money, I bet. Some of the kids around here are too lazy to work, and they sit around doing drugs and drinkin'. Probably thought that no one was living here. Man, is Julie going to be pissed off."

We looked around the place and saw that nothing else seemed to have been bothered. A close examination of the front door showed tool marks where someone had slipped a flat pry bar between the door and the jamb and popped the spring lock. I decided I had better call the sheriff's office and report the break-in. I dialed them up on the landline, and the dispatcher said someone would be out within the hour and asked me not to touch anything.

I opened the fridge and retrieved a couple of cans of soda, and Bud and I went outside to sit at the picnic table and wait.

"Bud, you mind if I ask you some questions about the local folks?"

"Sure, Mr. Cabrelli. I'll answer if I can."

"For starters, call me John."

"Okay. Bud's good for me. I hate Arvid. That was my great-grandfather's name on my mother's side. I bet he hated the name too."

"So, tell me about Julie. What's the deal with her? Yesterday she thought I was a prowler and damn near shot me with a shotgun."

Bud broke out in a big smile followed by a booming big man laugh, "You sure are lucky. Usually she doesn't hesitate much. I am surprised she didn't shoot," he said. "Julie is my cousin, but we were raised together. She never knew her dad, and her mother pretty much tried to drink Namekagon County dry. One night on the way home from the bar, her mom crashed her car into a tree and that was it. Julie came to live with my family. We were cousins, but she was more like a sister.

"She was way better in school than I was, and she helped me out a lot. Book learning and I just never got along, but she got me through. When we graduated, she went off to school at Eau Claire to become a teacher. I knew she would be a good one 'cause of how good she did with me. It's not because I'm not smart, I am real good at figurin' out things, it's just that books and me, well... She was at college two years, and then one day she showed up back home with all her stuff. She had this old car that I kept running, and it was packed to the roof. She told us she had run out of money and left school. My dad asked her about student loans, and she just said startin' out in life with a bunch of debt wasn't for her. She worked all that summer at the lumberjack show at night and at the co-op during the day. She sure was set on saving enough money to go back to school. She never went out, not even to the movies. She cashed her checks and put them in the bank. I think she was getting pretty close to what she needed, because she told me that she had applied for a part-time job at the student center and was pretty sure she would get it. Then late in the summer, my mother took real sick, and by fall, she had passed on."

Bud paused and looked out onto the lake. It was dark blue and calm. I could feel the sadness of past sorrows sweep over him.

"I'm sorry, Bud."

He just nodded and continued. "Julie took over running the house for dad and me. My dad kept telling her she needed to get out and see the world, that taking care of him and me was no job for a smart and pretty young girl. She'd have none of it. She was sure we couldn't take care of ourselves. When Christmas came around, Julie started taking some online courses through UW-Superior. She took care of us, worked two jobs, and still had time to study. My dad was in his eighties, and he had smoked pretty much all his life. It finally took him during the winter. He got pneumonia and never recovered. He had a paid-up life insurance policy when he died, and he left that to Julie and the house to me. The policy wasn't very big, and the house wasn't much, but Julie and I were thankful for it. He had lived a good life, and he was a good dad to both of us. She went back to school at the start of the summer session. She must have worked like a dog because it didn't seem like anytime at all a year had passed, and she was back home with her diploma.

"She was all excited about a special school they opened in Namekagon County for kids like me that don't do good in regular school. She wanted to teach there. Anyway, her first day home she drove out to the school to put in an application. The school was in an old town hall building about a mile off the highway. Guess there was no one around because it was summer, so she headed back into town and went to the school administration building. She went in and asked about the school. The woman in the office told her that it was going to close. I guess the teacher had quit, and even though they had a notice out for the job for a month, they had no takers. Julie applied right then and there. They called her within a couple of days, and she got the job. She became the lead and only teacher at Northern Lakes Academy.

"She's been working there ever since. Some of the kids are pretty hard to deal with, but she likes them and they like her. She got hooked up with your aunt and uncle three or four years ago. Heard that they had a cabin that no one was living in on their property. It was only five miles from the school. She went and talked to them, and they agreed to rent it to her if she would help with the chores around the place.

"She really loved your aunt and uncle. They treated her like family. They talked her into moving into the main house when Rose got sick. Her room is up on the second floor. It's pretty nice. It's big and has a window that looks out on the lake and a big whirlpool tub in the bathroom. She really likes it.

"She's pretty sad that she has to move out now that you're selling the place and tearing it down."

"I don't know anything about tearing the place down, Bud. I am pretty overwhelmed by all this right now, and I haven't really had time to give any of this much thought. I am working on trying to figure things out, but I haven't gotten very far."

"Well, it's your house now, and if you want to tear it down, that is your business. That's what I told Julie. She didn't like to hear it much, but that's the way it is."

At that moment a marked sheriff's car pulled into the driveway and came to a stop by the table.

The deputy got out and walked up to us sitting at the picnic table. He reminded me of many of the rural deputies I had met over the years, lean and fit. He walked toward us with a confident stride. A cop in the city has backup no more than a minute or two away. In a rural county like this, it could take an hour before help got to you. Deputies learned to pretty much handle everything on their own. This guy looked to be in his forties, and the hash marks on his sleeve showed he had over twenty years of service.

"I am Deputy Rawsom from the Namekagon County Sheriff's Office. You called to report a burglary?"

"That's right, Deputy. Let me show you."

"And you are?"

"John Cabrelli. I just inherited this place from my aunt and uncle. This is Bud Treetall, the caretaker."

"Pleased to meet you, Mr. Cabrelli. I already know Bud. How you doing these days, Bud?"

"Real good, Jim. I'm ready anytime to start helping with that deck you want to build. Just let me know."

"Don't worry, Bud. I'll be getting a hold of you."

I showed him the tool marks and the desk. He looked carefully through the contents and saw that while the search of the desk appeared to be random, it had, in fact, been done in a very thorough fashion. Every envelope opened. All contents removed.

"Well, whatever they were looking for was something that would fit inside an envelope. Could be money, but that doesn't explain what I found over here."

The deputy held up the three 100 dollar bills with a note clipped to them: "Bud, porch repair."

Nope. If they were looking for money, then they would not have left this behind.

The deputy measured and photographed the scene. He bagged some of the desk's drawer handles and a smooth heavy glass paperweight.

"They would have had to touch the drawer handles, and it looks like they used the paperweight to smash some of the desk. Surfaces are good. We might be able to get a print. We don't have the most hi-tech lab here, but our guys are pretty good working with what they have."

As the deputy was packing up to go, he turned and asked me, "Not that it's my business, but you have any plans for the place?"

"Honestly, I just got here, and I haven't had much time to think about it."

"I'd love to have a place like this. That's one of the best musky lakes in the state. The back of your property joins up with the national forest. You could walk for miles and miles and never see a paved road. I've got a little English cocker that I hunt grouse with behind here, and we've never been skunked. Places like this are awful hard to come by. But like I said, it's not my business. Here's my card. Any more problems or questions, just give me a call."

"Thanks, Deputy," I said.

To Bud, he said, "Catch you later and say hello to Julie." Then he got in his car and drove out.

Bud and I went in and straightened up the mess. We tried to turn the desk over, but one leg was about broken off, and it wouldn't stand. So for the time being we propped it up with some cement blocks Bud retrieved from the shop.

I asked Bud about the $300. He said he had repaired the porch just before Nick had been hit by the car and never bothered to submit a bill. I gave it to him plus another $100 for fixing the dock. He was thrilled.

"Well, John, I gotta get back to town; got a job to do over at the old feed store. They're converting it to a restaurant, and there's about three ceilings in there over the original one that have to come down before they can get started. I gave you my number. If you need anything, call."

"Thanks, Bud, I will."

He jumped in his 4-door Japanese car cruncher and drove out.

• • •

The taxpayers of the great state of Wisconsin spent a pile of money training me to be an investigator.

Based on that training and my vast experience, it was crystal clear to me that something was amiss regarding me and my aunt and uncle's property. I had no way of knowing what that might be, but when something like this doesn't make sense, it is usually because you don't know the whole story.

Why the strange visit from Officer Lawler, and why would he think I was trying to fly under the radar of the local cops? What was he was worried about? How come Attorney Anderson was so panicked when

I didn't jump at the property offer? And mostly, why the hell were the lawyer and the tough guy cop communicating about me? Who trashed Uncle Nick's desk and what were they looking for? This was no random burglary. I have never met a burglar that would pull three hundred cash out of an envelope and drop it on the floor.

But most importantly, who ran Uncle Nick down? Accident or murder?

A good cop is blessed and cursed. They are blessed with a will to bring the world back to order. They are cursed with the need to follow everything they come upon to its natural end, regardless of where that takes them. A lazy cop is just putting in time. A good cop is there because it is the only place for them. I was a good cop, and there was no doubt in my mind that something was wrong here, and I had no choice but to figure it out to my satisfaction.

I started with the papers that had been dumped out of the desk. Mostly just bills, check stubs for my uncle's patent royalty, a few cards from friends, a funeral notice from Aunt Rose, and the vet bill from when they had their old Chesapeake put down. There was a tax bill for the place, and it took my breath away for a moment. Property taxes were not cheap in the Northwoods. I found an envelope addressed to Uncle Nick with a return address of a law firm in Minneapolis. I decided that the right way to go about this was to match whatever contents I could find to the right envelope if there was one. I laid stacks on the counter and some on the desk and started. After three hours, I had done a pretty fair job of connecting the dots. Mostly nothing was out of the ordinary—mostly that is. I found another envelope from the law firm. This one also matched up to nothing I could find. Mean anything? I didn't know.

It was getting late in the afternoon, and it was about time for Julie to return home. I did not want to be in the house when she got there. I hoped we could have a civil conversation. The house was not neutral ground.

I went into the shop and could not believe what I saw. The place was immaculate. Toolboxes on wheels covered one wall, along with a lathe, a drill press, a couple of welders, and other tools. The adjoining wall had a workbench from one end to the other. On another wall was a gun and fishing rod rack, both full, as well as three tall file cabinets. I was fascinated by my uncle's workplace, and it took me back to some of the best times of my life. One wall had two big windows that looked out on the lake and the woods behind.

I could just see him sitting there looking out while he worked on his projects. I loved the house, but I fell in love with the shop. I could have stayed put right there for hours, but I needed neutral ground. So I took a fishing rod off the rack and headed out to the boat dock. On the rod there was a lure, a Mepps No. 5 gold spinner black bucktail, his favorite. He used to say, "There is no fish in freshwater that will not succumb to the charms of the Mepps French spinner, a truly brilliant design."

I cast out and around to where a mostly submerged log poked its end out. I was retrieving it slowly through a weed bed when *wham*. A beautiful smallmouth bass had clobbered the spinner and jumped straight in the air out of the water. I was twelve again and having the time of my life. I actually giggled. I didn't even know I could giggle, but I did. I brought the fish to hand and unhooked the spinner, gently put it back in the water, and it was gone in a flash. I turned around, back to shore, and was greeted by none other than Julie Carlson, hip canted to one side, staring at me.

"You giggle like a girl," she said.

I was as embarrassed as I could be.

Trying to recover, I said, "Did you see that bass? It was an easy three pounds. It flew out of the water. God, it was great. That would make anyone laugh."

"You giggled," she said, and turned and walked away, sitting down at the picnic table.

I walked over and sat across from her. "Julie, I think we had better talk."

"What's to talk about? I am moving out, and you are going to do what you are going to do to this place. Case closed, end of story, end of the need for conversation between you and me. So unless there's something new that you need to share with me, I am not interested."

"Are you always this charming?" I asked.

"I have student papers to grade and packing to do, so I would like to get to it."

"Well, before you go in, you should know that somebody broke in here while you were gone. They trashed my uncle's desk and threw all the papers around. They didn't bother anything else. If they took something, I don't have any idea what it was. It must have happened right after you left this morning, because your cousin Bud was out here pretty early to fix the boat dock."

With that, she bolted to the door of the house and ran in. She did a rapid run through and finally ended up back by the desk.

"It was probably kids looking for money or something they can sell to get money. Drugs are a curse here. Drugs, high unemployment, and time on their hands are a recipe for trouble," she said.

"At first look, that's what I thought."

"But not anymore?"

"Nope, I found $300 paper clipped to a note for Bud. If they were looking for cash, I can't imagine they would have passed that up. Anything else look different to you? Anything else out of place as far as you can tell?"

"Except for the desk, it looks like the way it did when I left this morning. Did you call the sheriff?"

"Yep, they have been here and gone. They took the drawer handles and a glass paperweight for prints."

"So, what is all this about now? Somebody breaking in, looking for who knows what. I can't wait to get my stuff and get out of this place." She suddenly screamed, "I hate this house. I hate this place!" With that, tears filled her eyes, and she ran out the door. Lucky I sidestepped quickly because, otherwise, I am sure she would have run right over me.

I sat down in my uncle's old chair, and I could see Julie out the window sitting cross-legged at the end of the boat dock sobbing by the look of the shaking of her shoulders. I thought, "This is one complicated shotgun-pointing, mad, ear-blistering, sobbing woman. I should just stay as far away from her as I can." But I am a good cop, and I have to follow everything to its natural end. My time with Julie Carlson was not at its natural end.

An hour passed, and I decided to take a chance. I grabbed a couple bottles of water from the fridge and headed out to the dock. She did not acknowledge my presence until I sat down beside her.

A long minute passed before she said in a soft voice that up until this point I didn't know she was capable of, "I hate it when I cry. I especially hate it when I cry in front of someone else. I really hate that I cried in front of you."

"That's okay," I replied. "I hate it when I giggle, especially in front of other people."

She burst out in a laugh. Her red-rimmed eyes sparkled like the lake water in the sunlight. Her shoulders relaxed, and she looked up at me.

"I am sorry that I have been less than cordial to you. This whole thing has been very difficult for me. I loved Nick and Rose, and I loved caring for them. They were two of the best people I have ever met. They were so kind to me. They treated Bud and me like family. We had Christmas and Thanksgiving and all the holidays together. I knew they were going to leave the property to you, and I thought it was the right thing to do. Even though I thought your absence in their lives was a pathetic comment on your personality. But your uncle stood up for you. 'John is a good man,' he would say. 'Someday when you meet him you'll see that.' Then I heard from your lawyer that you intended to sell the place, and they were bringing in heavy equipment to knock down the buildings. I asked the lawyer if I could make an offer on the property, and he just laughed at me. Then he told me that you wanted me to pack my stuff and be out by next Friday."

"I can understand your feelings," I told her. "I think Nick and Rose were lucky to have you. You need to listen to me and actually hear what I am saying though. I am not your enemy. I love this place too. Whatever Lawyer Anderson has been telling you did not come from me. I didn't even know you existed 72 hours ago. I am assuming I actually do have something to say about selling this place, and I am not even close to making any decision. You do not have to move. You can stay put until we get this all figured out. You're right. I should have come to see them, but I didn't, and that will be my sadness to bear forever. It's no excuse, but when you're fighting demons like I was, you can't do much else."

"We heard about the little girl on the news. Nick stopped watching the news or reading newspapers after that. He did not want to hear what they were saying about you. I'm sorry, I shouldn't have brought that up. I wasn't ... I didn't mean anything by it."

"Julie, several million people saw that on the news. It was a terrible thing. It is still a terrible thing. It was and still is my worst nightmare. The memory tempers any happiness I have ever had or will have. I am trying to move on. The best I can manage is one small step at a time."

"I'm sorry. I didn't mean to bring up bad memories."

At that point an outside bell on a post let us know the house phone was ringing.

I asked her if she needed to answer that, and she said she probably should because it might be one of her students or a parent. When she was about halfway to the door, the ringing stopped, only to begin again a few seconds later. She went in and came back out.

"John, it's for you. It's Derek Anderson. He says it's urgent."

I walked in and picked the phone. "Hey, Derek. What's up?"

"John, you are not going to believe this. The buyer just upped the offer to two million dollars, if we can close within 10 business days."

"Two million dollars? You have got to be kidding me."

"Think of what you could do with that, John. I am drawing up the final papers right now. How soon can you get here?"

Sometimes I honestly don't understand what makes me do the things I do. It just seems like the right thing at the time, and I go for it. Common sense does not seem to have much to do with it.

"Derek, don't worry about the paperwork. The place isn't for sale. I'm going to be staying around for a while, so I'll be in to finish up with my uncle's estate. Thanks for your work, Derek. Sorry to disappoint you, but it is what it is."

There was silence on the other end. Then Attorney Anderson almost snarled, "You have no idea what a fool you are and what a big mistake you've made. The people that want that place do not understand the word *no*. You'll see. You will come around to their way of thinking."

"Later, Counselor," I said, and I hung up the phone.

Julie stood staring at me, her pretty blue eyes the size of saucers.

"John, you just turned down two million dollars for this place?"

"I guess that's what I did, didn't I? Never let it be said that the Cabrellis didn't birth no fools."

"Oh my God, John. That is a fortune. I can't believe you just did that."

"Huh? In the not too distant past, you were chewing me out for selling the place, even though I didn't know I was. Now you're looking at me like an idiot for turning down two million bucks. You're going to have to excuse me if I am a little confused."

"I just can't believe you did it. Why would you care what I think? I can't believe it." ∎

CHAPTER 11
Cabrelli

Julie and I talked about her staying at the house with the break-in and all. She assured me that she would be fine and that she was going to put the shotgun by her bed. As I was mulling it over, the phone rang again. This time it was Bud. He was on his way out to stay for the night to make sure everything was okay.

Julie laughed a little. "Bud, I am going to be just fine.... Oh well, okay, if it makes YOU feel better."

"So Bud is coming out to stay tonight?" I asked.

"Yes, he sure is," she laughed.

"What's so funny?"

"Bud, as big and strong as he is, wouldn't hurt anyone. He has the sweetest soul of anyone I have ever met. He just doesn't have it in him. I am the dangerous one," she said.

No doubt.

I jumped in my rented jeep and headed back to town. What's two million dollars? I knew I had done the right thing. I also knew something else. I was home. I had found my place. I knew the minute I'd sat in Uncle Nick's chair, the minute I saw the lake and walked out on the dock. I was finally home, and two million was a small price to pay. Maybe here the demons would finally leave. Tomorrow I would start taking care of all that needed taking care of. I called Laura once

I got cell service, and she answered on the second ring.

"Hey, Cabrelli, I was just going to call you. That case of ours just settled. They saw the information you uncovered and went into a quick conference. They are giving our client what we asked. The risk for more is too high if they go to court. Good job, John. You're the best. How are things going up north?"

"That's what I called about. Things are going really well up here. So well, I am going to stay for a while. I don't know how long but for a while anyway."

"Are you quitting the firm?"

"Let's call it a leave of absence. Just give me a chance to get this figured out."

"John, if this is what you want, I am good with that. You are always welcome back here. Our caseload is pretty small right now anyway because I had booked six weeks for the trial. Elizabeth and I have been thinking about doing some traveling. Now might be a good time. I am gonna miss you, John. Stay in touch, and remember, don't sign anything until I look it over."

"See ya, Laura, and thanks."

All of a sudden I realized how hungry I was. I really didn't feel like fighting a crowd, and this time of year every place in Musky Falls was crowded. So I went to the Log Cabin and got a chicken dinner to go, based on the sign that said their fried chicken was the best north of Highway 10. After I got back to the hotel, I ate my dinner and was asleep in about two minutes. It's amazing how turning down two million bucks can wear you out.

• • •

Morning dawned like it only can in the great Northwoods—clear as a bell, air full of the sweet scents of the northern forest. I felt good, happy. I put on my Badger t-shirt, red shorts, and running shoes, and after a stretch, I headed out for a run. I ran down the road shoulder and then on to a bike trail headed toward town and a cup of coffee at Crossroads. I have always been kind of a plodding runner. I am definitely not built for running marathons, but I can run, and today I felt light, and running felt good.

I ran past the giant musky and was looking up at it when I should have been looking forward. A squad car pulled into the driveway I was about to cross, and I ran into it hard. I wasn't hurt, but it stunned me for a second. Officer Lawler exited the driver's side and walked over to where I had run into the car. He started to run his hand over the spot and look at it from different angles.

"I guess there is no damage, Cabrelli. You're real lucky, though. As hard as you hit it, I'm surprised there is no dent. If there was, I'd have to charge you with damaging public property. That would be a shame, but you know, the law is the law."

I could not believe what I had just heard, and the second before I rose to take the bait, I remembered the rules of the game. I had played it myself with gang members and general criminal elements in my beat. Push them until they jump, then come down hard. I took a breath.

"Jeez, sorry, Officer. I didn't see you. I was busy looking at the huge musky. I'll be more careful in the future. Catch you later."

I went around the car and started out again. Just as I was leaving, I heard Officer Lawler's final words of the day, "You just go ahead and run along now, kid killer. Stay around here, and you and me, we will have our day. Yes, we will."

I ran on and picked up my pace, demons chasing me once more. I hoped I could outrun them.

• • •

Crossroads was pretty packed, but I managed to get a cup of the daily brew and find a spot at a wrought iron table outside. The coffee was good, but my mind was elsewhere. What the hell was the deal here? Why was this cop pushing on me? Was it just my reputation? I could understand someone not liking me, but usually they had to get to know me first. This guy had a real issue, and he was going to push it until he got what he wanted. I could've gone to the chief and complained, but that would probably only make certain that every cop in town had it out for me. Nope, one jerk like Lawler was worth plenty of people not paying special attention to me.

The run back to the motel was uneventful. I took a shower and then tried to call Bud on his cell. It went to voicemail, then I remembered he had stayed at the cabin last night and called there. He picked up.

"Bud. It's John. What are you up to today?"

"Not much this morning, John."

"I was wondering if you could help me get the boat in the water. I thought I'd like to tour around the lake and maybe throw a cast or two."

"Sounds like a plan. I'll start getting everything together. You on your way?"

"I'll be leaving in ten minutes. Any problems last night?"

"Nope. All's quiet."

"Good. I'll be there shortly." ∎

CHAPTER 12
Cabrelli

Little did I know that at the same time I was getting ready to head out to the cabin, there was a very heated meeting going on behind closed doors at Attorney Derek Anderson's office.

It seems, as I learned later, ol' Derek was getting his head handed to him by the fellow who was so interested in my property. It must have been an ugly scene because people who saw the lawyer afterward said he looked shaken and scared. The lady who runs the moccasin store next to his office ran into him as he flew out the office door. She greeted him, and the only thing Anderson had to say was, "Get out of my way."

He jumped into his car, took off fast, and headed out of town. At that point I didn't know it, but he was a man treading water as fast as he could to keep from going down for the third time.

It used to amaze me how people got themselves into things so deep, so fast. I understand now that things happen, and sometimes they start out as a leisurely Sunday drive down a country road, and before you know it, you're racing 100 miles an hour, white-knuckling it all the way. Most of these problems start out simple—like in Anderson's case, it was greed. The problems quickly become more complicated—like greed, extortion, and—well, I guess I am getting ahead of myself here. We'll come back to that later.

I was excited to get to the cabin and out on the lake. The jeep did run great and had a substantial feel to it. Man, from Italian loafers, pressed jeans, and a fancy Japanese sports car to work boots, a sweatshirt, and a jeep. Things do have a way of changing.

I pulled into the cabin and Bud was backing the trailer with the boat loaded up to the lakeshore.

I walked over and he asked, "John, could you tell me when the trailer tires just touch the edge of the water? That's as far as we can go before we get ourselves into trouble."

He slowly, expertly, backed up until I gave him the signal to stop. Then the agile giant jumped out of the truck, up onto the trailer, and released a latch on the trailer tongue just under the boat. The trailer bed and boat started to tilt up. Bud grabbed hold and lifted. As soon as he got about a 45-degree angle, the boat started to slide down on the rollers underneath it.

The motor was locked in the up position and I saw why; the boat was descending at a significant angle, and the water was not all that deep. Bud guided it with expert hands, and soon the boat was free floating at the end of the twenty-foot rope he had in his hands.

"Here, take this rope and walk over to the dock and pull the boat in while I get this trailer locked down and the truck moved. Man, these tilt-bed trailers are really something. If you know how to use 'em, you can launch a boat just about anywhere."

I pulled the boat over to the dock and took in the attributes of my uncle's trusty craft. A 14' F7 Alumacraft, powered by a 15-horse flat top tiller Evinrude engine, an orange gas tank, oars, and a life jacket. I was sure it was the same boat I had fallen out of many years before.

Bud finished his chore and came walking over.

"That is just about the perfect boat for these lakes," Bud said with authority. "A tank of gas lasts forever, and they don't draw much water, so you can get in shallow places where the fish hide. Even though it's only 14 feet long, don't let that fool you. These boats are built to take any kind of water if you know how to handle them.

"They are getting to be collector's items. Nick didn't think anyone had ever made a better boat. That little 15 horse will push you along as fast as you want to go."

I couldn't wait to get going, and Bud could see I was anxious.

"John, do you know how to run this thing?"

"I think so, but how about a little refresher?"

"No problem. Just hop in the boat. Ah, don't step on the seat. Step on the floor in the middle and get comfy back there by the engine. That engine is old but it runs great, and it takes a gas and oil mix in the tank. There are a bunch of bottles of two stroke oil in the shop, so if you need to gas up, just add one to the six-gallon tank. I filled it up this morning, though, so you won't need gas anytime soon.

"Now flip that lever that says 'lock' and push the motor down so the lower half is in the water. You can run that motor two ways, deep drive like it is now and will be most of what you use, or if you reach down in the back and pull that other lever, it'll come up to shallow drive in case you're going around someplace where the water is a little bit skinny. You don't want to leave pieces of your prop on the bottom of the lake.

"Now put that flat toggle looking switch on neutral, pull that choke knob next to it about three-quarters of the way out, and pump up the bulb on the fuel line until it gets real hard. Now on the tiller handle turn it to 'start.' Here comes the big moment. Grab hold of that t-handle stickin' out of the top and give it a sharp yank. When the motor starts, push in the choke. Let it warm up a minute, and then you are on your way."

I grabbed the t-handle and pulled the rope. A sputter, nothing else.

"Give her another one, John." I did. Same result.

"Pump up that gas hose a little more."

I pumped until there was no pump left and gave it another sharp pull. This time I was rewarded as the engine sputtered and coughed to life.

"Push the choke in," Bud instructed.

I did and the engine settled down to an even purr. I was absolutely ecstatic.

"There you go, John. You take it easy and have fun. I brought these down from the shop," he said, and he handed me a fishing rod and the tackle box, "in case you decide to throw a cast or two. Did you pick up your fishing license?"

"Sure did. Stopped at the Happy Hooker Bait Shop on my way over."

"I don't know what you have planned tonight, but this is Musky Fest weekend, and there's a lot of stuff going on in town. Matter of fact, that's where I'm going now to help setup. Julie and her kids are coming over to help too. I guess they have a booth this year again selling t-shirts and sweatshirts as a fundraiser."

"What time does it all start?" I asked.

"About one o'clock before things get going, but it goes until midnight with the street dance and band. You should come down and check it out."

"Thanks, maybe I will, and thanks for all your help, Bud. I really appreciate it."

"No problem. Catch ya later."

As Bud walked toward his truck, I slipped the little motor into reverse, backing out from the dock. When I got myself headed in the right direction, I clicked into forward and slowly cracked the throttle. The little boat responded like a dream, and just like that, I was planed up and skipping across the calm water of Little Spider Lake. I headed northwest out of Gillich's Bay and looked at my surroundings. The names of those special places flooded back to me: Hannah Bay, Heinemann's Resort, Musky Run, Clear Lake. I wish I could put into words what I was feeling, but in the simplest form, I was happy and free with the wind in my face, going back to visit the best times of my life. The boat handled well, and I opened the throttle all the way.

On my right, I saw something on the water and realized it was a loon. I slowed down to look and saw that she had two chicks riding on her back. As I reached the end of Little Spider Lake, I remembered the secret passage. As you approached, it appeared to be an impenetrable shoreline. But once you got real close, you could see that there was a short S-shaped channel that took you right into Big Spider Lake. I slowed to "no wake" and passed through. It was as big and wonderful as I remembered. The water just shimmered in the dozens of small bays while a slight breeze resulted in a small chop in the center of the lake. Off to my left was Candy Island, a place where my uncle and aunt and I would pull up for lunch. Dead ahead was Picnic Island, my favorite. Out from Picnic Island was a rocky bar that went out over a hundred yards under water. It was where I had caught my first musky, a 24-incher that leaped from the water and danced on its tail. I was upset when Uncle Nick told me we had to release him, but back then the length limit was 36 inches, and this guy didn't make the cut.

I also loved to put on my mask, fins, and snorkel and explore the rock bar. Uncle Nick and I used to circumnavigate the island trying to propel ourselves forward using only our hands lest we kick up sand that would compromise the water clarity. We would find ourselves swimming along with huge smallmouth bass, hundreds of little bluegills, and occasionally a musky. We had a contest to see who could find the best treasure, mainly in the form of lures hung up on the rocks and broken off by fishermen.

When I came upon the island, I saw a buoy that warned of the rock bar. The wind was blowing the right way, so I shut the motor off and drifted in. I started to relearn my casting skills as I pitched my lure along the edge of the bar, each cast bringing new hope. I was about to float into the island shore but decided to throw one last cast. As I was reeling into the boat, and just as I began to pull my lure out of the water, there was a splash and a swirl as a big musky made a grab for my spinner. I was too fast for him though and pulled it safely back into the boat. I watched as the fish swam back toward the rock pile, no doubt laughing that musky laugh.

Then I remembered: *"Figure eight,"* Uncle Nick had said. *"Figure eight your lure in the water at the end of each cast. Those muskies are tricky, and they like to hit right by the boat. A figure eight gives you an extra chance."*

The motor started on the first pull, and off I went through the channel to Fawn Lake and into a bog channel that would take me to a huge culvert under the road and into North Lake. The channel was full of beautiful plants, a small patch of carnivorous pitcher plants with their enticing flowers, leatherleaf, bog rosemary, and tamarack trees. My aunt Rose used to collect some of the plants every year from this spot to dry and make an herbal tea that she used to cure the common cold later in the year.

I had always pretended that this was a prehistoric river. My uncle, who was a keen student of nature, explained to me often that nature was a community to which we belonged, and to be a successful and respectful participant in this community, a person needed to know the members. To this end, he spent a great deal of time taking little side trips to introduce me to our neighbors, both flora and fauna. It was as if my memory had been triggered and reactivated by this boat trip. Somewhere my mind had stored these long ago learned facts, and now given the opportunity, they leaped to the forefront.

I was a ten-year-old kid again responding to a question that had an answer of which I was certain. "Johnny, what is the name of that plant?"

"Pickerelweed, Uncle Nick. Pickerelweed!" I blurted.

"You got it, Johnny. It is pickerelweed. Do you remember what likes to hide in the pickerelweeds?"

"Bass and big muskies!" I replied.

"Then I think we better throw a couple of casts here just in case someone is home."

And with that, Uncle Nick handed me my rod, and I became a hunter on a prehistoric river, a bass and musky hunter.

In the channel the water had turned more of brown color compared to the lake I had just left. I knew it was caused by tannin, a dark stain released by the tamarack trees. I remembered what I was taught, that while people tend to call any place that is a wetland a swamp, a true swamp had to have trees. This was a true swamp, and tamaracks were always Aunt Rose's favorite, the needles turning smoky gold in the fall.

Carefully I piloted my boat through the large culvert into North Lake, watching thousands of small minnows in the water doing whatever minnows do. For some reason North Lake was always special to me. Maybe because of its wildness, or maybe it was the trees growing right down to the shore, or maybe it was knowing that if I got out at the end of the lake and started walking north I would end up on the shore of Lake Superior. The lake had not changed at all. It was the same as I remembered—untamed, its dark waters placid today, a wild place to be sure.

In the sky above an eagle swung around lazily, looking for an unsuspecting fish on which to dive. It was a mature adult resplendent in its white headedness, dignified in its flying. This bird was a fine representative of our country's symbol.

By this time the sun had risen almost straight above me, maybe a little after noon. I turned my little ship around and headed home. I never got over half throttle on the way back. I was content to go slowly, feeling the soft breeze, the warm summer sun, revisiting times past. Something was different; change was afoot. I could not remember one time in the last many years that half throttle and John Cabrelli had been used in the same sentence.

I pulled into the dock with expert seamanship, managing to clobber only one of the upright posts pretty good. It took the blow well and saved me from telling Bud that he had another one to straighten out.

A feeling of apprehension came over me as I stepped onto the dock and walked toward the cabin. From the outside, everything seemed okay, just like yesterday. I started to turn the doorknob and realized that I had done this many times before—turned the knob with my left hand while holding my gun in my right, ready for whatever was on the other side. No gun today, just me. I could feel the adrenaline course through me, my muscles tensed; I felt like a trap ready to spring.

I swung the door open and looked left, right, and straight ahead all at the same time. I walked in, watching every way I could. Everything was in its place, all things in order. I breathed a relieved sigh and waited for the adrenaline letdown. Old habits die hard? Paranoid? Nuts? Maybe one or all three.

My only intention in coming in was to see if the place was okay. I had no intention to do any snooping. After all, I would not want Julie Carlson snooping through my stuff. There was a heavy padded chair and footstool next to the fireplace. So close in fact that the hearth served as a handy end table.

On the hearth was a book on top of a file folder. The folder was about three inches thick, and I doubt you could have stuffed another sheet of paper in it. The book was a new release by Dana Stabenow, an Alaskan mystery writer. I opened the file and found student writing and research projects. I paged through them and saw that teacher Carlson had taken the time not just to grade them but write individual comments on each. Her comments were not critical but constructive, very positive in general. Meant not to scold but to help.

She had written to one student, "You can do better than this and you usually do. I know things have been tough at home lately. How about you and I sit down together after school one day and fix this up? Here is my cell phone number. Again, remember day or night if you need something, call me. ~Ms. Carlson"

The shotgun-toting Julie Carlson, as my old academy instructor used to say, is an enigma wrapped up in a mystery. I put things back as they were, locked the door, and took off. ∎

CHAPTER 13
Cabrelli

I cruised back into town and could not believe the number of cars. Tourists lined Main Street, meandering along carrying plastic bags emblazoned with the store logo from their last purchase. As they walked, many of them dined on donuts, ice cream, cheese fries covered in chili, and of course those heart stoppers all Wisconsinites love, deep-fried cheese curds. A significant portion of Main Street had been blocked off. Craft vendors and others were busily erecting their displays inside of white tents. I finally found a place to park down by Crossroads, and since I was there, I decided to get a cup of coffee to go.

The place was packed. A family standing in line ahead of me was ordering specialty coffee drinks. Low fat, no fat, half fat, loco mocha decaf latte yoko ono, with whipped cream and cinnamon. They all sounded the same to me.

When I got up to the counter, the harried girl actually smiled when I said, "Today's special brew, medium to go, and leave some room for cream." She handed me a cup. I paid her with a five and put the change in the tip jar.

"Hope you survive the day," I said.

"I will," she smiled. "Off at four, street dance tonight."

In the few minutes it had taken me to park and get a cup of coffee, it seemed like the number of people had doubled. Everyone was walking along, stopping in the shops, looking for the treasure they couldn't live without. In Northern Wisconsin, I was sure, the folks couldn't wait for the tourists to get here and couldn't wait for them to leave. There were other businesses around the area, but a beautiful destination like this lives and dies with the tourist dollars.

I came upon a group of seasoned citizens all wearing Lions Club shirts. Must have been about eight or ten of them. Each one had taken it upon themselves to give instructions to a younger guy who was trying to back a truck up with an attached boat and trailer to a designated spot next to the Lions' booth. Signs on the boat indicated that it was to be raffled off as part of a charitable fundraiser. The driver had his hands full trying to avoid kids and parents weaving in and out around him, trying not to crash the boat into the club trailer, and trying to listen to each of his coaches. He took it all in with a smile and eventually got the boat into position. The old guys wiped their brows, breathed a sigh of relief, and, exhausted from their combined efforts, they agreed unanimously that they had earned a reward and headed off to the beer tent leaving the driver to unhook and put up all the signage by himself as well as set up the table to buy the tickets.

I stepped up. "Hey, can you use a hand?" I asked.

"Sure could. I need someone to raise this trailer jack while I put blocks under the tires and tongue. Got to get it real stable for all the people that'll be crawling in and out for the next couple of days."

I cranked down the jack onto a board and raised the front end. He put two timber blocks underneath and angle cut blocks in front of and behind the tires. At his command, I cranked the jack back down, and the trailer came to rest solidly on the blocks instead of the jack.

"That jack would have held up just fine," he said, "but the city street guys hate it when the jack leaves a big old divot in their blacktop. Thanks, I appreciate your help. Name's Luke," he said, and he held out his hand. He was clean-cut, trim, and wearing a brand new Lions Club shirt, the next generation of community leaders.

"John Cabrelli, Luke. Nice to meet you."

"You live around here?" he asked.

"I don't know. I didn't, but I might now. It's actually complicated."

Luke had no interest in my complications, and with another, "Thanks again," he headed off to finish his work.

I turned around to head out to Main Street again when I walked smack into a gray-haired grizzly-looking guy dressed like a biker, with a well-worn leather vest and chaps, an earring, and tattoos. He was one of those guys that you could tell had been there, done that, and had lived to tell about it. He looked me square in the eye and, although I thought I had the right of way, he didn't yield or move to go by.

In a gruff and demanding voice, he asked, "Did I hear you say your name is John Cabrelli?"

Immediately, "What now?" came to mind.

"That's me."

His grimace turned to a twinkle in his eyes, and a big smile cracked through his beard-encrusted face.

"Well, son of a bitch, you must be Nick's nephew from down in Madison. The one that used to be a cop. I knew you'd be coming. My name is Ron Carver. I was your uncle's running buddy. We were best of friends. I'm happy to finally meet you," he said, and he stuck out his hand, giving mine a strong grip and a hearty shake. "I'm glad you're here. We got a lot of talking to do. You going to be around for a while?"

Taken totally off guard, I said, "Uh, yeah, I am planning on staying for a while, until I get things figured out, anyway."

"Tell you what, Johnny. I got to get into my store over there. In the jewelry business. This is a big weekend for us, and the girls are swamped. So I gotta go help out. The festival is over Sunday afternoon, and while I am very anxious to talk to you, it's gonna have to wait till Monday. Where you stayin'?"

"At the Lodge Motel out on B. At least for now."

"Why aren't you stayin' at your uncle's place?"

"Right now the place is occupied. Julie Carlson is living there."

"That cute little Julie Carlson is still stayin' there? Man, then that's where I'd be stayin'," and he laughed with a cackle. He picked up a pen and pad from the Lion's Club table and took down my phone number. "I'll call you on Monday, then you can let me know what works."

We shook hands again, and he walked off and went inside the jewelry store.

What a character. Just the kind of guy Uncle Nick would like.

I continued my journey, sipping away at my lukewarm cup of coffee. There were vendors for everything, from funnel cakes to metal heron sculptures. All pretty much folks from around the general area selling their wares out of a tent instead of from a brick-and-mortar storefront. They greeted one another, praising the good weather and the big crowd. Everyone seemed to be in a festive mood.

I walked and looked and visited briefly with folks. When I came to the end of the street, I saw shotgun Julie standing up on a step ladder hanging a banner from a white tent.

The sign read "Northern Lakes Academy: Hands On, Feet Wet, Learning Through Doing." I walked over and saw that the tent was abuzz of semi-organized chaos. While Julie was trying to hang the banner, she was also instructing a bunch of kids, her students I assumed, on laying out t-shirts, sweatshirts, brochures, and raffle tickets. It was a unique form of multitasking.

I stood far enough away from the ladder so that if she decided to kick me, I would be safe.

She looked down at me and then continued to hang the banner, asking one of her students for another bungee cord. With the cord in place and the task completed, she climbed down and directed two of her kids to fold the ladder up and put it away.

She was dressed in jeans, a dark green Northern Lakes t-shirt, and a ball cap that read "Take a Kid Outdoors" with her ponytail pulled through the back. Ron was right, Julie was really cute.

She said, "I see you made it in off the lake. Bud was just here and told me you got the boat going this morning. Did you have a nice ride? Perfect weather."

"It was better than a nice ride. God, I love those lakes," I replied. My mind began to drift, to relive the wonders I had seen. I stopped myself. "Anyway, it's just what I needed. I take it these are your students? What do you guys have going here?"

"Running a school like mine requires that we do public education about the school as well as raise extra funds to support our efforts. Musky Fest is when we sell most of our t-shirts and sweatshirts. Every year the kids come up with new colors and some design modifications, but always the same logo. We buy the shirts all locally and have them printed. The company that does the work holds on to our bill, giving us a chance to sell enough to pay for it. First thing the kids have to do is sell enough to pay for their own tees and sweats. That's their official school uniform."

"How many kids do you have?"

"Twenty-five officially. But we also have a couple of drifters that come in and out. So sometimes more, never less."

"What are the grades?"

"Middle school, seven to nine, but we're trying to add a high school. We sure have the need for it, but not everybody in the community thinks it's a good idea."

"So what's the deal with your school that's so different?"

"You know, John, I'd love to sit and chat with you, but as you can see I'm little busy getting everybody here going in the right direction."

Just as she spoke, I heard calls for Ms. Carlson come from the two opposite corners of the tent.

"I will be right there kids. Just hold on. How about I turn you over to two of the kids, and they can fill you in."

She looked around, and then called, "Danny and Anna, will you come over here, please?"

Two kids trotted over, a tall girl with long blonde hair, streaked with purple and a big smile and a boy who couldn't have weighed 60 pounds soaking wet with perfectly combed straight hair wearing a new school t-shirt that came to his knees. "Whazup, Ms. Carlson?" asked Danny.

"Danny and Anna, this is Mr. Cabrelli. He is interested in knowing about our school. I thought it would be good practice for you to give him your presentation before we officially open the booth."

"Sure," bubbled Anna with a little giggle. And she and Danny took me over to a display board that was covered with pictures of the kids and their school.

Anna started by saying, "Northern Lakes Academy is a project-based school where all learning is tied back to our natural resources."

Then Danny added, "It is a public school that anyone can come to. You don't have to pay extra, and you get to do a lot of different things than if you were in regular school. It's not like a school for dummies, it's just …" he started to get a little flustered.

"What Danny means is that some kids don't do well in regular school. It doesn't mean they aren't smart. It just means that they learn better other ways than sitting at a desk. Some kids that come are just looking for a challenge," Anna explained.

I remembered my talk with Bud, a guy that was smart in a way that would be difficult to find its way to a school desk.

"Before I came here, I hated school," Danny said. "I never even showed up most of the time. But I sure like it here. I get pretty good grades too. You can just ask Ms. Carlson. Are you her boyfriend?"

Anna looked mortified, "Oh my God, Danny, shut up! That is so inappropriate."

Quickly she got them back on track, and the presentation continued, flawlessly, although Anna stayed within arm's reach of Danny, I am sure just in case corrective measures were required.

They described the activities and projects they undertook during the course of the year, and it was fascinating. Reading, writing, and arithmetic all tied back to the outdoors. At least one field day a week, regardless of weather, was spent outside working on a community or restoration project.

"This is Northern Wisconsin. I know the weather can get a little tough sometimes. Do you still go out then?" I asked.

Danny piped up, "There is no bad weather, just bad clothes. I mean like when it's cold out, you got to wear clothes that will keep you warm. Or if it's raining, you gotta have a rain suit. You know, you gotta dress right. Otherwise, you will be miserable, and Ms. Carlson doesn't care. She just says, 'Next time maybe you will dress for a field day.' I mean, I don't think she'd let you die or anything. One day I didn't dress warm enough, and we were out clearing a snowshoe trail, and it started to snow like crazy. I got so cold I about froze my ass off."

"Danny!" Anna shouted.

One should not encourage bad behavior in children, and the belly laugh that I let loose could be construed as condoning Danny's choice of words, but there just was no stopping it.

With that, Anna made it clear the presentation had come to the end. "Well, thank you for asking about our school. We hope that you will come and visit. Here are a brochure and a schedule of events. The public is always welcome. If you want, you can also buy a t-shirt or sweatshirt over at the other table. The t-shirts are $15, and the sweatshirts are $30. Thank you again."

She smiled, grabbed Danny by the arm, and pulled him away where I am sure she burned his ears.

The dozen or so kids working the booth were each engaged in their own tasks. Some unpacked sweatshirts and t-shirts, while others arranged school brochures. Julie was like an orchestra conductor, turning here, looking there, directing one student and turning 180 degrees to direct another in the same breath, keeping the kids on task.

The part of the student body I was observing would be tough to categorize. Along with Danny and Anna, another boy was at least six feet, wearing a flannel shirt with cutoff sleeves, a mop of hair that looked like it was cut after somebody put a bowl on his head. One girl had pink hair and a huge nose ring. The friend she was talking to stacking up brochures had jet black hair, jet black eye makeup and lipstick, and was wearing black clothes. One boy looked Native American. Another boy and girl looked Asian. This group was as diverse as it could be. In my old beat, this could have been the beginning of street fights, broken windows, and burning cars. Here they were just working together, having fun, being kids.

I stepped up to the other side of the table by the sweatshirts. "Anna told me the sweatshirts are $30 and the t-shirts are $15. Is that right?'

"Yup, that's right," said a boy with a mohawk and pants hanging down.

"I'll take one of each, extra large."

I handed him the cash, and he gave me the shirts. Electric blue tie dye, my favorite.

"These are some good looking shirts," I said to my salesman. "Where did you get them?"

"Just down the street at Mystery Bay Graphics."

"Where exactly is that?"

"Just walk down this street here about two blocks. Then turn at the Quick Mart and go another two blocks. It's right at the end of the street. It's got a real big sign."

"Thanks, buddy," I said as I started to walk away.

"Thank you, and my name is Anthony."

"See you around, Anthony. I'm John."

I walked down to Mystery Bay Graphics. It was only about twice as far as Anthony had told me, but it was a nice walk. I went inside and saw that the counter was manned by an older guy wearing wire-rimmed glasses trimming up some kind of design on paper.

"Can I help you?" he asked.

"Did you folks do the clothing for Northern Lakes School?"

"Sure did. Do it every year. By the looks of what is under your arm, I see they must have corralled you. Man, that blue tie dye is bright."

"How much do they owe you?"

"Nothing right now. They pay it off as they sell sweatshirts. We have a deal worked out. My wife and I like those kids and their teacher. We don't mind helping out."

"They do have a bill that needs to be paid eventually, right?"

"Oh yeah, sure, right. We wouldn't be able to stay in business very long any other way."

"I want to make you a deal. I want to pay the whole bill, but I don't want them to know it was me that did it. You think we could work that out?"

He smiled. "I am sure we could, and now would be a good time to pay it because my wife is out running errands and, well, she can be kinda a talker."

"Then let's get to it, my friend, before she returns."

"Let me bring this up. Okay, well, they ordered 75 sweatshirts and 100 t-shirts ... let's see, they are tax exempt, so you don't have to pay the governor, and we give them the biggest discount we can. The total comes out to be $2,100."

You may at this point question why I would just plunk down a couple grand for some kids I had just met. I can't explain it. It is just me.

"Do you take Mastercard?"

"Sure, of course we do, and I would be glad to take yours, but my wife does the books, and when she sees your name on the credit card, I am afraid your secret will be out. She is faster than the Internet at spreading the word."

"I'll be back."

I headed over to the bank. After five minutes with the teller and a quick swipe of my bank card, I had an envelope full of cash and hiked back toward Mystery Bay. My route back took me past the Northern Lakes booth, and when I neared it, I saw none other than Officer Lawler, leaning up against a tent post, in full uniform, looking cool, looking dangerous, talking to Julie. As I got closer, I could see that she was trying to have none of it, and this was not lost on her kids. I decided to see what was going on.

Just as I got to them, the big kid in the flannel shirt stepped up beside Julie and said to Lawler, "Leave her alone, you creep. Can't you see she doesn't want to talk to you? Leave her alone."

"Nathan, please be quiet. I can handle this," Julie implored.

Lawler was feeling like a bad boy, feeling tough, and he gave Nathan his most withering stare and, quick as a cat, reached out and grabbed him by the front of his shirt and pulled him face to face.

"You got something to say to me, you little shit? How about you and I head down to juvie and we take the long way? You've been there before. Matter of fact, that's where I heard your old man got his start. Might as well get ready to follow the family tradition."

I saw it coming. Youthful indiscretion responding to hurt and anger. Nathan balled up his fist and prepared to swing hard at Lawler's head. I stepped into it, got between them and took the shot on my jaw meant for Lawler.

Lawler, Nathan, and I were face to face to face. I worked my way completely between them.

"Come on, Nathan. Lawler back it up. This is no good here."

The look on Lawler's face said it all: he wanted to show me just how dangerous he was right then and there. Good news for me, bad news for him, the commotion had begun to attract a crowd, and there were plenty of witnesses. Lawler took it all in, stepped back a little, and gave the kid a shove.

"Mind your own business, Cabrelli," Lawler snarled. "I've got more important stuff to do than waste my time with trash like you." He turned to walk away, but as he passed me he intentionally knocked the big envelope I was carrying out of my hand to the ground, and about half of the money fell out. His interest in me was immediately renewed.

"What's this, Cabrelli? Where did all the cash come from? Nobody carries that kind of cash around ... unless they are doing something illegal. Like maybe selling drugs. You a drug dealer? You selling drugs to these kids here?" He was on a roll. "That money looks like evidence of a crime to me. I am going to have to take it with me until we get some answers."

I'd had enough.

"Lawler, you have not one ounce of probable cause to touch that money. It is mine, it is legal, and I am going to put it back in the envelope. Just leave it be. Don't make this worse than it already is. Walk away Lawler. Walk away."

It wasn't going to happen. He didn't mind threatening a kid, but taking on me would be a different story. He just couldn't back down; dumb, tough guys never can. He took a step toward me. The battle was imminent, when the voice of the Lord called out in the form of the Musky Falls Chief of Police Donald Timmy: "Stand down, Officer Lawler. Back up."

Lawler backed up a step and the chief walked between us. "What the hell is going on here? Where did all this money come from?"

"Drug money, Chief. I caught this guy with it. I think he might be a drug dealer, and he was hanging around these kids," Lawler said.

The chief looked me up and down. "You're John Cabrelli, right?"

"I am," I responded.

"Is that your money on the ground?"

"It is."

"Seems like a lot of cash to be walking around with. Any special reason you might have that much cash?"

"Chief, there is nothing illegal going on here with the money. Give me one minute to talk to you alone and I'll explain."

"Sounds like a good idea to me. That work for you, Lawler?"

"Whatever you say, Chief, but I wouldn't believe a word he says."

I explained the whole story to the chief. He seemed satisfied but asked me to stick around.

I picked up the money and put it back in the envelope.

The chief had words with Lawler, and then he swaggered off down the street to attend to his more important duties.

The crowd that had gathered dispersed at the chief's urging, and in a couple of minutes, all was pretty much back to normal. Nathan walked up to me sheepishly (with Julie's urging) and said he was sorry that I caught the punch he'd meant for Lawler.

I told him, "Nathan, I'm not sorry I caught it. Hitting a cop, even a jerk like him, is a felony. It would ruin your life. Besides, it didn't hurt that much." My face had already begun to swell.

"Mr. Cabrelli, my squad is right across the street. How about I give you a ride to ... where you're going."

"Thanks, Chief. I would appreciate it."

I said goodbye to Julie and the kids, and we took off.

• • •

During the short drive to Mystery Bay Graphics, the chief didn't say much. I walked in and settled the Northern Lakes account. The owner smiled, thanked me, and told me how much he loved cash.

The chief waited outside. I got back in the car, and he locked eyes with me. He was probably close to retirement, and had the look often worn by career cops. A big man, still looking pretty fit.

"John, I am going to tell you something. I don't know what good it will do either one of us, but what the hell. Your uncle Nick was a good man and a good friend of mine. His death has affected us all. In some cases like this people want to find a reason, punish someone for their loss. They see things that aren't there. When he got run down, I was all over that case, but because it happened in the county, it is the jurisdiction of the sheriff's department. They were cooperative and did a fair investigation. After you put everything together, it looks like just a hit and run, no premeditation. There are a few loose threads, but until the driver is caught, it'll be tough to tie those up."

"Who did it, Chief?"

"I really don't know. All I do know is that rumors about his death have been flying around this town for months. People claim it had to do with his property and his unwillingness to sell to the mine. Others say that he stole some other inventor's idea and made a fortune off it. I've looked into all of them and none hold any water. If there was something there, I would have found a lead. I know that much. The other thing I know is there are a whole bunch of people I don't trust too much that have been very interested in your arrival and intentions. This is a small town, and a good chief keeps his ear to the ground at all times. There is something going on, something big, and who knows, maybe Nick was involved in some way, and it got him killed. If that's the case, it might do the same for you if you aren't careful."

"Is your boy Lawler involved?"

"Hard to say. He's pretty much an asshole all the time. Never goes far enough to get canned, but he's always right on the edge. He does seem to have taken a special shine to you. If he's a problem, I'll straighten him out, make sure he backs off. Want me to talk to him?"

I thought for a second. If he was involved in my uncle's death, I wanted him free to make whatever moves he was going to make.

I really needed to know what his relationship was with Anderson, and how I figured in.

"No thanks, Chief. I'm not worried about him."

"Whatever you want."

"Chief, can I ask you about someone else?"

"Sure, go ahead."

"What is the deal with Ron Carver?"

The chief let out a short, gruff laugh. "So Ron found you, did he? Let me tell you about Ron. He is a piece of work. He was Nick's best friend and is a close friend of mine. When you get to know him, you're never going to forget him. He's a hell of a good man. When you talk to him, you'll find out that he is convinced that Nick was murdered. But like I said, everybody has their own ideas, whether there is any evidence to back them up or not."

I got out and the chief started to drive off, but before he pulled all the way out, he put his window down and said, "John, by the way, I have a copy of the report you're looking for waiting for you on my desk. Figured you might want to see it. Stop by anytime to get it."

Uncle Nick had been murdered, maybe by accident, maybe intentionally, his life taken from him by an unknown person or persons. And finding out who did it was not a conscious decision on my part as much as it was a natural part of the chain of events. ∎

CHAPTER 14
Cabrelli

It is a rare criminal investigation that benefits from the passing of time. Minutes can make the difference between success and failure. As hours pass, you watch the case come together or fall apart. The role of a good investigator is to know when to switch course, to decide which leads to follow now and which ones can wait. The wrong call and the case can slip away: critical evidence disappears, witnesses become harder and harder to find. Most often, within a couple of days the die is cast, and you have what you have.

To investigate something that happened months ago is daunting, but not impossible. The first thing you have to do is find out everything that the first investigators found: read all the reports, look at the evidence, check to see if there were any stories in the papers. Then make a list of your principals: the victim, any witnesses, the investigators, the dispatchers, close associates, friends, and anybody else you think might have a connection to the case or even a small bit of information. In a dated and unsolved crime, you are always looking for the rock someone didn't turn over. Sometimes it is a piece of information that someone had and never thought important, or maybe it's just two seemingly unimportant pieces put together. Once you have all you can get, it is time to try and move forward. This will require you to develop a list of questions that you think you need to have answered. There is only one way to do this—talk to the witnesses and investigators.

Uncle Nick's hit and run had been identified as just that, a hit and run, an accidental act in which the driver had fled the scene. Usually this happened because the driver was drunk or because there was some other mitigating factor. Regardless, a hit and run is a homicide. The difference is huge. A hit and run is most often an unintentional, negligent act, whereas a murder is an intentional act, requiring premeditation and planning driven by motive.

Reexamining someone else's investigation that was technically still open because the perpetrator remained at large is a road paved with potential problems. The word of the day in such a case is *tact*. When you start looking closely at the work of others, they feel like they are being second-guessed, and most often they are. That tends to make them unhappy and less than cooperative. You can expect your reception to run the gamut from helpful to downright hostile. Unless you meet that good cop, the one who believes in what he or she is doing, the one who is never afraid to share information to help someone looking for the truth, the one for whom getting the bad guy is priority one, then your reception will be different. For that cop, it doesn't matter to them who gets it done, as long as it gets done.

I went to the chief's office and, as promised, there was an 11x17 manila envelope waiting there for me with my name on it. The clerk looked at my ID and then handed it over. It was thin. I needed to be in the right frame of mind before I read it, so I decided to take it back to the hotel. On the way, I stopped at The Outfitter clothing store and bought a couple of shirts, cargo shorts, and other items of clothing more suitable for the weather and my current activities than what I currently had, actually doubling my current inventory of casual attire.

At the hotel I could barely keep from opening the envelope, but I knew better. Something this important needed all my focus, all my attention. Waiting a little longer would not hurt anything. I decided to lie down for a while before going back downtown for the night's festivities.

I was tired but couldn't sleep. There was too much going on inside my head: Uncle Nick murdered, a rogue cop pushing hard to get me to jump, the inevitability of what would happen if he kept it up, the property, and a million other things. I gave it a good twenty minutes, got up, took a shower, put on my new clean clothes, and headed back to town. As the day progressed, the crowds had thinned a little. In the middle of Main Street at a cross street intersection, steel barricades were being set up. The street was open to all, but they were fencing in the area where they served the beer, and you needed an ID bracelet to get in.

The band was unloading instruments and sound equipment, moving items here or there around the stage, testing amps and mics for sound. A bass player wearing plaid shorts, an orange bowling shirt, and heavy black framed glasses got his stuff ready to go and treated the pre-concert crowd to a wild guitar solo that charged everyone up. The drummer joined in and people started moving toward the concert area. I saw a sign for the world's best steak sandwiches and headed over. I left the vendor's window with a huge steak sandwich, an order of onion rings, and a soft drink. I found a spot at the nearby picnic tables and started in. I'd had no idea how hungry I was, but the pile of food was gone before I knew it. It may not have been the world's best steak sandwich, but it was damn good.

Full and content, I sat and watched the crowd and volunteers as they finished the final setup for the night's show. People were moving in toward the stage as the crowd grew, ages ranging from babies in carriers to elderly with walkers. Everyone was smiling with laughter and good cheer being the order of the evening.

The stage and crowd came alive as the band let out with a great rendition of Elvis's "Wheels on My Heels," followed by an Elton John oldie. After the song, the band leader leaped to the front and yelled, "Hello Musky Falls! Hello Musky Festers! We are the Gonzos! We hope you're ready, because we are bringing it on!"

The crowd cheered, totally into it. The next song, Neil Diamond's "Sweet Caroline," had everybody singing the refrain—including me if you want the truth. It was too much to resist, and I found my way out into the crowd, getting quickly caught up in the mood and the music.

The band was great, made up of family members from Northern Wisconsin who played the festival and fair circuit in the summer and on weekends. They appeared to be having as much fun as everyone else. As people got livened up, dancing broke out in small pockets in front of the stage. Little kids were going at a rate that adults find difficult to comprehend. Dads and moms were dancing with kids, a couple in their later years were dancing cheek to cheek, teens and young adults were dancing but making sure to maintain their cool. Next to me were four girls kind of line dancing in place. They sang along with every song and knew all the words.

As I was watching the band, I felt a tug on my arm. I turned around and saw it was Julie.

"Hey, John, buy you a beer?'

"Sure," I said. "Where is your entourage?"

"They finished up for the day about an hour ago. Some of them will show up here, but if they do, it's on their own or with parents. Trying to supervise kids next to a beer tent at a street dance falls outside of my teaching duties."

We walked over to the beer concession area, and with a nod, the gatekeeper let us pass. Julie ordered two tap Leinies, and we headed off to the picnic tables. Our spot was close enough that we could still enjoy the band, but far enough away that we could actually carry on a conversation without shouting.

"Thanks for the beer, teacher. It was very nice of you."

"I'm the one that needs to be thanking you, John. I can't imagine how bad things would have gone had you not stepped in between Nathan and Lawler. How's your face? It looks a little puffy but not too bad."

"Nothing to worry about with me. I've been hit a lot harder than that and for not near as good a reason. Besides, my face can always use a little improvement."

She laughed, and it almost sounded like singing.

"I am sorry we got off on the wrong foot."

"You mean like sticking a shotgun in my face the first time we met?"

"Well that would be one thing, but in my own defense, a girl has got to protect herself, and I had no idea who you were and why you were in my house. What I am really talking about is my attitude after I found out who you were. There was no excuse for it. Your aunt and uncle had nothing but praise for you. I knew they were both good judges of character and should have trusted in that judgment. I was very close to them, and I miss them every day. For some reason I thought you were going to be some slickster showing up to take things over, change things for the worse, destroy what was left. Then I saw that car and those shoes and, well, what would you expect?"

"I'm just curious. Your kids wore every manner of clothing today. Do you judge them on how they dress?"

"No, of course not. In your case, I was just looking for reasons not to like you. The shoes and sports car were just convenient. The truth is, I thought the shoes were actually very stylish. Although I did enjoy it immensely when you stepped in that puddle on your way to your car."

"You saw that, huh. It was like you wished it upon me and then it happened."

"Anyway, your new hikers look good and are way better suited to hanging around up here. I just want to make sure you understand how much I appreciate what you did for Nathan. If he had hit Lawler, that would have been it for him, and Lawler would have made sure of it. He is such a jerk. I don't know why they don't fire him. Most people around here do not like him, and he seems to thrive on it."

"Not like it's my business, except that it did ultimately result in me getting clobbered. Why was he bothering you? What was the deal?"

"There's not much to tell. He sees himself as every girl's 'dream come true man' and can't understand why I would not be interested in dating him. He is further perplexed by the fact that I actually find him disgusting, and he interprets that as me playing hard to get. I avoid him as much as I can, but whenever he gets the chance, he shows up, and getting rid of him is, as I am sure you observed, difficult."

"Julie, do you think he's a dangerous guy? I mean really dangerous?"

"I don't know exactly what that means. He carries a gun and has a very aggressive attitude; he seems pretty dangerous to me."

"Some people want to appear dangerous. The more they try to look that way usually the less dangerous they are, but not always. Some want to appear dangerous, and they truly are. They spend their life pushing others into confrontation, just waiting for the chance to land on somebody with both feet."

"Well, I can tell you that he has had a couple of run-ins with people around here that have been really scary. Lawler and some other guys like him hang around at the gym over on Third Street. They like to lift weights in the front window to impress passersby, I guess. Anyway, he was working out one day with a couple of his buddies when a group of college kids from Eau Claire, after a few at the Moccasin Bar, stopped at the window to look in. One of the kids was a big guy on the college football team, and he started pointing at Lawler and then began jumping around and acting like a monkey. Lawler and his crew walked out of the gym and onto the sidewalk to confront the kids. The story going around was that Lawler pushed hard to get the kid to take a swing at him. When finally he swung, he missed Lawler by a mile, but it was enough to open the door. Lawler hit and kicked him until he was lying on his side on the ground trying to cover his face."

"Jeez, how did the kid end up?"

"He spent five days in the hospital here until he was transferred down to Eau Claire. I'm not sure about all that was wrong with him, but I heard he had to have facial reconstructive surgery, and he had a serious concussion. The kid's parents raised holy hell and demanded that Lawler be arrested. That didn't happen. Lawler and his guys swore that this big football player initiated everything and that the only reason Lawler even went out to talk to him was to tell them to have a good time but not cause any trouble during their visit to Musky Falls. Besides that, even the other college students said that the football player took the first swing. It must have been bad though, because one of Lawler's friends, Joe Larken, a pretty tough guy himself, threw up at the side of the building after it was over. You never see them together anymore."

"Sounds like at the very least, he likes to whip on those he can whip on. Do you have any idea what Lawler and Derek Anderson might have in common? They seem to be front and center in my life right now, and I'm not exactly sure why."

"Derek Anderson is also a creep, but other than that connection I don't honestly know what they could have going on together. I can't imagine they hang out with one another."

"Well, keep it in mind. If you think of anything, let me know."

"I will, although I'm so busy with the school, I'm kinda out of the loop in town. But if I hear something or something comes to mind, I will let you know."

"Thanks, I'd appreciate it. Can I get you another beer, Julie?"

"Nope. One is pretty much my limit, but don't let that stop you."

We visited for a while longer, and I could see that she was getting tired. I could also see she had something on her mind. Finally, it came out.

"I am really tired and want to get home, but there is something I need to know."

"Spit it out," I said.

"When do you think you'll know what is going to happen with your aunt and uncle's property? I was scheduled to be out of there today, but based on what you said, I haven't finished the move yet. I'm just moving back into town with Bud, so it's very flexible. I'm not trying to influence your decision. I just like to know."

"Honestly, I don't know. The property is not for sale, and I told Anderson that. He didn't take it very well, by the way."

Julie's look was quizzical, a combination of a smile and eyebrow raised in suspicion.

"I am sure not. I'd bet there is a pretty hefty commission on that sale. One thing Derek would never want to miss is the chance to make a buck."

"I'm planning on staying here indefinitely, at least until I get everything squared away. Right now the hotel is okay, but I'd like to find someplace better, a little more permanent. But I don't have any plans yet."

"Well, you could move out to the lake, and I could move to town like I planned. After all, you own it."

"I thought about that, but right now you should just stay put. I have got to have some time to process all this."

She looked at me with trepidation and said, "The house is plenty big. My rooms are upstairs, and you could move into the downstairs. I don't think it would be a problem. I lived there with your aunt and uncle for quite a while."

"Interesting idea," I said. "That is just what Ron Carver suggested to me this very day as a perfect solution."

Julie laughed. "So you met the one and only Ron Carver. That guy is a piece of work," she said and laughed again. "Just to clear your mind, I am sure that my idea of us both living at the lake and his are going to be way, way different," she said and shook her head, "That guy."

I was enjoying her laugh when the light on the back of the beer trailer was blocked out by a looming hulk. We both jumped and were much relieved when Bud sat down with a beer.

"Hey, you guys. Whatchya been up to?"

"Not much, Bud," I said. "Just taking in the sights and the sounds. How about you?"

"I've just been running around like I do every year. The generator they wanted to use at the outdoor pavilion wouldn't start, so I got that going. The chamber sold ten more spaces for tents on Main than they thought they did, and when two tents try to occupy the same space, well it gets a little tense. I helped them move the tents to another spot even better than the one they were fighting over. Just lots of little stuff, you know. I did hear that there was some problem over at your booth, Julie. What's the story with that?"

"Lawler stopped by. Need I say more?"

Bud's usual smiling face turned into a scowl. "Was he bothering you again?" he asked.

"Bud, Lawler bothers everyone, not just me."

"You know exactly what I mean!"

"Lawler is nothing to worry about. I never even gave him a second thought."

"Well, he better not let me catch him bothering you anymore."

This was no idle threat. Bud was dead serious. I couldn't imagine the havoc a guy like him could cause if he had a mind to. If Lawler tried anything on Bud at an event, it would be significantly different than beating up a half-drunk college student. I did not wish any trouble on Bud, but I couldn't help but smile a little at the thought.

Julie quickly changed the subject and defused the situation.

"Bud, I am beat. Let's get going back to the lake."

"You still staying out there, Bud?" I asked.

Julie answered for him. "He is convinced that I need protection from whoever broke in, and nothing I am going to say is going to change that."

"I just think it's better to be careful, Julie," Bud responded.

"I know. Thanks, Bud."

They got up to leave, but before they did, Julie asked, "What have you got planned for tomorrow?"

"I thought I might come out to the lake, do a little fishing maybe, or go for swim. I don't know."

"The weather is supposed to be great. Bud and I will be in town all day, so you'd have the place to yourself."

Goodbyes said, they walked off in the direction of Bud's truck. I walked back to the hotel for a good night's sleep. ■

CHAPTER 15
Cabrelli

I was up early and went over to Crossroads for a cup of coffee and a scone. The free continental breakfast at the motel was still available, but after a day or two of whole-hearted indulgence, I began to feel a little less enthusiastic about the sausage patties, biscuits and gravy, and the waffles made in the flip-over cooker.

My timing was excellent, as Crossroads was not busy yet. I got a cup of coffee and picked up a copy of the *Namekagon County News*. There was a little morning chill in the air, just like most mornings in the Northwoods, but I still opted for the outdoor seating. The paper was full of news about Musky Fest; at the time it went to press, the Lions Club fishing contest already had 75 entries, and the sizes of the fish were listed.

The one that caught my eye was a natural Musky, 52½ inches and 29 pounds. In the picture, the lucky angler was holding the fish out in front of him as far as his arm would go, making the fish look a lot bigger in relation to him. He needn't have bothered, as it was a big, beautiful fish without his help.

There was also a schedule of the remaining Musky Fest events. Today, Saturday, was packed full with more live bands performing in the street, a magician, clowns, a skit on the history of Cal Johnson's world record musky, and another skit on the history of Louie Spray's world record musky. I could remember even when I was a kid that there was strong disagreement on who actually held the world record; apparently it had not yet been resolved. There was also a talent contest from 1:00–3:00 featuring dancing, singing, and baton twirling. Carnival rides opened at 10:00 today.

The festival also had events set for Sunday, concluding with a parade. Uncle Nick and Aunt Rose always took me to the parade. They would set folding chairs up early to reserve their space. They usually tried to get a spot right in front of the bakery, making me a happy boy. To this day, I love a good donut.

Sunday started out with a 5K run and an around-the-block Minnow Run for the little kids. Next came a casting contest for kids and adults. I was excited for all of it.

• • •

With coffee in hand and the newspaper left for the next reader, I went over to the Chamber office. There was a very bouncy and exuberant young lady who was glad to register me for the run. She took my t-shirt size and informed me that check-in was at 8:00 a.m. in front of the bank on Main Street.

I fired up the jeep and drove east to the lake and had only driven a couple of miles out of town when Bud and Julie passed me on their way in. Climbing a hill in front of me were a group of serious bicyclists, spandex clad on ultra-light bikes, moving fast, seeing the country with pedal power.

As I passed them, the leader gave me a thumbs-up sign. I guessed, unlike bike riders in the big city, they actually appreciate it when someone gives them the right of way.

The rest of my trip was blissfully uneventful, allowing me to enjoy the beauty of the north. I turned onto the road leading to the cabin. There on the edge of the pavement was a living, breathing dinosaur. The creature was intent on finishing a hole it had begun in the gravel. With no traffic to worry about I just stopped in the middle of the road and watched. The very large, mature snapping turtle paid me no mind and continued unperturbed with her business. As a youngster, I had watched this very scenario play out before. The snapper would dig the hole, then lay her eggs in it. Once done with the egg laying, she would cover the hole back up and go back to her wetland home, the eggs left to hatch on their own and the baby turtles left to dig their way out. My uncle and I had surveyed many turtle nests that we'd found on our walks.

After the eggs hatched there would be a hole with eggshells. We would examine the eggs and, from the way they were spread about and from the evidence of the remaining yolk, we could tell whether they'd hatched or whether some skunk or raccoon had dug them up and made a breakfast out of them. Most of the nests we'd found had eggs that had been eaten, but every once in a while, we'd find one that had successfully hatched, helping ensure the survival of the species. The snapping turtle itself is a formidable beast. I smiled at the memory of a goofy guy that lived down the lake and sold my uncle bait. He was missing the tip of his pointer finger. The story goes that he was poking a big snapper one day, kind of teasing it, trying to get it to snap. He got his wish but was a little slow, and the turtle bit the fingertip clean off.

I let the turtle be and drove on in, parking next to the cabin.

There was a note stuck to the door.

John,

The walleyes are really hitting up at the boys camp. I put a couple dozen minnows in a bucket sitting in the water tied to the dock. On the dock, next to the bucket is a small box of jigs. Tie one of those on, hook up a minnow and drop it in the water right at the end of Boys Camp Point. A fresh walleye dinner tonight would sure be great. Julie can cook fish better than anyone I know. We should be back about six or so.

Good luck,

Bud

I walked down to the dock, and sure enough, there was a small plastic box with half a dozen jigs in it, each with a different colored tail. Hanging from the pier post was my uncle's old minnow bucket, a galvanized thing with all sorts of small holes in it and a snap-lock lid. I knew it would keep the minnows alive and well for a long time.

My uncle was always building something or working on a project. As a result, about 100 feet from the house he had built a wonderful shop building, plenty big for good-sized projects but small enough to heat with wood. I had loved working with Uncle Nick on projects in the shop. It was his place, a place where he had his stuff, a place where he could express himself with his hands. It also served as a good place for him to go when Aunt Rose wanted him out from under her feet. I unlocked the shop and went in to get the rest of the gear needed for my fishing expedition. While I felt a little self-conscious snooping around the house, checking out the shop didn't bother me anymore. I just loved the place.

A big wood stove occupied one corner. It had a strange octopus-looking ductwork thing on top of it, running up to the ceiling and then into different pipes that ran to each section of the shop. Next to it was a woodpile with perfectly split, perfectly stacked firewood, probably at least two years old. When I was ten, and Uncle Nick and I were splitting firewood, he told me that the wood we were spitting would keep us warm when I was twelve. Cutting wood was an adventure. We always cut either standing dead trees or ones that were already on the ground that were still solid. Uncle Nick could put a notch on one side of a tree, cut through from the other side, and the tree would fall exactly where he wanted it to fall. I loved to hear the rifle shot crack as the tree began its descent.

He used to ask me the same strange question every time we went wood cutting: *"Johnny, if a tree fell in the woods and nobody was around to hear it, do you think it would still make a noise?"* I always answered yes, and he always agreed with me, but went on to say that some folks would disagree. I never figured that one out.

I walked over to the fishing rod and gun rack. The rods were out in the open, but the guns were behind a locked welded steel gate. I tried my keys in the lock, but it wouldn't open. I figured Bud probably had a key, and I would get that from him later.

The tools in the toolboxes were all in their place; they showed signs of being well used, but also well cared for. Good tools, the kind that come with real lifetime warranties. Nick had no use for crappy tools.

Over the workbench I saw a picture of him and me standing behind four wooden duck nest boxes we had built. I must have been about thirteen or fourteen. Each year we would build a couple and put them up in trees along the flowage, hoping the wood ducks would find them.

There were several file cabinets. They were super heavy duty and had a "fireproof" label on the upper left-hand corner. I thumbed the latch and pulled the top one open. There, on top of a book lying in front of the files was a revolver and next to it a box of ammunition. I pulled the gun out and opened the cylinder. It was fully loaded. I recognized it. When my department switched from revolvers to auto-loading handguns, the old wheel guns, while still serviceable, didn't have much value. Uncle Nick asked me to get him one. I did, a stainless-steel Model 66 Smith and Wesson .357 magnum. One of the best guns ever built. I even scored him four or five boxes of ammo from the range officer and a high-rise belt holster. While there are bigger calibers, .357 has a long history as a proven butt kicker. I knew Uncle Nick often carried it with him on hikes in the woods.

I looked through the file tabs on warranties and instruction and service manuals for every piece of equipment he ever owned. These alone filled the first and second drawers. The third drawer had folders filled with magazine articles, photographs, newspaper stories, and ads all pertaining to pieces of equipment or some task performed by equipment. He had made pages of notes for each folder. Glancing over the notes, I could see that the intention of the files became clear; they were ideas about helping improve a product design or inventing a product to perform a task.

The rest of the drawers, except for one, were filled with tech manuals, drawings and designs, and step-by-step processes on doing certain things. The remaining drawer was filled with firearm cartridge reloading books, data sheets, and binders with targets inserted. Each target had the load data, caliber, and firearm in the corner. I had forgotten that Uncle Nick was a handloader and loved creating his own ammunition. He always felt his handloads were superior to the factory stuff.

As I was looking through the bottom drawer, I noticed it did not come out as far as the one above it. I reached in the back to try and get it loose and hit an obstruction. I could not see what it was exactly, so I grabbed a flashlight off the bench and looked in. In the back of the drawer, I saw a small door fitted with a combination lock. I couldn't quite figure it out until it dawned on me. This was the door to a small safe that went through the back of the file cabinet and into the wall. Ingenious. No one would ever find it here, and even if they did, it would take some serious effort to get at it and have any chance of getting it open.

After some inspection, I saw that the drawer could be released by two latches, one on either side in the back. I flipped them and the drawer came loose with a click. The heavy, fully-loaded drawer slid out easily, and when it reached the extent of its forward travel, it pivoted to the left, out of the way, giving clear access to the vault door behind. Now with the drawer clear, I noted two other things. First, there was a small switch that, when flipped, turned on a light that illuminated the space. Second, below the switch was a magnetic holster, and in it was another gun. I pulled the gun out and saw it was a loaded Walther PPK/S .380.

Two loaded guns, one file cabinet, and a secret vault definitely got my curiosity going.

Uncle Nick had something he wanted to hide and reason to believe that someone might try and take it from him.

When you are investigating something and in "hot pursuit," investigative procedure and experience play into your decision-making process, but whatever is happening at the moment most often dictates the next move you make. A crime that occurred months—or for that matter even years—in the past requires a much different approach. A smart investigator thinks things through before they run off trying to figure out what happened. You should keep an open mind and consider all possibilities. In this case, a veteran law enforcement officer was pretty convinced that it was an accident. Uncle Nick's best friend and my gut told me something else. That coupled with the fact that my reception upon arriving in Musky Falls was confusing at best and sinister at worst made me consider only one possibility: Nick Cabrelli was the victim of premeditated murder. I intended to turn over every rock in Namekagon County to find out who was responsible.

Today though I was going fishing. Fishing is one of those great productive activities that allows plenty of time for thinking, and I had a bunch of thinking to do.

I closed up the file cabinet, but before I did, I removed the little Walther and put it in the pocket of my cargo shorts. The revolver was a more formidable weapon, but the Walther's compact size made it a better choice for concealment. Old habits die hard. It's better to have a gun and not need one than to need a gun and not have one. I grabbed the tackle box, a PFD, and two fishing rods. One was for the jigs and minnows Bud had provided, and the other was set up with a No. 5 Mepps Spinner in case I decided to cast for one of the denizens of the deep.

The boat was loaded, and much to my happiness, the motor fired up on the first pull. While it warmed up, I filled the container bucket with water and put the other part of the minnow bucket in it, depositing them on a flat spot on the deck. I grabbed the box of jigs, and soon my little boat and I were skipping across the water. Another day in paradise with a little breeze, clear skies, and the air temperature already in the 60s.

There were a few other boats on the water, today being Saturday and all, but it was not what you would call crowded. Water skiing, tube riding, and other tow-behind activities were limited to the hours of 11:00 a.m. to 3:00 p.m. The set times let the fishermen fish and the skiers ski during peak times.

I was across from a place called Bear Paw when I cut in toward the boys camp. There were two boats anchored off the point within a few feet of each other, and I figured they too were looking for a walleye dinner. I shut down to idle and came up to a spot near the other boats, but not so close that they would think I was encroaching on them. I quietly lowered the anchor, which took a fair amount of rope with it, and I judged the depth to be about 25 feet. As I was getting my gear operational, the question about the other boats' presence was answered when one of the guys set the hook and soon brought a beautiful walleye to his net.

Ever the trained investigator, I noted that the tail on the jig he was using was a very bright chartreuse. Chartreuse was indeed one of the color choices Bud had included.

I hooked the minnow up and dropped it over the side of the boat allowing it to free fall with an open bail. When the line went slack, I knew I had hit bottom. I closed the bail and reeled up two turns. Then I began the jigging motion of pulling up on the line and letting it settle back down, repeating the rhythmic motion, hoping to entice a fish into biting. I noticed the guy in the other boat was jigging very slowly, rod tip up, rod tip down, and I tried to copy his technique.

Sitting there fishing, I couldn't help but think of my uncle. I wished that I had spent more time with him in his later years. Being back here, I realized all that he had taught me—his kindness and sharing his love of the outdoors. I could not change what had happened no matter how much I wanted to. I could do one thing though. I could bring his killer to justice, and that is just what I intended to do. Whatever it took, Uncle Nick would have justice.

Wham! All of a sudden, my rod tip bent, and I realized my bait had just been attacked. More out of reflex than planning, I set the hook and could feel the unmistakable jiggling pulling of a fish on the line. I reeled up and with my hand net scooped a two-pound walleye into the boat. Its golden green sides shimmered in the light as it flopped around. I carefully hooked it to my stringer, avoiding the sharp little teeth. The stringer was attached to the boat, and I dropped it, fish and all, into the water, keeping the fish alive and fresh, as nothing is better than fresh fish for dinner.

From then on, the action intensified. The dinner bell must have wrung because my boat and the other two seemed to have fish on the line more often than not. The small ones went back, and within two hours I had four fish the perfect size for eating, the biggest I would guess weighed about 3½ pounds.

The other boats around me had done at least as well, and anchors were coming up. I pulled in my stringer and lay the fish in the bottom of the boat. The motor popped right off, and I took off back to the cabin.

This time I landed with a far lighter crash than last. Once the boat was secured, I tied my stringer full of fish off the dock.

As I started to walk up to the shop to get the fish-cleaning supplies, I felt the weight of the Walther in my right cargo pocket. It felt both strange and familiar. There had been a time in my life when I would go nowhere without a gun. It became part of getting dressed. But since I had left the department, and even though I had a retirement ID and could carry, I had not carried. Memories of the past still plagued me often at night. I would see the shell casings for my gun eject and tumble slow motion to the ground. The shots and screams pierced my sleeping ears. Angelina Gonzalez's face smiled at me. These memories would always be a part of me. I felt I deserved them.

I didn't stop carrying a gun because I thought the gun was evil, even though that seems to be the common sentiment among those more enlightened folks. I just no longer had it in my heart to be the hand that guided the gun. I had destroyed enough. Any more destruction caused by me was certain to kill me. I am not a mean person, a fighter yeah, but I don't have a black heart. Some may disagree. But I had picked up the Walther without thought and had put it in my pocket, where it would stay for now. There was just too much trouble in the air to ignore it.

I unlocked the shop and, after a brief search, located a wooden block with cut slots filled with three different knives. I pulled out the first one, a fillet knife. It had a brown wooden handle and a long flexible curved steel blade, the edge razor sharp. My uncle had taught me the art of filleting fish years ago. His knives were always honed to perfection, as he maintained that "only dull wits use dull tools." Tucked off to the side by the knives was a flat board with a clamp attached. The board bore the scars of countless knife cuts and was worn down in the middle where most of the action took place.

I took it to the picnic table and set it on the end. The clamp slid under the edge of the table, and I screwed the tightening bolt in, and it clamped securely to the table.

After doing a less than stellar job on the first fish, I really took my time with the others and ended up with eight fillets ready for the pan. I brought them into the house, half-filled a bowl with cold water, submerged the fillets, and put the bowl in the refrigerator. I went back out to the table and picked up the fish remains and threw them in a bucket. Then I worked my way along the shore to a little trail of rocks that led out into the water, terminating in a fairly large one with about five feet square of exposed surface, and there I spread the guts and skeletons. Back at the shop, a quick spray down with the garden hose cleaned up the cutting board, knife, and table. I was setting everything out to dry in the sun when I noticed something out of the ordinary.

On Madison's Lake Mendota it is not uncommon to see 25- to 50-foot cabin cruisers plying the waters with weekend captains cruising and partying on a boat that has all the comforts of home at a price that probably cost more than a lot of homes. On Spider Lake, at least from my memory and from what I had seen around, cabin cruisers such as those were not nearly so common. But here about 50 yards off my dock idling was a huge boat by Spider Lake standards: thirty feet if it was an inch, not a full cabin cruiser, but one with a low cabin that took up the front two-thirds of the boat. The sleek black hull and the throaty rumble from the inboard engines just said *speed*. The cockpit was open and occupied by a man and a woman. He was dressed in shorts and a polo shirt, she in a very small bikini bottom and t-shirt. The man was looking right at me, and as I stared back, he made no attempt to look away.

I waved as is the courtesy. He did not wave back, but responded by hitting the throttle, and the boat virtually leapt out of the water and took off toward Big Spider, blasting wake against the shore, pounding my little Alumacraft. Another strange visitor, but to be expected in the land of strange visitors Musky Falls was turning out to be.

Yup, for now the Walther would stay right where it was.

• • •

Time on the water both refreshes you and wears you out. The events of the last few days had worn on me a little, and I decided to hop into the hammock, which I saw hanging between two huge red pine trees. I crawled in and stretched out in, *oh-h-h ah-hhh*, comfort. I listened to the distant sounds of boat motors and the noise of Spider Creek behind me. I don't even remember falling asleep.

The crunching of gravel and the noise of a truck engine brought me back to semi-consciousness. I opened one eye and looked in the direction of the sound. The familiar truck stopped, and the engine was turned off, and Bud and Julie jumped out.

They walked over toward me.

"Hey, John, did you get to go fishin', or have you just been swingin' in that hammock all day?" asked Bud.

I couldn't help but smile and swung my legs out without rolling the whole works.

"As a matter of fact, Bud, not only did I go fishing, but I also caught and cleaned enough fish for a delicious supper. I believe you said Julie was a master walleye chef given the raw materials, which are now in the fridge in a bowl of cold water. I am looking forward to dining." My stomach was growling.

Julie laughed that laugh and said, "Come on in, boys, and let's see what we can cook up."

Once in the house, she pulled out the walleyes and looked them over. "Did you fillet these with a chainsaw?" she asked.

"It's just the first one. All the others are much better. I was kind of rusty," I responded perhaps a bit too defensively.

"I guess they will do for our purposes." She got to work and told us to get out of her way. We took the hint and grabbed a couple of cold beers and went out to sit on the porch.

...

"How did everything go in town today?" I asked Bud. "Any Lawler sightings?"

"Yeah, that jerk was around all day. I stuck pretty close to Julie's school booth to make sure he didn't bother anybody. He kept eyein' me but stayed clear. Jeez, I don't like that guy."

"You are a good judge of character, Bud."

We sat and talked about fishing and the lake and the land when Bud got a little distant. I could tell something was on his mind and outright asked him.

"Oh it's nothin', John. Really, it's nothin.'"

"Does it have to do with me?"

"Well, yeah, I guess it does."

"Then spit it out, Bud. Don't worry about it."

"Well, Julie said I shouldn't. She said that I should wait a while until you get settled. But I kind of have to know now."

"Bud, what's up?"

"Well I got a job offer to be the maintenance man at Lost Lake Lodge. It's a really nice place and the new owners have got a lot of big plans. Anyway, they heard that I had lost my job here for your aunt and uncle and heard I was lookin.' So they found me and asked."

"Sounds like a good opportunity. Good pay?"

"Oh, yeah, good pay, health and dental insurance, and paid vacation every year. It's a pretty good deal."

"So what do you need to ask me about?"

"Well, I've been working here, and I was just wondering if I did lose my job, and you didn't get around to telling me yet. I know you haven't been here long and been real busy, but I just kinda gotta know, pretty soon or right now, if you know. If you don't know I can wait, I'm not trying to push you. I'm sorry. I shouldn't have said anything. Julie is going to be so pissed at me."

"Slow down, Bud. Take a breath. I really never thought about it yet, but I can see why you would want to know. Have you been getting paid for the work you've been doing since my uncle died?"

"Yeah, well, kinda. Derek Anderson writes me a check once a month. It's about half of what I usually get, but he says that's all that the estate allows for. I don't argue with him. I don't like even talking to him."

"Tell me what you are owed, and I will take care of it first thing on Monday, and Bud, I am very happy to do it."

"That'd be real good. I could use the money. What about me working here anymore? There is always a lot of stuff that needs doing. I mean I do the boats, the tractor, and fix what needs fixin'. I do the forest management plan. If you had to hire those things to be done it would cost more than I do. I can tell you that."

"The last person you have got to convince is me. I am going to see my old buddy Derek on Monday after my meeting with Ron Carver—"

"You're meetin' up with Ron Carver!? That guy is a dandy. He and your uncle were best buds. Tell him I said hello."

"Anyway, I am meeting with him and Anderson. I plan to hash everything out then, so if you can wait until Monday afternoon for an answer, that will work. If not, and you take the other job, well, congratulations. They are lucky to have you."

"Nope, Monday's good. That'll work fine. Ah, don't mention this to Julie, okay?"

"No problem. My lips are sealed."

· · ·

"You know, John, there is another storage building down at the end of that little sand road. That's where the tractor is. There are also a couple of old trucks and a really cool jeep. I always helped him keep it all running. I just checked on everything about two weeks ago. Didn't drive them, but everything started and ran. I think the old jeep may need a new battery 'cause I had to jump it. Everything else, a little choke, hit the key, and they started right up."

"How far is it?"

"Oh, just down the trail, maybe 100 yards. You just can't see it because it's hidden by the trees."

"Let's walk down there," I suggested.

"Sure," Bud said. "You're going to really like all that stuff."

We both got up and started heading down the trail when Julie came to the door and announced that dinner was ready. Two hungry men can do an amazingly fast about-face when tempted with food. Direction reversed, we walked into the house and were met not by smell but by aromas.

Bud was almost drooling. Julie pointed to our places at the table, and we both sat. There in front of us was a pile of golden brown walleye fillets, breaded and pan fried. Next to that was a loaf of bread and a stick of butter. A large bowl contained a mixed salad of some kind. It all looked so damn good.

Bud is not a shy eater and reached for the bread.

"Bud, not yet," Julie said, "First the prayer."

We bowed our heads.

"Thanks, Lord for the gifts you have given us—the fish from the lake, the sun overhead and the clean sweet air we breathe. Thank you for our friends and family. Amen."

We dug into one of the best, most familiar fish dinners I had ever had.

"Taste familiar?" asked Julie.

"Yeah, it sure does."

"It's your aunt Rose's secret recipe. She taught me how to make it, and since then, I never make fish any other way."

What a perfect night it was. We had white wine from a local vineyard. Julie regaled us with stories of the kids and sweatshirt sales. I told them I had registered for the run, and I was surprised to find out she also had.

"I run it every year. A bunch of my students run with me. They have a contest to see who can beat me by the most. I'm in pretty good shape, but youth will trump conditioning every time."

"Truth is, I'm no sprinter, but I will plod along behind you and the kids. Are you running, Bud?"

"Nope. I save all my running for when something is chasing me."
He laughed heartily at his own joke, and so did we. "I am going to
help set up barricades before the race and take 'em down before the
parade. I think that will be enough exercise."

• • •

The night had flown and was coming to an end based on the
sleepy eyes of my dinner partners. I said I'd better get going, and to
my pleasant surprise, Julie asked Bud to clean up a little and offered
to walk me out to the jeep.

About halfway there she said, "A funny thing happened today.
When we closed the booth, I added up all our sales and went over to
Mystery Bay Graphics to pay our bill. When I tried, the owner told
me our bill had already been paid in full. When I asked who paid it,
he wouldn't tell. His wife walked out of the back and I asked her. She
said she didn't know. I asked whether the person wrote a check or
paid with a credit card so I could get the name and thank them. Turns
out the person paid cash. It seems a small bit coincidental that when
that creep Lawler knocked that big envelope out of your hands it was
full of cash. Also, when you rode off with the chief, you were going
toward Mystery Bay."

"You think I paid the bill!?" I asked, trying to sound incredulous.

"The thought did cross my mind."

"Julie, thanks for thinking of me, but honestly I am just not that
nice."

"I didn't think so." She turned and headed back to the house and
didn't say another word.

• • •

I drove off in the jeep toward town. A couple of miles from the city
limits I had to slow for a squad car alongside the road with its lights
flashing. Another car was pulled along the shoulder. I slowed as I
passed, and *bam*! I heard a gunshot. I slammed on the brakes and got
ready to move out when I looked at the deputy.

He was standing there talking to someone like nothing had happened. Then I saw the deer on the side of the road.

The driver had hit a deer, and the deputy had ended its suffering.

I arrived back at the hotel and went straight to my room. The envelope with my uncle's file stared up at me where I had put it on the desk. Not today, Uncle Nick, not tomorrow, but I think Monday I shall begin, and I won't stop until I reach the natural end. ∎

CHAPTER 16
Cabrelli

I was downtown by 7:30 in gym shorts, a ratty old t-shirt, and my running shoes. I had left the Walther in the glove box of the jeep, as concealing it in running shorts would be impossible. Already the crowd of runners, walkers, and well wishers had begun to fill the square. I stood in line at the table and checked in. The race volunteers gave me a water bottle, a number to pin on my shirt, and a race t-shirt. The shirt had a drawing of three cartoon muskies together, apparently line dancing. It was really clever. The back of the shirt listed all the local businesses that sponsored the race. I stepped off to the side and out in the street, barely missing colliding with two very fit pre-runners. You know, those guys who warm up for the race by actually running the race, in spandex pants, no shirts, no body fat, and fleeter of foot than I have ever been or shall ever be. Then I took off my ratty old t-shirt and put on my new race shirt. I looked at my old shirt and wondered what to do with it. A trash can a couple of feet from me solved the problem.

I couldn't help looking through the crowd to see if I could catch a glimpse of Julie, but no such luck.

In my meandering around, I found myself trapped smack in the middle of an exuberant family of brothers and sisters, moms and dads, aunts and uncles, grandmas and grandpas. They were all geared up to run the race. The eldest member, a distinguished looking and very spirited gentleman they called Uncle Jimmy, asked me if I would take a group picture for them. I agreed and was handed a half-dozen individual cameras and phones. I fumbled through the serious smiling shots and the hilarious ugly faces and bunny ear photos. We visited for a bit while waiting to line up for the race. Their family had been coming to the same place every year since the oldest of them here was a baby, over 60 years. Originally from Madison, they now also came from Houston, Texas; Spokane, Washington; and Los Angeles, California. They had continued an unbreakable tradition that had become a touchstone in their lives.

I had taken a continuing education class a few years before involving the sociology of the family. The professor maintained that one of the things that had caused erosion in the fabric of society was the loss of tradition. How many families were held together by tradition? How many families fall apart for lack thereof?

The only tradition I really ever had in my life was my summers on the lake. I had let that tradition get away from me. I had lost it for a time. I promised myself then and there to never lose it again. Musky Falls was a good place for tradition to begin anew. The race announcer gave the call of five minutes to race time, and the crowd began to move toward the starting line. There was lots of good-natured jockeying for the best position. Suddenly, the crowd tightened up and moved over to the left in an almost involuntary wave. The reason was sharks had just invaded the school of fish. Half a dozen iron pumpers dressed in wife-beaters moved through the crowd toward the front. None other than officer Lawler led them. He spotted me immediately and, of course, walked over.

"Nice day for a run, Cabrelli," he sneered as he looked me up and down. I didn't respond, and he laughed and walked away.

I did notice one thing: he had a big surgical scar on his right knee, possibly from his former days as the high school football standout that never made it. Anyway, it was good information, something I needed to take note of.

The race announcer called the ten-second countdown and, just before the gun, Julie Carlson elbowed her way in next to me. I looked over, and the gun went off. She took off like a rabbit chased by a group of kids, her students Nathan, Anna, and Danny among them. As I have said, I am no sprinter, but I am durable and good for the long haul, and I took off with my plodding pace as most of the crowd disappeared in front of me.

The run took us through the streets of Musky Falls, uphill and down. All along the route well-wishers cheered us along. After the first mile I found myself gaining ground on a few of the other runners. My first big move came as I passed the group wearing t-shirts from Weight Loss Extreme. Then I passed some parents with children in strollers and began to work my way up. Two pregnant women were my next target, but each time I approached them, they would speed up. I finally dropped back hoping not to be the cause of or a participant in an early delivery on the race course.

After mile two I was still lumbering along and began to routinely pass the former runners, now walkers. Although setting a rapid pace by my standards, I had not caught a glimpse of Julie or the kids, or Uncle Jimmy or any of his crew. Mile three was gone and I turned the corner to the final stretch. Ahead of me I saw what from the back appeared to be a herd of rhinos running through the middle of everyone. It was Lawler and company.

Personal victories often have little or no value to the world around you. It's because they are, well, personal.

The opportunity does not present itself often, and one must be prepared to take advantage when the chance comes your way. I did that day. With a burst of deeply hidden speed, I ran up next to Officer Lawler, smiled at him, then blew his doors off. He responded with a visceral noise and a burst of speed of his own. Before I knew it, we were neck and neck, running hard into the home stretch. He was so close to me I could smell his animal sweat. The crowd was yelling, and the announcer said, "Here comes one of Musky Falls's finest in a dead heat. Who will cross the line first?"

The wonderful photo family, who had now been joined by Julie and Bud, were screaming their lungs out for me. I pulled ahead of Lawler and crossed the line, beating him by a couple of yards. Ever the sportsman, as I slowed after crossing the line, he continued and ran into me from behind, knocking me to the pavement. He was quick to respond to his overt act.

"I am really sorry, Cabrelli. I wasn't looking, sweat in my eyes. Let me help you get up. Boy, you ran a heck of a race. I hope you are okay."

I am sure he fooled some in the crowd but not many. As a result, the tone of things became instantly more somber. I got up on my own, my knee bleeding from road rash, my elbow throbbing from the fall. I turned and walked toward the friendly crowd and raised my hand with an "I'm okay" wave; they burst out in cheers.

At that point I doubled the number of items on my to-do list. Find Uncle Nick's killer and kick the shit out of Officer Lawler.

Julie brought some medical wipes from the registration table and gave them to me to wipe off the blood.

Uncle Jimmy from the photo group turned out to be an emergency room physician, and he gave me a once over including a range of motion exam on my arm. He pronounced me fit and offered me a chocolate donut as medicine. We shook hands, and I limped away.

Lawler was nowhere to be seen, but Chief Timmy was and walked over. "Cabrelli, do you really think you need to aggravate that guy to get his attention?"

"You mean by beating him in a charity fun run, Chief? Or getting blood on his street? The last time I checked, winning a race was not just cause for hitting someone from behind. Maybe it's different in Musky Falls. Do you have some different bullshit laws here, Chief, that I should know about? Because if you do, let me hear them now. I don't want any more surprises."

"Settle down, John. I don't blame you for being mad. Our laws are the same here as everywhere else. So is my job, and among other things, it involves keeping the peace. You pimping Lawler is not a road to peace, whether you are in the right or not."

I started again and caught myself. It wasn't the chief that was the problem. Giving him hell would accomplish nothing. Bud and Julie were next to me, and we walked off toward the coffee shop together.

Julie, apparently never at a loss for an opinion, chimed in. "I know you don't want to hear this, but the chief is right. Lawler is a bad guy and getting him all worked up is not going to make anyone's life better. He is clearly looking for a reason to hurt you. You don't need to help him along. Just ignore him. Hopefully he'll get tired and go away."

"He's not going anywhere, Julie. He was waiting for me when I got here. He knew about me long before I knew about him. He's part of this thing, whatever it is. I'm not going anywhere either so whatever happens, happens. In the meantime, I am not going to go out of my way to avoid him, but I am not looking for a fight either."

Julie and Bud both took off, and I walked back to Main Street to get myself a seat for the parade. The casting contest was still going on, and it was fun to watch. A boy about twelve plunked the wooden lure they were casting right smack dab in the middle of the hula hoop laying on the ground. He won a gift certificate at a local sporting goods store and was smiling from ear to ear.

In the distance I could hear fire whistles and band instruments. The paraders were lining up, and the announcer gave the five-minute warning for the start. Everyone was asked to clear the streets and stay back from the curb.

The parade began right on time with the whirring whine of an antique fire siren, and old engine number nine led off. Number nine was a perfectly restored 1930s model fire truck. The back of the truck was filled with well-wishers who threw the first of many pounds of candy to be thrown to the crowd.

The parade had it all. Shriners riding mini-bikes in formation and a clown riding a weird wobbly wheeled bike. The Musky Fest float followed an open convertible with the mayor and his wife sitting on the back. Seated on the float, waving to the crowd were the Musky Queen and her court. Interspersed in the parade were three different drum and bugle corps. Each group stopped in front of the grandstand and played a number.

It was just as I remembered. Kids running out to grab candy thrown from the floats. Everybody waving, everyone smiling.

Even the boy and girl following the horse-drawn wagons with scoop shovels had smiles on their faces.

Then much to my happy surprise, I saw a big pickup truck wrapped in ribbon and banners, manned by several kids all wearing electric blue tie-dyed sweatshirts. Somehow they had lashed down a canoe on top of Bud's racks, and there were three kids in it, one fore and one aft paddling, another in the middle waving an American flag. Those students that weren't riding were running along handing out school pencils, candy, and brochures about Northern Lakes School. As they passed the grandstand, the announcer gave them a super plug and called them the national award-winning Northern Lakes School and everyone cheered. By the looks of it, if Julie Carlson ever quit teaching, she would have a great future in marketing.

Watching the parade let me be a part of the world that is dwindling away before our eyes. For that moment, a display of community pride, simple laughter, and the proud Musky Court replaced the insane hyperactive nonstop, on-demand entertainment we have come to expect. Being there, even just sitting on the curb, I was part of the parade, part of an event that was real. Will a tree make a noise if it falls in the forest and no one is around to hear it? Is a parade even possible without people lining the streets? I was disappointed when the last fire truck passed. This year's parade and Musky Fest had come to an end.

I lingered downtown for a while to watch them take things down. The unseen injuries sustained in being knocked to the pavement began to make themselves known in the way aches and pains do. My leg was throbbing, as was my arm, and my back had begun to stiffen where I had been hit. Nothing serious though, according to Doctor Uncle Jimmy; all would heal on their own without further medical intervention, so I needed to persevere. Perseverance over any kind of pain is the only way to survive in the world. Get over it and get going.

I also noted a post-run aroma emanating from me. That particular odor is fine when among a large group that had run the same race.

However, when walking among those freshly showered and in town for the day, it became a bit more noticeable. I walked back to the jeep and drove to the hotel.

• • •

For whatever reason, instead of turning right to the hotel, I turned left and headed toward the lake, soon rolling down the highway as if on my way home.

I pulled in and saw that Bud and Julie had not yet returned.

Back in the shop it only took me about a minute to find a snorkel, mask, and fins. The day had warmed to the eighties with clear skies. There was a small sandy area just a little way from the cabin where I used to swim. I walked over and waded in. The water was cool enough that it made me stop for a second to get used to it. I put on the gear. The underwater world was waiting.

You know, you never think about it: we are busy walking around on the dry earth, driving cars, talking to people, and on and on. We drive by lakes and rivers, but we only look at them from the surface. Below the surface, though, is another whole community occupied by species that if moved to our world would perish, just as we would perish if moved to theirs. I couldn't stay, but I could visit.

I swam carefully using only my hands to propel and avoid kicking up a sediment cloud that would obscure my vision. I investigated an old rock and timber pile that had been part of a dock more than a century before.

Hundreds of bluegills and sunfish swam around through the weeds, some as big as my hand. Others were only an inch or two long, perfect miniatures of the bigger fish. Crayfish hid in the nooks and crannies of the old structure, waiting for a passing snack. At the far end of the old pier was a school of minnows. While the bluegills and sunfish moved this way and that, based on individual desire, the minnows moved together in formation, communicating directional changes telepathically.

As I swam along, I saw something shiny on one of the submerged logs, and I took a deep breath and dived down to see what it was. Stuck in the log was a six-inch long fishing lure with about a foot of line still attached. I wiggled it loose and headed for the surface. It was a silver Rapala Countdown, a good musky and bass bait. I swam it back to the shore, and once it was shallow enough, I stood up and began to do the fins on your feet backward walk toward shore. I turned around to walk back out when I saw Julie coming down the hill toward where I was snorkeling.

"What a perfect day for a swim," she proclaimed. "Get rid of the day's grunge and grime and cool off." With that, she stripped off her t-shirt, exposing a conservative one-piece suit, and dove in. No testing of the water for this girl. Total immersion was her style. With strong strokes, she headed across the lake.

I took off my gear, threw it on shore, and followed her. She slowed until I caught up, and then we swam together all the way to the opposite shore. We stood on the bottom, water up to our necks, and took a break before swimming back. The exercise and cool water did wonders for my aches and pains. The knee stung a little but not for long. We came to our home shore and climbed out. She picked up a towel and dried off, while I stood and drip dried, not having thought to grab one.

I couldn't help but glance at her in the swimsuit. She was slim and fit, and her physique matched her personality perfectly.

She must have caught me looking and wrapped herself up in the oversized towel.

"How are your knee and arm?" she asked.

"Good. That swim was just what the doctor ordered. I feel a lot better."

"You better come back to the house and put some antibiotic cream on that scrape. It's looking kind of red already. Clean it up and cover it for now, and it should limit any chance for infection."

We walked back up to the house. On the way she surprised me.

"John, I thought about it, and I want you to move into the house. It's your house and you have been very kind not to throw me out on my ear. Eventually, though, I am going to have to move, and I'm pretty much packed up now, so I might as well get it done. Bud will be glad to have me if for no other reason than to clean his place up. It's not that it's a total pigsty, it's just that, well, he is a man. You know."

I wanted to be offended at the sexist comment, but I couldn't be. Some things are just true.

"I thought about it too. I don't want you to move. I'm going to meet with Anderson tomorrow if everything goes as planned, no bumps in the road. You can stay here, and I'm going to keep Bud on as the handyman. I do have a proposal. You can continue to live in the main house, and I'm going to move my stuff into the cabin. There is plenty of room for me there and it will be tons better than staying at the hotel."

"No. John, I will move into the cabin, and you should stay in the main house."

"Sorry, Julie. Not open for negotiation. If you don't like the terms, you can move into Bud's place. I'm not changing my mind."

She reluctantly agreed.

I smeared antibiotic cream on my knee, got into the jeep, and drove back to town for my last night in the hotel. The evening passed uneventfully, and after a quick dinner down the street, I collapsed into exhausted sleep, not waking until seven the next morning.

I did not bounce out of bed. I noted numerous issues with parts of my body that were loudly complaining when I moved, not just from Lawler's cheap shot, but also my usual jogging legs as stiff as wood from the unaccustomed sprinting. A hot shower did little to help, so I got on my running shorts and t-shirt and headed down to the hotel jacuzzi. I grabbed a cup of coffee from the breakfast bar. The jet-powered hot water felt great and restored a portion of the flexibility that I had recently lost. I sipped my coffee and stared out the huge bay of windows that faced Lake Musky Falls. An old couple joined me. They had been coming up here every year for a month around Musky Fest for 20 years, and God willing they would see 20 more. Tradition.

I got up to leave and kind of hobbled out and the old guy said, "I see you're walking a little stiff. Sure is hell to get old isn't it?"

"Old? Who's old?" I replied. He just chuckled and turned back to his wife.

Dressed and ready, I was a little early for the meeting with Anderson so I stopped by the body shop to check on the status of my car. It was in the garage on a low rack, with the right front fender removed. The owner came out and told me that they were waiting for the parts and expected them sometime the first part of the week. After that, a few hours to put it back together, time to paint it, and it would be good to go.

"I bet driving that jeep is culture shock after cruising in this little hotrod," he mused.

"Not really. The jeep runs great and is pretty comfortable. I kind of like it."

"Well, I'm sure Doc O'Malley down at the garage would trade you even up anytime you wanted!" he laughed.

●●●

I drove over and parked in front of the attorney's office. The street was pretty empty and amazingly clean; litter left from the huge crowd and all the tents and booths were gone.

The office was already open, and I walked in.

The receptionist was not smiling and clearly not in a good mood. "Good morning, Mr. Cabrelli. Did you have an appointment this morning?"

"I don't, really. I was just hoping that Derek could work me in so we could finish things up."

"I'll ask him, but I don't think it's going to work for him today."

She stepped into the inner office, and I heard Derek tell her to send me in.

"Hi, John, good to see you. Enjoying your time in Musky Falls?"

His professional conversational tone was not consistent with his appearance; he looked like hell. He was pale and drawn with dark circles under his eyes. His shirt looked like he had slept in it; there was even a stain on the front like spilled coffee.

Normally when you see someone looking like that you might ask about their health. I really didn't care enough to ask, so I plowed forward.

"I am having a great time. Really enjoying myself. I ran in the fun run yesterday, did some fishing too. It's been nice. Thanks for asking. I think we have some paperwork to finish up on my uncle's estate, I would like to get that done as soon as we can. I was hoping we could figure out a schedule this morning."

Clearly a man with a burden, he asked, "I don't suppose there is any chance you have reconsidered selling?"

"No chance, Counselor."

"Kind of what I thought. Everything else is ready to go. A few signatures and we are done. We can take care of it right now if you want."

He lined the papers up; they had sticky notes where I needed to sign. I picked up the pen and stopped. Laura's words came back to me: *Don't sign anything until I read it.*

"You know, Derek, I don't want to be insulting, but I think I should have my lawyer look these over before I sign anything."

When I said that, he began to look even worse than just a minute before.

"John, I do not see why that is necessary. This is a very simple matter of closing out an uncontested estate. I actually am representing you in this case and your aunt and uncle posthumously. I have reviewed everything, and all the paperwork is in order. Delaying any further seems like a waste of everyone's time. Let's just sign the papers and be done with it. I am a very busy man, and I have had to put other clients on hold while we settle this."

"I'm sorry for the inconvenience, Derek. I will give you the fax number, and we can fax them over right now. I am sure that she will take a look at them and get right back to us."

"No, I'll send them via email, John."

My gut feeling took over. "Derek? Give me that stack of papers, the same ones you wanted me to sign. I will take them someplace to have them faxed over."

"No, no, we'll do it. I'll take care of it this morning."

"Sorry, Counselor. Give me that stack of papers, now."

His receptionist came to the door and said she was going to the post office. I briefly looked her way. That's when Attorney Derek Anderson accidentally knocked a full cup of coffee over onto the documents, soaking them completely.

He yelled at his assistant to bring in some paper towels, but he was not nearly as upset as he should have been. As a matter of fact, he looked kind of happy, like a guy who had just dodged a bullet.

I didn't know what to say. Once again he was clearly up to something.

I did the only thing I could. "Derek, my lawyer's name is Laura Davis. She will be getting in touch with you." With that, I got up and left and didn't look back. I called Laura on her cell and relayed the events.

"You are a smart guy not to sign anything, John, whether you think the guy is on the level or not. It's too bad that you didn't get the papers before he destroyed them. There was something there that he didn't want me to see. Anyway, I will call when they send me something. How is it going there otherwise?"

"Even with all the drama, this is a good place. I am enjoying myself. Like I'm on vacation."

"Good, you deserve some time off. Enjoy it. I am looking forward to you coming back. Elizabeth and I are going on a cruise to do some diving and sightseeing. We lucked out and found an open suite on a great boat. I will be out of cell range, but I can respond to emails. We're going to leave in three days. Hopefully I will get the stuff from Anderson by then. John, I have to take this other call. Talk to you later." She hung up. Back to her high-speed life.

●●●

Next stop was Ron Carver. The store was open, but the staff said he had not yet appeared. His schedule, they said, was variable. He came and went when he wanted. They had no idea when to expect him today. He would be in, but *when* was anybody's guess.

I sat on a bench on the street. I was not at peace at the moment. Today was the day I was going to begin. Read the report and go from there. I wanted to get the stuff with Anderson all straightened away before launching my investigation. I needed to reduce the number of things requiring my attention and preservation of thought. Clearly that was not going to happen today. Anderson's shenanigans had again changed the game. One thing I was sure of was that ol' Derek was up to his neck in this thing and had reached the point of desperation. He looked bad, he was nervous, and he'd tried some sort of flim-flam to get me to sign something that I shouldn't. He did not appear to be the same man that I had so recently shared deep-fried cheese curds and beer with. He was a desperate move maker trying to fix something by doing something else wrong, but just digging himself in deeper and deeper.

I was absorbed in my own thought when the sound of a speeding car brought me around. Anderson was in his car driving fast north out of town. Before taking any time for rational thought, I was on my feet running on my board-stiff legs to the jeep. I fired it up, backed out, almost pulling a Bud, and before I knew it, I was in hot pursuit. I had lost sight of Anderson's car but jumped on the main highway north. Edging well over the speed limit, trying to gain a visual. I moved in and out between the other three or four cars on the road and caught sight of Anderson.

Vehicle surveillance is very tricky to do well. It would be easy if you could just park on somebody's bumper and just keep up. The problem with that is that they know they are being followed and are most likely going to alter their course. What you want to do is follow them from far enough back to watch them and from close enough not to lose them. A surveillance using several vehicles is always the best way to go: one car breaks off after another takes a position, significantly reducing the chance that the person you're following will figure things out. A one-car operation requires skill on the part of the pursuer, knowing when to drop back, use another car for a shield, or when to close the gap.

The first problem I faced was that Anderson was going like a bat out of hell, in excess of 80. The speed didn't worry me, but another car traveling that fast coming up behind you is a tip-off, especially if the pursuer is driving a vehicle known to the pursued. We traveled a very fast ten or so miles, when, without signaling, Anderson turned left onto a small blacktop road. The road was really a private driveway flanked on either side with two fieldstone pillars and a heavy steel gate hanging between them. As I cruised by, I saw the gate open for Anderson. I tried to get a glimpse of what lay at the end of the drive, but the property was heavily wooded and didn't reveal a clue. I continued down the highway at the speed limit. About a mile past where Anderson turned, I found a sand road that ran off into the trees. I slowed, pushed the button to activate the four wheel drive in the jeep, and pulled in. Although some distance away, the sand road ran in the same direction as the driveway Anderson had taken.

The jeep crawled along without spinning a tire. The road was just a fire lane cut through the brush to act as a fire break and access point for fire equipment in the event of a forest fire. It appeared to have been recently mowed by a brush hog, so there were no trees or heavy brush to stop my progress.

I came to the crest of a hill and stopped. Below I could see a good-sized, fast running river, probably the Namekagon. The view was spectacular, a river running its course through a dense northern forest community. I looked in all directions, and to the south I saw what appeared to be the peak of a house roof. I went down the hill and walked over to get a better look.

It was a house all right, 10,000 square feet of logs and stone set as close as possible to the bank of the river. Anderson's car was parked in front on a circular driveway. A massive porch extended off the back, part open, part closed in. It was the kind of place you see in beautiful home magazines. One accoutrement that you rarely see in beautiful home magazines are two guys walking a foot beat around the house, armed to the teeth.

Security, two guys meant to be visible, would be a deterrent to the casual trespasser. Armed with AR-15 type rifles, they could also lay down a pretty good field of fire as the first line of defense. If there were two outside, chances were damn good there were a couple more inside. As much as I wanted to get a closer look, I knew that it was likely they also had some electronic surveillance gear in place. I should have, but hadn't been, looking for it on my way in, but I was pretty sure it was there.

I didn't need to push my luck at this point; a body left in these woods would be subject to immediate conversion from a human life form to usable sustenance by all manner of creatures, the process beginning minutes after death. What would be left would be hard to find if anyone was even looking.

I had learned a great deal, and while assumptions are often dangerous, sometimes you just have to jump.

After his meeting with me, Anderson had left his office and driven 80 miles an hour to this house. The house was huge and expensive, and one could assume that the owner was pretty well off. Very visible and obviously armed security staff furthered that notion. I think that whoever it was in the house, Anderson and I shared some common interest.

It was time to go. I walked back to the jeep, and a second too late I noticed a set of heavy lugged boot prints in the sand by the driver's door.

I spun around and was faced by a guy who had an AR-15 pointed at my midsection. He was 30 feet away, no distance at all for a rifle, but enough time for him to get a shot off if I made a move.

"You are on private property. What are you doing here?"

My brain was pretty quick on its feet. "I'm new around here and I thought this might be the road to the public landing on the river. I guess it's not. Do you have any idea where that landing might be? I would like to do some fishing. "

He said nothing.

"Well, I'm sorry about the trespass. I'll know better next time. I will just get in my jeep and get out of your hair," I said, reaching for the door handle.

"Don't." One word conveyed many things, and the way he said it stopped me cold. "You are going to walk down the hill toward the house the way you came. You are going to do it right now."

This man was serious. I could see it in his eyes, and I could feel it. "If I don't?"

"You make your own choice. You are going down to the house. I really don't care how that happens. No more talk. Get moving."

"Just let me get my wallet out of the glove box, and I will come along peaceably," I said.

At that point, he raised his shirt, and I saw my little Walther tucked in his waistband.

We set off at a slow pace toward the house. He never got any closer to me or any farther away. If I had made a move, it was not his intention to try and restrain me with physical force. The way he had it set up would allow him only one solution for any perceived indiscretion on my part—a very permanent solution.

Everyone was on alert when we got to the house, no doubt alerted by the radios connected to the earbuds they were wearing. They gathered around me, none too close, all making sure they were out of the other one's direct line of fire. Pros. Their faces remained expressionless as we walked toward the front door.

When we reached the steps, the door opened and out stepped the man I had seen on the massive power boat on Spider Lake. Off to the side behind him was my beer drinking buddy and lawyer, Derek Anderson. He looked as though he could melt into a puddle at any moment.

"Mr. Cabrelli, how nice to finally get to meet you. My name is David Stone. Welcome to my humble home. Won't you come in? Candace was just going to bring Anderson and me a cold iced tea on the deck. I hope you can take a minute to join us."

"I don't think I have much choice," I said glancing around at the guards.

"Don't give them another thought. I pay them well to be very serious about their jobs. That includes dealing with trespassers. But you're not a trespasser anymore. Now you're a guest. Stay or go is your choice."

Go was the right choice. Stay is what I did.

The house was incredible. A huge stone fireplace dominated the center of the room. It was open on two sides. On each side above the openings were heavy thick mantles crafted of rustic wood.

On the mantle on one side was a beautiful bronze sculpture of a man and a dog in a boat, battling enormous waves with only a paddle. The other had a shoulder mount of a gigantic moose above it, an antique flintlock rifle below. The walls were tastefully adorned with what appeared to be original oil paintings depicting outdoor and wildlife scenes. It was one large room that contained a dining area, kitchen, living room, and a library.

Looking up, I saw that the ceiling was open, and the next floor was contained within an elaborate but still rustic wooden railing.

"Quite a place you've got here, David. I don't know that I've ever seen anything like it."

"Well, John. Can I call you John?"

"John's good," and because sometimes I just can't control myself, I was tempted to say, "John's fine, but just don't call me Arvid." I didn't, although it seemed like a funny idea at the time.

We walked out to the rear deck through the center doors in an enormous glass wall that had a stunning view of the river. The deck was covered, and there was a seating area on a smaller section that was built out far enough to be above the river. We sat there and were almost immediately served iced tea by Candace, who turned out to be the woman I had seen in the boat with David. She poured our drinks and then left the room, leaving just me, David, and Derek sitting. Derek drank his tea in about one gulp and refused to make eye contact with me.

"John, I am really sorry that we had to meet like this. I want to tell you upfront that I was following the advice of counsel. As a result, I had put off getting together. Now that we are here though, we should talk. I am the person that is interested in buying your uncle's spectacular property. I did not know you, and sometimes it's best if a man in my, my ... let's say position, allows others to negotiate on their behalf. It seemed that it was unlikely to be an adversarial situation, so I agreed to allow Anderson to handle the sale since he was already handling the estate. Needless to say, he has not been successful in his endeavors to this point. So it is high time we get together, mano a mano, to work this thing out."

Mano a mano: I never liked the saying. Whenever I heard it I always felt like the next thing we needed to do was get up and pee on the closest tree.

"What can I do for you, David?"

"It's really more about what I can do for you, I think. First, a little history. I have long lusted after your aunt and uncle's property. Just prior to his accident, we had almost worked out the details of the purchase that would ensure financial security for him for the rest of his life. His dear Rose had passed away, quite a woman she was, and he had been talking about doing some traveling. The place had become somewhat of a burden for him to take care of. There is always much to do when you have land. He had hired a local dullard to help him, but I think the man was more of a hindrance than a help. He even took in a boarder to help with chores, although I again don't think she did much. I shouldn't say that. She did manage to bilk him and your aunt, for that matter, out of a fair amount of money that was supposed to go to a local charity or school for the underprivileged."

"Are you talking about Bud Treetall and Julie Carlson?" I asked.

"I think those are the right names. Anderson, are those the right names?"

Anderson barely muttered a "Yes."

David gave Derek a flint steel look that told him all he needed to know; sit up, straighten up, and do it now. Derek responded as best as he could, which was still none too good.

"As I was saying, your uncle and I had worked out a deal that would provide him with a lump sum and then monthly payments, with interest of course, over the next ten years. He was very excited. In fact, he asked if I knew the name of a good travel agent. I was glad to give him the direct number for the one I use myself. She said he called her the next day and began discussing potential destinations.

"Just prior to us signing on the dotted line, Nick had that terrible accident. It is a miracle that he lived as long as he did after being struck. Damn tourists come up here, sit in the bar, drink until they can't walk, then think that since they aren't at home it's fine to drive. Unfortunately, it happens all too often. The last I heard, they still don't have any suspects. What a shame. Nick was a real asset to this community. So that brings me to you, as the sole heir. Any further negotiations will be between you and me. I'm sure that Anderson here would be glad to draft up any paperwork after we reach an agreement."

"Well, David, as I told Derek, who, by the way, told me he didn't know who the buyer was, I am not interested in selling. As a matter of fact, I intend to move into the place."

Stone looked at me with a practiced smile, but his eyes were reptilian cold, "I know. That's what Anderson told me, but I don't think you really understand how badly I want the property. I understand that my last offer was not enough to interest you. So let me ask you, what would interest you? I am a very wealthy man, and I am sure we can reach an agreement. If you are determined to relocate up here with the kind of money I am willing to pay, you could buy something very, very nice."

"That being said, why don't you buy some other place, David? Why overpay for this property when you could buy any other?"

"In this case, no other property will do I'm afraid. Your property is the one I want."

"On that we are of like mind," I said. "No other property will do for me either."

He locked his eyes on mine. They were cruel and angry. But in a second his smiling façade had returned. He got up and said, "The boys have brought your jeep around and returned all your property. Thank you for your time."

As he turned and started to walk into the house, I said, "Hey, David. One question before you go." He stopped and turned around. "What was the name of the travel agent that you had Uncle Nick contact?"

He was briefly caught off guard but recovered quickly. "I am sorry, John. I don't recall. I recently changed agents." He quickly turned on his heel and disappeared into the house, ending the possibility of any further questions.

The look on his face confirmed I had caught him in a lie about the travel agent.

I got up and walked to the door. Derek remained seated, slump shouldered and looking down. I got in the jeep and drove out. As I approached the gate, it swung open, allowing me to leave. On the road, I immediately checked the glove box. The little Walther was there, minus the ammunition. ■

CHAPTER 17
Cabrelli

I drove back into town and stopped at Ron's jewelry store. In a parking stall in front of the store was a full-dress, made-in-Wisconsin Harley Davidson motorcycle, a two-wheeled advertisement that said Ron Carver was in. I parked and walked by the cycle. It was immaculate, chrome and leather all polished to a sheen. The gas tank had a custom paint job, flames trailing back from either side, joining in the middle to create a vortex.

Chrome exhaust pipes ran along the side and out by the back wheel, the chrome a little discolored from the heat. There are motorcycles and there are *motorcycles*. This one was really something, made for the open road.

I walked into the store and saw that Ron was holding court with his employees. He glanced up at me and gave me the sign for *just a minute*. The jewelry cases were full of every kind of jewelry imaginable. Hundreds of pairs of earrings, necklaces, and rings were all perfectly displayed in lighted cases. From plain silver bands to stone-encrusted pendants, it was all there.

At the end of the counter, I saw a different kind of display—a Plexiglas case that held custom knives. Not your run-of-the-mill hardware store fare, these were each handcrafted with the utmost attention to detail; locking folders and fixed blades dominated the selection. But down in the corner were several elegant little pocket knives. The handles were made from varied materials ranging from wood with beautiful grain to what looked like ivory. There was one that was a single blade about three inches long, and its handles were made of some type of highly figured wood. The blade was long and slim with a small "up" curve at the tip. It was a beauty. I needed to remember to ask Ron to let me take a look at it.

Ron Carver did not just walk into a room, he took the place over with his gravel voice, barrel chest, white beard and hair. His voice boomed, "Johnny boy, I see you made it to see ol' Ron. Come on, let's get out of here and go get a beer or whatever. We have got to talk."

With that, he walked out of the store, across the street, and into the Fisherman Bar. He never looked back to see if I was following because he was the kind of guy that just assumed I would. And if I didn't, he wouldn't care. He had a strong stride and seemed to be a little bowlegged. He walked like a man that meant it and left a wake of vibes that said "mess with me at your peril."

He slid into a booth, and I joined him.

A cute waitress hustled over to us.

"Hi, Ron! Do you want the usual?"

"I would, sweetheart. Have the cook grill up another steak sandwich for young Johnny here, too, and get him something to drink."

I ordered a Diet Pepsi and Ron laughed.

"I gotta say, Johnny, it's good to see you. You probably don't remember me from when you were a kid, but I was around. Back then I was too busy building up my business, working all the time. Even then, your uncle Nick and I were best friends. He and I had independent streaks that really don't require much social support. Besides that, we were both incapable of listening to chitter-chatter small talk. So we found that each other's company suited our needs just fine.

"Your aunt Rose, though, just wanted to kill us sometimes. She was always doing something, organizing this and organizing that. If there was a good cause that needed a friend, Rose was the girl. She would tell Nick and I that we needed to show up at these fundraising events. She told me that it would be bad for my business if I didn't. She told Nick it would be bad for his health if he didn't. We tried it for about a year, but social butterflies we were not. We didn't cause any trouble, at least not much, but some people are just not made for social small talk. Rose got tired of talking us into going, and we got tired of going about the same time. She was a smart one, that Rose."

Ron stopped for a second and took a big sip of his beer. I could see in his blue eyes that his remembrance made him revisit the sense of loss he still felt. Sadness that never really goes away.

"So get this, one night she had us both in monkey suits and was taking us to the hospital fundraiser. Christ, every time Nick put on a tie I was sure his head would pop. His goddamned face would get so red. Well anyway, we get there, and before we walk in, Rose says she has a deal for us. We don't have to go to any more fundraisers if we are willing to make a cash donation to the cause. We could buy our way out of jail so to speak. We didn't even bat an eye, 'How much?' Nick asked as he reached for his wallet. 'Not so fast, boys,' Rose replied. 'Nick, your donation cannot come from our household account or savings. It needs to come out of your shop/gun/gear fund. Ron, I don't care where yours comes from.'

"Jesus, I thought Nick was gonna have a stroke right there. Rose was raiding his private little cash account, the account he had held sacred, the walking-around money he had gleaned from this and that. Aunt Rose had him. A continued life of chitter-chatter or a decrease in the net value of his most valuable cash resources. I didn't much care what your uncle did. I was not going to miss my chance and I went for it. 'Sounds good to me, Rose. How much?' 'We will start with ten times the event ticket price,' She answered. Tickets for tonight are $25 each, your donation would be $250.'

"It was a no-brainer. I had a blank check in my wallet and wrote it out with a pen she just happened to have. Nick, however, was just standing there looking like a deer in the goddamn headlights. I knew he had been saving for a new milling machine for the shop, and this would put a dent in things, but he was more worried about the long-term consequences; Rose did a bunch of charity work, and it wouldn't take long for him to feel the pinch. She took my check, waved goodbye, grabbed Nick by the arm, and dragged him toward the door. They almost got inside when Nick stopped stone dead. He didn't say a word. He turned his back to Rose and pulled out his wallet. From a side compartment he pulled out some hidden bills, he carefully went through them, put some back, and handed Rose two hundreds and a fifty. She kissed him on the cheek and went inside. That Rose was quite a gal. She loved Nick and tolerated me. What more could you ask for?"

Ron got a misty, wistful look in his eyes, "Yeah, Nick and I had some great adventures. They don't make many guys like us anymore. I miss him. I haven't had a decent piece of blueberry pie since Rose died. She used to send us out into the bush to collect wild blueberries. Nick had these antique blueberry scoops he bought at the flea market, and they worked perfectly. In a good year, we would collect a couple of big buckets full. Then Rose would turn those into pie sent from heaven. God, I loved her blueberry pie for breakfast."

Ron jogged my memory, and I said, "I used to love her blueberry pies too. I remember her putting a big scoop of West's vanilla on top. I picked blueberries, too. We used to go out to Bear Island, and they were thick. One time out there, I was picking on one side of the island, and Uncle Nick was on the other. For every blueberry I put in the bucket, I ate two. By the time we got back in the boat to go home, I had reached my blueberry saturation level, and I was looking a little green, but I was happy. Uncle Nick just laughed at my almost empty bucket."

We just sat there for a moment. I was thinking about the picture Ron had painted of my uncle and aunt. I longed to see them once more, just one more night by the fire, one more piece of pie. Just a few more minutes to make up for time lost.

"Enough reminiscing, Johnny. We got a lot of ground to cover and work to do. You and I are going to find the son of a bitch that ran him down. I got some pretty good ideas about where to start looking. There's a fair bunch of snakes in the woodpile around here. We are going to light it on fire and smoke them out. We'll make them pay, Johnny. We are sure as shit going to make them pay."

Steak sandwiches, a Diet Pepsi, and a glass of the darkest beer I had ever seen were served.

Ron ate like a man who was in a hurry but really liked what he was eating.

"This dark beer is a local brew. They don't sell much of it, but there are a few locals that won't drink anything else, so they keep it on tap. You can damn near get a spoon to stand straight up in it. It's kind of like a meal all in itself. You ought to give it a try next time you're drinking beer. It will put hair on your—"

The waitress interrupted, "Can I get you boys anything else?"

Neither of us needed anything. She put our check on the table, and as she turned her head to look at Ron, I noticed the beautiful sparkling earrings she was wearing. "So, Ron, what time are you going to pick me up tonight? I'm looking forward to that motorcycle ride you promised."

"Around six or so. Looks like it's going to be a nice night for it," he replied.

"See you then, handsome," she said, as she sashayed away with a little glance back to make sure Ron was watching, and she wasn't disappointed.

We finished up and walked back out on the street. Ron suggested we go back up to his store. He had an office in the back that could be accessed from the showroom or the alley behind. The office was a mixture of hi-tech and log cabin. A bank of five super high-resolution security cameras were above a desk that was against what appeared to be one-way glass, making it so we could see everything going on in the store, and no one would know we were watching. In another corner, a fishing vest and wooden handled net hung on an antique coat rack, and a fly rod leaned against them. Hanging from another one of the hooks was an old cowboy belt and holster, made of black hand-tooled leather and adorned with silver conchos. In the holster was a vintage Colt single action army revolver with what looked like real ivory grips. Leaning in a corner beneath the coat rack was an

AR-15 style rifle, made of black metal and plastic with a high capacity magazine sticking out the bottom. There was a well-worn leather recliner, and next to it a small table with a pile of magazines on top. A flat screen TV was mounted on the wall across from it. The remote control for the set was duct taped to a pine board about four inches wide and two feet long.

As I looked at it, he said, "I kept losing that remote. Haven't lost it once since I taped it to that board."

Then Ron added, "I knew that you would come here and help me look into what happened to Nick, so I waited for you. I know some things I haven't shared with anyone. The fact is, I don't know who to trust, so in that case, it is better to keep your ears open and your mouth shut. Now that you're here, it's time to get moving. I just needed a little backup."

I started to speak, but he shushed me. "Listen to what I have to say first. Maybe it will answer some of your questions."

He paced back and forth. "First off, they said there were no witnesses to the murder, and I am calling it murder because that's exactly what it was. There were two witnesses, Nick and the bastard who ran him down. I don't know about anybody else. No one came forward anyway."

In a sense, perpetrators and victims are witnesses. This becomes most evident when there is more than one perp who rats out his or her buddy. The perp becomes an eyewitness—happens more often than you would think. Honor among thieves is not alive in today's criminal population.

"Your uncle didn't die right away. He had sure been killed but hung on for a while. He saw the driver. He saw the truck. He wasn't himself, but even half there Nick was smarter than anyone else around here. It took him a while, but the story he gave me is one helluva lot different than what the cops came up with.

"The truck was a white Ford Expedition. I brought in pictures of every truck I could find, and he picked it right out. Then I showed him a color chart from one of the dealer brochures, and he pointed to white.

"He was getting weaker by the minute, but he wanted to tell me as much as he could. However, both of us knew that the end was close.

"Here is what I figured happened: Nick walked over to the café to have a cup and a little breakfast every day, rain or shine, 90 degrees or minus 20. He liked the place because the food was good, the coffee was strong, and the joint opened at 5:00 a.m. He loved to walk. I think it helped heal his mind after Rose died. His route took him along the lakeshore, then to a trail that paralleled the highway but was 100 or so yards off. The trail is in pretty good shape because it sees some semi-regular use mainly by locals on ATVs and snow machines. Nick loved watching wildlife, and he'd write in his notebook about every different kind of bird or critter he saw. He read a bunch of stuff by a guy named Leopold and really got into something called phenology. Anyway, he took very detailed notes about everything he encountered on his walks."

"Do the police have the notebook?" I asked.

"Hold on. You're getting ahead of me. The answer is they don't have it, I do. We'll get to that. Just let me finish."

"Okay, sorry."

"Here is what he was able to tell me about the day he got run down. He was just taking his normal walk, spotted a bird that he hadn't seen before, and was stopped on the trail looking at it through his field glasses. When he got to the road, he stopped to record his sighting, and that's when he heard the truck. It must have been coming fast. He was in damn good shape, but he couldn't move quick enough to get out of the way. He said the truck aimed right at him, but he couldn't see the driver. He had no doubt the guy was out to get him. That's the last he remembered and pretty much the last thing he spoke, except for the words, 'My journal.'

"I went and talked to the sheriff and gave him the information I had. He listened to me and then called an investigator in. I think they already had their mind made up that it was an accidental hit and run. I felt like they were just trying to humor me. I did my best to convince them. Before I left, I asked if they had recovered Nick's journal, because I was sure when his nephew, you I mean, got here that you would want it. They looked over the evidence list and found no mention of a journal, and neither one recalled ever seeing one.

"I was pretty pissed off when I left there. The next morning, I hauled my ass out to the scene of the accident and started looking around for myself. After about an hour, I saw something yellow mostly buried by leaves. By God, it was his journal. He used these notebooks with waterproof pages so it was still as good as new. I put it in my pocket and kept looking around, but I didn't find anything else.

"When I got back here, I started looking through the notebook and found a notation made two days before the accident. A couple of the seasonal lake homes had been burglarized, so the sheriff put out a notice in the paper and on the radio asking folks to write down the descriptions of any strange vehicles or people they saw in their area. Pretty much everybody participates in the Northwoods neighborhood watch anyway and especially when they put out a special alert.

"Nick had come upon a white Ford Expedition parked off the road, where it was out of sight. His hiding spot was on Nick's trail. He must have thought things looked suspicious because he wrote down everything he could remember. And if Nick was anything, he was a detail man. As soon as the driver saw Nick, he slammed the truck in reverse and took off. I figure the sonuvabitch was looking things over, figuring the best place to take out your uncle. He got a little confused and pulled into the wrong trail. Nick saw his killer two days before he was run down. This was no accident; that bastard was stalking him."

"Did he get a plate number?" I asked.

"No plate on the front, and one of those temporary cardboard plates on the back. It was covered with mud, and he couldn't make out the letters or numbers."

"Did he report the truck as part of the watch program?"

"I would think he would have, but neither Chief Timmy nor the sheriff's department had record of a report," Ron answered impatiently.

I didn't interrupt anymore and listened to the rest of the story. My uncle was murdered, premeditated, intentionally killed. The weight of the situation settled squarely on my shoulders. I had nothing to say. In fact, neither of us spoke for a while, keeping our heads down and avoiding eye contact to avoid the possibility of sharing feelings.

Our quiet was disturbed by a low but audible beeping. A red light at the bottom corner of one of the screens had started to blink triggered by an employee. On the screen, one of Ron's salespeople was showing a customer a tray of rings.

Ron and I looked closer and backed up the video. You could see that the customer had passed his hand over the ring tray and selected a ring from the back row. When he brought his hand back with the ring he had selected, two of the previously filled slots in the front row were now empty.

"My people are trained to be cool in these cases. No one will do anything to spook the thief. They just go on like nothin' happened."

Ron hit the speed dial on his cell, notified the dispatcher of the situation, and gave a description of the thief. Then he told me to follow him, and we ducked out the back door and came around to the front, lingering on the corner like a couple of tourists. The guy walked out of the store, and Ron blocked his way.

At that moment, a squad pulled up. The thief, a thirty-something man with a goatee and a spider tattoo on his neck, did the look around—fight, flight, or give it up. Ron reached his hand inside his leather jacket and turned it back a little just so the guy could see his hand on the butt of a gun. The sight of the gun helped make up his mind for him, and his shoulders slumped as the cop approached. He emptied his pockets, and there were two of Ron's rings worth a couple thousand dollars. The dude was up from Chicago on vacation and figured he would make a few extra bucks while he was here. The cop cuffed him and put him in the back of the car. Ron said thanks to the cop and sent him off with a "Book 'em, Danno."

"We are always on the lookout for thieves," Ron said. "It's a big problem during the tourist season. They come up or over from the cities figuring that small towns are easy pickings. We all got wise to this long ago. It was your uncle Nick, actually, who helped us design a surveillance system, and Chief Timmy held training during the winter for business owners and staff. Each counter has a hidden switch. When one of the girls sees something they don't like, they push the button, and the camera locks into a frame-by-frame save mode. Usually I'm in the back working, so I monitor like I did today. If I'm not here, one of the others usually is.

"Our little town lost tens of thousands of dollars to thieves every year before these systems. Now it's about a tenth of that. I tell my people to never confront anyone and call the law. A couple of years ago, the gal from the leather store went nose to nose with some guy from the city whose pockets were full of her stuff, and he pulled a gun. Not worth dying over something like that. There's not one damn thing in my store that's worth more than my employees. The D.A. here doesn't screw around with these guys either. Many a big city shithead has found himself cooling his heels in the Namekagon County jail for six months. Our local criminals don't care for the big city boys, so they don't enjoy their stay very much."

I was pretty sure that while Ron forbid his sales staff from confronting a thief, the same rules did not apply to him. He was not the kind of guy to watch his merchandise go walking off down the street.

We went back in the office, and Ron got right to it. "So what are we going to do now. What's our next step?"

"First off, I'm hoping you could answer a couple of questions for me."

"Shoot. I'm all ears."

"There are some people around here that are really interested in what I am doing or not doing. You've been around a lot longer than I have, so maybe you can help me understand. I have got to ask about my uncle's choice in lawyers. He was always a remarkable judge of character, yet he ends up with Derek Anderson for a lawyer. What is the deal with that?"

"That's an easy one. Derek was working as a junior partner for Jonas McMann, a lawyer in town forever. Jonas was a honest and hardworking gentleman. He was still sharp and practicing law in his late eighties but took on two associates to help him with the day-today stuff. One of the associates, I don't remember his name, lasted about a year or so and moved on. Derek was from the general area and stayed.

"Jonas used to love to fish fall muskies. With him, you better make sure you had your legal problems all fixed up before fall. If not, they'd have to wait until winter. One day, he was out musky fishing, and when he didn't come back by early evening, his wife called the sheriff. A warden found him in his boat a little while later. He had passed on. Interesting thing, he still had his fishing rod gripped in his hands. The warden saw that the tip was jiggling and hand lined it in. At the end of the line was a very tired, but still healthy 50-plus-inch musky. The warden gripped the fish, worked the lure out, and watched it swim off. Nick told me that he was surprised that more people didn't keel over when they had a big musky on the line. So, Derek just took over the practice and most people who had Jonas for a lawyer stayed with him."

"Is he your lawyer?"

"Nope. I never liked him much, and when Jonas died, I went to a friend of mine in Spooner."

"Did Uncle Nick say anything about working with Derek? Derek did all the estate planning, and I assume he and Uncle Nick had to work together quite a bit."

"Nope. That's not right. Jonas did Nick's estate planning. I know because I was a witness to the signing of the papers. I am also listed as the executor in the event that something happened to you. I was supposed to take care of distributing his assets to various things he thought were worthwhile. The property was to go into a trust, and he was pretty specific about its disposition if you weren't around. He agreed to do the same for me. Matter of fact, he pushed me pretty hard to get my planning done. As I recall, at the time he was greatly concerned that my penchant for riding my Harley fast over these backroads would soon be my undoing."

"Do you have kids or other family, Ron?"

"No kids that I know about anyway, and I am not married at the moment. That could change any day but I am between wives right now."

"Does 'change any day' mean you have someone special in mind?"

"Not really, but you never know what I am going to do until I do it."

• • •

"Derek was the one that first contacted me about my aunt and uncle. He was pretty cordial to start with but was really pushing me to sell the property. When I told him I wouldn't, our relationship went straight downhill. He obviously had a vested interest in the sale of the property. Clearly, he has his own agenda. I finally got to the point where I hired my own lawyer to work with him. I am getting strange vibes. There's something else going on with Derek that involves me. I don't know what it is, but I think it has to do with the property."

"What did he tell you about the property?"

I went over everything thing I knew or suspected up to that point. Ron was an attentive listener and didn't say much during my recount of the activities. After I had finished, he began asking me questions. That's when I learned something very interesting about Ron Carver. His outward appearance would fool many people into thinking he was just an old rounder, battered by the storm of life, likely unable to string enough words together to make a sentence. They would be wrong. When Ron asked me questions, it was apparent that not only had he been listening but could recount every word I had spoken verbatim. His questions were clear and succinct and in better chronological order than they had been when I presented them.

"So Derek Anderson brought you an offer to purchase the property and recommended that you sign off and take the money?"

"Correct."

"Did he share with you the name of this most anxious buyer?"

"He told me he didn't know. He said he was working on behalf of another law firm. That was another lie. Subsequently though, I have met the guy. His name is David Stone."

"David Stone!? David Stone is the guy who wants the property?"

"That is what he said his name was."

"Johnny boy, I am going to have the girls make up a fresh pot of coffee. When I get back, I need to hear the whole story. Don't leave anything out. I want to know about Stone and anyone else you might have met since you arrived. You've no doubt met some dangerous characters when you were a cop, but it is unlikely that you've ever met anyone as dangerous as David Stone, for he is truly a dangerous man."

A few minutes later I was telling Ron everything I could think of about meeting Stone, Lawler, the chief, Julie, and Bud. I found that recounting all that had happened since my arrival helped me sort things out. The back and forth discussion that followed blew some of the mist away, and I could see the events more clearly. My investigator's eyes became focused. The conclusion was simple. David Stone was running this show. Anderson and probably Lawler were doing his bidding for him, trying to get me to sign while scaring me off at the same time. Carrot in one hand, stick in the other. Stone didn't get to be a wealthy businessman by spending money foolishly. If he was willing to pay more than the property was worth, it wasn't for his dream home.

Ron didn't know much about Lawler. He had heard lots of rumors about the guy but didn't know much else. Chief Timmy was a good man and usually a good judge of character, just like my uncle. But he had hired Lawler, and Uncle Nick had hired Anderson. Two good men hire two bad men, and the bad men have some sort of unknown relationship.

Coincidence or pieces of the puzzle?

I didn't tell Ron about the safe hidden in the file cabinet. I sensed I could trust him but felt it best to keep some of my cards close to my chest.

Stone, Lawler, and Anderson were our three principals of interest that we knew. The driver of the Expedition was still unknown. At least one of them had something to do with Uncle Nick's murder; maybe they all did.

We didn't have a motive. The property was clearly at the center of this, but that didn't explain why killing Uncle Nick would get them any closer to owning it. Money is a powerful motive. I had seen store clerks shot over the fifty bucks in their register. Someone getting killed over millions is not very hard to believe. Nick wouldn't sell. Maybe they thought I would just take the money and run. Maybe now they intended to kill me, too. There were too many complications, too many pieces of the puzzle missing. I still needed to know two things: what they were looking for when they trashed the desk and what was in the safe.

Ron had some business to attend to, and we both needed a break. I was going to go out to the lake and move what little I had into the cabin. Before I left, I needed to catch up with the insurance man.

Dennis Targett was in and sitting at his desk, putting new line on a musky-sized fishing reel. I felt like he was genuinely glad to see me.

"Hey, John, pull up a chair," he said. "I can't stop now or I will be fighting line loops forever. Changing out your line often is a requirement on a musky rig. Those big boys really stress fishing line, and nothing will make you sicker than to have your line break when you set the hook on a big fish."

He was talking to me but focused on his line winding technique using every digit available to guide the line onto the reel. He had a clever way of using his thumb to keep tension on the line making sure it was wound on tight.

"Lot of folks use this new braided line, and it does seem to last longer. I am a monofilament guy. I think it's harder for the fish to see. It doesn't last as long, but I think I catch more fish. What kind of line do you like?" he continued.

"I don't know that I currently have a preference. I'm just using the gear Uncle Nick had set up."

"Hmm, you should probably change that line out. I'll send you home with a spool of my favorite stuff. It's called Newton's Ghost. Best stuff I ever came across. Small company but a top-notch product."

He finished with his new line and held the tag end in place with a wide rubber band around the reel, and then set it off to the side. He opened a file drawer and pulled out a file that he laid on the desk.

FIGURE EIGHT. A NORTHERN LAKES MYSTERY

"Your uncle had a life insurance policy that he had paid up years ago. It had a pretty good cash value, but I don't think he needed the money, so he never asked about cashing it in. He had an option of reinvesting the dividends to pay additional premiums and up the value. That's what he did, and the company just did it automatically. The value is substantial, and your share comes out to just about $200,000. The remainder goes to the other beneficiary."

"Other beneficiary?" I asked.

"You were the only one listed for a long time, but somewhere along the way your uncle filed a change directly with the company. He could have done it right here, but for some reason, he decided to work directly with the home office. I have a copy of the form right here," he said as he slid it across the desk.

I looked at the form, and it took my breath away. Uncle Nick had filed a change of beneficiary form three weeks before he was run down. The person named would receive a half a million dollars upon his death. It wasn't the money that took my breath away. It was the timing of the change and the name of the new beneficiary: Julie Carlson.

Targett pulled the form back. "Are you okay, John? Would you like some water or something?"

"Does she know? Does Julie know about this?"

"She sure does. We finished up the transfer paper a while ago. Yours is the last disbursement."

I didn't, I couldn't, respond. A dark cloud smothered my mind. Julie Carlson had deceived me. She played me like the fool I was. Why had I even come to this place? I must have been delusional to think that Musky Falls was some kind of nirvana. How stupid could I be? Moving from one place to another doesn't change the world. Deceit, heartache, and evil are everywhere.

I barely heard Dennis as he told me that by signing the document of receipt I would authorize them to electronically transfer the money to any account, checking, savings, or investment. They just needed the right account number. I gave it to him and signed a check release form. The money would be available within 24 hours.

We shook hands, and I stumbled out the door. I got into the jeep and drove over to Musky Falls Autobody. They were just pulling my car out. I parked the jeep in the lot, and they handed me the keys to my car.

"Good as new. No bill either. Dennis took care of everything. If you want, you can just leave the jeep here. I have to go down to the garage a little later, and I'll drop it off."

"Thanks," I mumbled. I got in, started the car, and backed out, then punched the accelerator as I hit the highway. I needed to get some answers and get them now. I was going to start with innocent, sweet, little treacherous Julie Carlson. I knew she'd be at school for the start of the summer session. It would be better for me to wait until she was home, but waiting wasn't happening. After driving the jeep, my car seemed like it had wings as I flew east out of town. ∎

CHAPTER 18
Hospital

Nurse Holterman walked in and told Presser that he had to leave. I protested that we only needed a few more minutes, but to no avail. Bill—who I believe is wisely terrified of her—got up and left.

"Mr. Cabrelli, the medical team led by Dr. Árnason will be in shortly."

The team blew into the room, checked my vitals, and mumbled words I didn't understand. They were joined by another new face, Dr. Jónsdottir.

"Mr. Cabrelli, Dr. Jónsdottir is a neurosurgeon. I sent all of your test results over to her. She found something of concern," said Árnason.

Jónsdottir, a pretty blonde, spoke with a slight accent that I couldn't place. "Mr. Cabrelli, when I looked over your test results, I saw that your infection was cleared up by the use of a broad spectrum antibiotic. Subsequent tests showed no further evidence of infection. However, I am very concerned about the weakness and numbness in your lower extremities. It indicates that there may be some serious neurological issues stemming from the bullet remaining close to your spine. In addition, there may be some localized infection in the bone next to the bullet. In my opinion, we should proceed as soon as possible to go in and remove the bullet associated fragments and deal with the infection. There are many risks, but I truly believe that this is the best course of action."

"How risky?" I asked.

"Mr. Cabrelli, you have been shot twice by a high-powered gun. The damage is as to be expected: significant. So far you have survived everything. Repairing damage due to trauma in close proximity to your spinal column is always risky. You're lucky that the bullet did not hit your spine less than a half-inch closer to the center. That would have likely resulted in a much more dire situation. There is always risk, but leaving the bullet is not an option."

"Anyone else want to weigh in?" I asked. "Come on gang, speak up. Since I am six years short of a medical degree, how about you give me some input?"

Doctor Jr., although often quiet in front of his seniors, was first. "I believe that Dr. Jónsdottir is right. The only course to follow is the one she has suggested. Either way, postponing the surgery or doing it now has an element of risk. I think we need to defer to Dr. Jónsdottir. You have been a fighter through this whole ordeal, but you are showing signs of fatigue and weakening. These will only get worse if your body tries to fight off yet another infection. Let Dr. Jónsdottir proceed with some additional tests to get ready for the surgery."

My answer was based only partly on what the doctors were saying. The need to tell my story had become paramount in my life. It was the only item on my bucket list. The truth needed to be told, wrongs needed to be made right, and the devil needed to get his. I was the only one who knew it all, and I had to get it out; a couple more days was all Presser and I needed.

"Do the tests. I'll wait."

"I think it is a wise choice, Mr. Cabrelli," said Jónsdottir. "I have some additional questions to ask you. The bullets, when they entered your body, would have carried with them microparticles of anything they had come in contact with. It could be pocket lint if they were carried in a pocket. I am most interested in whether or not you had blood from someone else on your clothing at the time of the incident."

"Yes, I had blood on my shirt for sure."

"How long before had you come into contact with it? Was it dried blood?"

"I am pretty sure it was still wet."

The smile on Jónsdottir's face turned to a frown at my answer.

She said, "The lab team will be here momentarily."

Everyone turned and left except for Nurse Holterman. She fixed her eyes on me and said, "Mr. Cabrelli, I have no intention whatsoever of allowing you to succumb to some mysterious infection and die on my watch. You have survived the impossible and shall continue to survive. You will maintain the stubborn and obnoxious attitude that has served you so well. The world cannot afford to lose men like you."

As she walked out of the room, she paused for a moment to say that Presser could come back in, and our time restrictions were temporarily lifted, providing we didn't abuse the privilege.

• • •

"Bill, we need to get to work. Skip some of the little stuff and get right to it."

"That will work to a certain extent, but the 'little stuff' is important. Everybody is going to read this story and have their own opinions. From the gang at the Moccasin Bar to the Lion's Club. Everybody is going to weigh in. Details are important."

"Let's get through the big story, and if I'm around, we'll fill in the details later."

The *if I'm around* part was no joke. Even though I had kept a pretty damned good game face on, I was a sick man. My strength was waning. I had noticed the weakness in my legs, the left one especially, but I thought it was just from being bedridden for so long. I removed the snap-on lid on my hospital issue water cup and found it very difficult. I doubt that I could have even racked the slide on my little Walther. I was just tired, worn out.

"Anyway, I was dumbfounded when I found out that Julie had deceived me. The time had come to take the bull by the proverbial horns."

FIGURE EIGHT. A NORTHERN LAKES MYSTERY

CHAPTER 19
Cabrelli

So as I was saying, after driving the jeep, it felt like I was low flying in my little car. There was little traffic so I kept the car at a steady 75. The landscape I had so enjoyed just days before was now a blur. Distance to be traveled. I slowed down before I pulled into the lot at school. All the kids were outside working on the garden or building benches and wood duck houses. I parked and walked over to Julie. She was down on her knees helping some students transfer small plants to a raised garden bed.

"Julie, we need to talk."

"Talk," she said with a smile.

"I know about the life insurance."

Her face went sheet white. She moved her mouth, but no words came out.

Although I was steaming mad on the trip out to the school, once we were face to face, her look said it all. I was no longer mad. I just felt betrayed and defeated. I had fooled myself that Musky Falls was a place that would bring me peace, happiness, and honesty. Now I found it was a place just like all others.

"John, if you could wait just a half hour, the kids will all be gone. Summer school lets out early, and they are cleaning up right now. I don't want them around when we talk."

My temper rose again. "I don't blame you for not wanting them to know what kind of person their teacher really is. I'll be glad to wait. I'm sure this is going to be worth it."

I walked over to sit at the picnic table next to the building. Some of the kids said "hi," but I was in no mood for conversation. Soon they had cleaned up and were all on the bus. Julie waved as they pulled out. She came over to sit across from me.

I have been told by others that at certain times I have a look on my face that is scary. It usually shows up just before hell is about to break loose. I don't consider myself some kind of super badass, but when this happens, there is no backing down. If you choose to start a fight, I may lose, but you will get all I have to offer and even more if I can find it. That must have been the look I had on my face when I glared at Julie.

She was at first startled, and then showed a look of fear. Then she stared right back, her eyes meeting mine.

"That hellish look on your face may scare others, but it doesn't scare me. If you want to talk, we'll talk. If you are going to yell and rant and who knows what else, I am leaving, and we can talk sometime later when you have settled down. You make the choice."

I told her we would talk now.

"When were you going to tell me about the life insurance policy?"

"I actually didn't know how to handle it. I was as surprised as you. I have never been in this situation before, so I didn't do anything. Besides, Dennis Targett told me that I didn't have to tell anyone anything. So I decided not to, until I felt the time was right."

"So you didn't think it was important to tell me that my murdered uncle had changed the beneficiary on his life insurance policy three weeks before he was run down and murdered? That sounds to me like it's something you wanted to hide, motive ..."

"Motive for what!? You stupid ass, you jerk! You actually think that I had anything to do with Nick's death? What the hell is wrong with you? You, the 'concerned nephew' that didn't even know that Nick and Rose were dead. You and all your crap about how this place feels like home. I never asked one thing from Nick and Rose. I loved them and cared for them. You were nowhere to be found. How dare you talk to me this way!"

She stood up and slapped me across the face so hard it felt like I was hit with a blackjack.

"I am staying at Bud's house tonight. I don't want to have anything to do with you. Stay away from me. That goes for Bud, too. We will be out tomorrow to get my stuff. Please let me know when you will not be there."

She got in her car and left, tires spinning, gravel flying.

My face burned from the slap, but more from her obvious hurt and anger.

She was right. Technically it was none of my business. Also, there really hadn't been a point where it would have been a good time to have broached the subject.

It was time to find out what the hell was going on. Things were no clearer than when I'd started. The first place to start was the safe in Uncle Nick's shop.

I pulled in, and the warm coming-home feeling had deserted me. I, John Cabrelli the cop, was on the case and going to run it down, take it to its natural end. Whoever the bad guys were, they were going down, starting now. Lawler, Anderson, Stone, whoever; their time had come. As my old precinct commander used to say, 'Your ass is grass, and I am the lawnmower.'

I opened the shop and pulled out the file drawer. The light lit the door and the safe dial. It was a sturdy safe with hidden hinges and what looked like a thick door, probably fireproof. Not a cracker box that I was going to open with a pry bar and drill. Safe combinations are usually in two categories. People use the combination that was assigned to the safe, or they change it to something that is easy to remember for them but personal information someone else would not readily know. On a safe dial numbered 1 to 100, the combination almost always had six digits. Right-left-right or the opposite.

Six digits, zero could be used. I sat at the workbench and picked up a notebook and paper, trying to put number codes into a usable sequence. The phone worked if I dropped the first or last number. I tried it both ways—no luck. The fire number was a short one. What worked was a birth date. I had Uncle Nick's and Aunt Rose's in my paperwork. I tried both—nothing. Then I tried mine, and the lock clicked. I turned the handle, and the door came open.

The safe was about two feet deep, and the opening was a foot square. It was three-quarters full. Before taking anything out, I looked to make sure no one was sneaking up on me. There was a workbench with a window over it that looked out on the driveway. I took the Walther out of my pocket, set it on the bench, sat down with the first two envelopes, and began.

The first was a business-sized white envelope with my name on the front. A note inside read:

Johnny,

If you are looking at this, it is because you are a smart boy, found the safe, and figured out the combination.

It also it means that I have gone on to join your aunt Rose. I can't wait to see her. I have missed her so much.

I don't know where to begin. There is so much to say. What is contained in this safe is mostly self-explanatory. As you will see, I ended up in the middle of things that I wanted no part of. I did not ask to be involved and tried to avoid it at every turn. They just kept coming, and I knew that they were not going to stop. Vince Lombardi said, 'The best defense is a good offense," so I began to look at the situation and started putting things in categories, just like developing an invention, common denominators, isolated factors, co-dependent factors, and so on.

I decided to do this after I had a long talk with myself. After Rose died, I felt like a ship without a home port. If I could wish something for you, I would wish that you would have a partner like Rose. She made me stronger, smarter, and a better person. Any success I have had in life has been because of her, not in spite of her.

When that little weasel Anderson came to me with the offer from Stone, I was very tempted. I have loved the north country and all it has to offer: its clear waters and fast running rivers and the big woods. Northern Wisconsin is a place like no other—a place where everyone can spread their wings and not touch wingtips. There comes a time when you have to look at the future, and this place is a lot to take care of. I thought about selling and almost did until I found out the truth. From then on, it was me against them. There is more to find out, but what's here ought to get you started. Be careful. I think these guys are dangerous.

I hope you have met Julie Carlson by now. I left a good portion of my life insurance policy to her. The amount should be enough to get an endowment started for her school. There is only one stipulation: she has to take a portion of the money to buy herself a new car. She hauls kids around in that rattrap of hers, and between Bud, Doc O'Malley, and I, we can barely keep it running. See that she does it. She's not too good at receiving gifts.

I believe strongly in what she is doing. Most of those kids have nothing, yet she makes them all feel special. I am convinced that her school is part of saving the world. Video games, cell phones, computers, and a couple hundred TV channels have made certain that kids will spend as much time as possible indoors. I believe with all my heart and mind that the health of our environment and the health of our human population are forever intertwined. Who will the leaders be that step up to protect what we have if their only exposure is a nature show on TV? I tell you who: it's going to be those kids at Northern Lakes. I hope you will get to know them. They are worth your effort.

Johnny, the rest is in the safe. I want you to know that Rose and I loved you like a son. You were a good boy and have become a good man. I know the pain you must have gone through. Just remember, you can't change what happened a second ago. You can only change what happens a second from now. Miss me and mourn me, but live your life. It is one of God's greatest gifts.

Uncle Nick

I put the letter down and wished that Julie was there to slap me again, just harder this time.

I am predictable to some extent. When I am feeling emotional pain, the best medicine for me is hard work. Idle hands or an idle mind or something like that is the devil's workshop.

I sat at the bench and opened the second envelope. In it was a letter from a private investigation/law firm located in Minneapolis indicating they were confident that the information they had developed was accurate and that there was little else to be found. Closing with a "call us again if need be."

The first document was a corporate charter. Attached to it was a flow chart. Attached to the flow chart was supporting information and several other corporate charters. The narrative was interesting and listed many names of people I had never heard of and companies with names I had also had never heard of. With one glaring exception. Following the flowchart and the narrative through several different corporations led me to the controlling owner of Northern Mining Company, David Stone.

Next was a permit application for mining and mineral exploration. The permit had been approved and was very detailed about what testing could take place and where. The permit had been issued by the Wisconsin Department of Natural Resources, U.S. Army Corps of Engineers, and Namekagon County Zoning. Attached to the permit was a high resolution aerial photo and a map. Each had areas delineated by various solid and broken lines. Two areas on each map were highlighted with bright yellow: the area along Spider Creek including this property and an area marked as Tribal Trust lands. After that was a huge tract of land marked as being owned by Northern Mining Company and another large tract owned by ST Trust. I am not a cartographer, but even I could see that the only access to the Northern Mining and ST Trust property was through my uncle's land, right down Spider Creek and all of the land on either side. The rest of the land surrounding their property was owned by the government and was listed as national forest or wilderness area. Even if they could come through the federal property to get to their site, that distance was many times that compared to coming through Uncle Nick's land, and by the looks of the aerial, it would mean crossing dozens of large and small rivers and streams. The only access point with enough space to run the heavy equipment they used for iron ore mining was through his property. Even if the tribe went along, it wouldn't get them there.

The firm had uncovered several other interesting documents: one report was marked "confidential" and "proprietary" and "possession of this document by an unauthorized party constituted theft."

It had two parts: a fiscal analysis and a geologist's report regarding the proposed mine area. The geologist's report was in-depth and involved terms and data sheets that were beyond me. It essentially said that the proposed mine site was a Precambrian "Lake Superior-type" sedimentary iron formation. The area contained millions of tons of marketable iron ore. In addition, it noted that it was the largest remaining site in Wisconsin. In the geologist's opinion, the site had sufficient quantities of taconite over a large area and that it was feasible to mine.

The fiscal report was enough to set you down. Initially the site would produce hundreds of millions of dollars in net revenue from the taconite. Contract terms were currently being negotiated with China to form a partnership that would ensure a ready market for the ore. Shipping via the Great Lakes would ensure economical transportation. The report was done as some type of document for investors. It had none of the fluff and baloney about community benefit that accompanies public documents. This was made for a select few big players that could risk a million or two. The bottom line was pretty plain: the mine would have net revenues over a twenty-year lifespan in the billions of dollars. A long way from shooting someone over fifty bucks at a convenience store, about a billion or two worth of motive. Any way you looked at it the mine was a big deal and was going to make a few people very, very rich.

Money is always one of the top three when it comes to motive. The more money, the less value a life that might stand in the way has.

Next was a group of documents inside a legal folder with a label that said Jonas McMann, Attorney at Law. It was several inches thick, and the first layer was correspondence between Uncle Nick, Jonas, and a lawyer from St. Paul. It was a back-and-forth correspondence regarding the sale of the property. It included three offers to purchase, each more than the preceding one. A letter from Jonas should have closed that issue, as it clearly stated after the third offer that his client did not want to sell, period. Don't bother us again.

The letters they got in response were ugly. It seems that under the authority of a thing called the Economic Development Act a government entity could move to acquire a property through condemnation. The final offer they would put forth was a permanent easement through the property. They offered a sizable sum for the easement. If the offer was refused they would proceed to initiate a condemnation procedure.

Lawyer McMann was an able researcher, and he studied the potential for their being successful if they were to proceed with the condemnation. The law that they were using was relatively new and one signed at midnight by the governor to serve the interest of a big campaign donor. It was a bad law that would be almost surely found to be unconstitutional. It, however, was the law. The people trying to buy the property had followed the progression required to move forward with such an action. In a nutshell, his opinion was that they would be unsuccessful in any attempt to acquire the property through condemnation.

The problem with that was that even if Jonas worked *pro-bono,* they would have to hire a law firm that specialized in these sorts of cases. Nick's defense would soon drain all his assets, and the opposition would just be getting warmed up.

Nick had written every branch of government and every law group that might be looking for a cause, to hang their sign up to fight injustice. From the looks of things, those that did bother to answer gave him little hope.

What had changed any thoughts about selling was next. The mining companies that were involved in the Northern Mining Company had a long history of mining in the U.S. There were pages of documents regarding violations of the Federal Clean Water Act and state water laws. Additional documents detailed fines and penalties that had been levied, and they totaled in the millions of dollars, which was a whole bunch of money, but nothing compared to billions in revenue. There were copies of news stories from around the country.

A common theme was easy to detect: the mine was built and operated; the operators were shielded behind a corporation; they extracted as much ore as quickly as possible; eventually environmental regulators would catch up to them and find numerous violations, most involving lakes, rivers, streams, and wetlands. The mining representative would refer issues to their team of lawyers, who would delay the process through legal challenges. They would eventually go to court and be found guilty and fined a couple of million dollars. The lawyers would file appeals and eventually settle. During all of the wrangling, the mine would continue to operate at a huge profit and continue to destroy natural resources. They would appeal to locals working at the mines and tell them how the government was trying to take their jobs by nitpicky environmental violations, thereby turning the public against the regulators. While this was all going on, just months prior to a settlement, the mine would be sold to another company. The new company would pledge to be a better citizen, and the whole process would start over. At least three of the buyers of these mines were ones listed in Uncle Nick's documentation.

There were two folders left. The next one I read was the most chilling. It was written by a hydrogeologist employed by the U.S. Geological Survey. It listed his credentials as well as various publications that he had been involved in. In his opinion, if the proposed mine was allowed to go forward as planned, the mining process would cause widespread contamination of both surface and groundwater. The proposed process had been used in several other places in the U.S. and Canada, and each case had resulted in significant and long-lasting environmental damage. Although it claimed to be cutting edge mining technology, it had never been used anywhere in the world that did not result in significant impacts. Attempts to pre-treat the contaminated water on site before being discharged into surface waters and wetlands had been unsuccessful and had resulted in significant damage.

In this case, the potential for disaster was incredible. The scientist from the USGS had included detailed maps of waterways that would be impacted by the mine. Most of them flowed directly into one of the largest bodies of freshwater in the world, Lake Superior. The hydrogeologist was willing to stake his reputation on the fact that the mine as proposed would cause long-term irreversible damage to one of the Great Lakes.

Should this happen, the north country would never be the same. The place Uncle Nick and Aunt Rose had loved would be destroyed, the splendor of the northern lake region lost—maybe forever.

The last folder was a little confusing. It was several pictures of a small bird. Along with the photos was a log that gave GPS locations, times, and dates that corresponded to the photos. As should be expected, the documentation was meticulous, likely part of his ongoing nature observations. There was nothing in that file that connected it to the mine. It must have been a big deal for him in his birding life to put it in the safe.

It looked like everything he could have done had been done. The mine was too big, too powerful, and had too many lawyers. The situation was just going to be another case of a little guy getting his butt kicked by a big guy.

So why kill him? According to his own lawyer, he was beat. Why not just wait him out? Tie him up in court until he ran out of money? And what was the deal with someone breaking into the house and trashing his desk? I had more pieces of the puzzle, but not everything. Something was missing.

• • •

When you embark on a great and all-consuming task, clear your plate, if you can, before you start. When murder is involved, and you are trying to find a killer, a clear head may be the only thing that keeps you from being another victim. It was with this on my mind when I saw Julie's car pull into the yard. I walked out of the shop and toward her. She turned to face me. Her eyes were red from crying. We were only a few feet apart staring at each other, her skin-blistering glare now replaced by something else. We were both exhausted. The events that had transpired had taken a toll on each of us in our own way. We were too tired to fight. I walked into the house and came out with two cold beers, opened them, and sat them down on the picnic table. She sat across from me.

"Julie, I'm sorry. I'm a jerk sometimes, and I can't help it. I don't try, but I sure do it well."

"No, John. I should have told you the truth upfront. I just felt like you would think I had manipulated Nick into naming me on the policy. I didn't want you to think I was another Derek Anderson. I loved Nick and Rose, and the last thing I wanted from them was money." Her eyes welled up with tears.

The nightmares I live with when I sleep are proof that there is no such thing as a do-over. But there is such a thing as a start-over. With Julie Carlson and I, a start-over was clearly needed.

So I said, "My name is John Cabrelli. Nick and Rose were the closest I had to family in the world. I am here because they have died, and I have inherited this beautiful place. Coming back here has been a blessing and a curse. I loved Uncle Nick and Aunt Rose. I was not as good to them as they were to me. I feel ungrateful. I wish that I could have spent some time with them, but that is an opportunity I lost. I hope they will forgive me.

"Since I arrived here, I have learned many things. The most difficult is that my uncle was murdered. The one thing I can do for him is find the person, or more likely persons, responsible and make them pay. To stop me, they will have to kill me too."

She blinked back her tears. "I am glad to meet you, John. I am Julie Carlson. I have heard a lot about you. I am a teacher at a local environmental school that serves kids who people call 'at-risk.' Nick and Rose were kinder to me and my cousin Bud than anyone in our life had ever been. Nick told me that he wanted to endow the school. We always struggle with finances. He listed me as the beneficiary of his life insurance policy and trusted me to use it to help the school. There are no other restrictions. The money is in my name, and Nick told me to use my best judgment. The only condition that he put on the funds was that I buy a new car that was four-wheel drive and big enough to haul kids to all the places I take them. All of the money is in an account at the bank downtown. I haven't used a penny. I loved Nick and Rose. I am going to help you find the killer, and nothing you can say will stop me."

So began my relationship anew with Julie Carlson, one of the best people I have ever met. I thought if I was ever lucky enough to find a girl like her, I'd never let her go. Fat chance. The John Cabrellis of the world never end up with the Julie Carlsons of the world, but a guy can still dream.

I took her into the shop and showed her the hidden safe, then the files that had come from them. As she went over them, I could envision her correcting student papers. I sat down next to her, shoulder to shoulder, and we went through things together. We didn't say much until she got to the folder that contained the photos of the bird.

"Amazing, these are photos of a very rare bird called the Kirtland's warbler. It is a federally listed endangered species. My students did a project on endangered species of the north, and this bird was one that originally lived in this area. These are GPS locations? Oh my gosh! Give me the mine map."

We spread out the mine map. Julie took one location from Uncle Nick's notes and scanned the first map, and there it was, a corresponding GPS, a few points off of Uncle Nick's but close enough. The locations he had noted were all within the proposed mine area and half of them on his property. Uncle Nick had found his ally with deep pockets, a government lawyer. Julie filled me in on some of the history of the Endangered Species Act, how successful legal challenges had been mounted against huge companies all in the name of protecting rare and endangered species. She relayed a couple of incidents that her kids had researched.

Presence of an endangered owl had darn near shut down the whole logging industry in the Pacific Northwest. Protesters on both sides had amassed in the hundreds. Those trying to protect owl habitat had gone as far as chaining themselves to the bumpers of logging trucks. The loggers who were trying to make a living and support their families fought back, and the controversy went on for several months before the federal government made a decision. They decided in favor of the owl and dispatched adequate law enforcement to make sure their ruling stood.

Probably on one of Nick's daily outings he had seen this unusual bird. Who knows whether he knew what it was, but being a very astute observer of wildlife, he likely did. The first date of observation preceded the correspondence with the law firm and investigator from the cities. It was his ace-in-the-hole card; he'd probably thought that just simply not selling would stop the project, but had found out later that it likely wouldn't. His lawyer and friend had said that there was no way to fight the mine's lawyers without going broke. But he had the bird. He must have known that they would challenge anything that he put forward without an over-the-top amount of documentation. He was acquiring evidence, building his case, and by the looks of things he was almost ready. If he wanted to stop the mine, bringing the full weight of the U.S. Department of the Interior against them was sure a step in the right direction.

Uncle Nick had them. He was going to win. They were going to lose out on billions of dollars. Somebody knew he had this stuff. They gave the information to someone high up from the Northern Mining Company who would decide they needed to do whatever they had to do to prevent this information from coming forward. Uncle Nick was about to shut them down, and they'd killed him to keep him quiet. The search of the desk had been an afterthought just to make sure his former cop nephew wouldn't uncover anything.

The burning question was who had Uncle Nick confided in? Who had he told?

Julie and I sat for a long while, each immersed in our own thoughts. There is always some feeling of satisfaction when you are working on a case, and the *why* has become clear. It is at that point that you can focus your efforts, and most often you will be successful in finding the bad guy or guys. My mind was buzzing, ready to go on the hunt.

There was no doubt that Nick had shared his information with someone. We needed to start with a potential list and then draw links between them and the mine. Nick's group of trusted confidants was small: Julie, Bud, Ron Carver, Chief Don Timmy, and that was about it. What about his lawyer, Derek Anderson? Would he have confided in him? It didn't seem likely that he'd liked or trusted him much, but there was a link between Uncle Nick, Derek Anderson, and the mine. Maybe in his conversations he had threatened David Stone with the release of the information unless he backed off. Certainly Stone wouldn't hesitate to make sure this information never saw the light of day. Maybe he contacted the U.S. Fish and Wildlife Service and told them what he had found. Maybe he had confided in one of his close friends, and they had sold him out. Money made normal people do strange things all the time.

The task became more defined.

• • •

Julie still had the contact information for the local USFWS biologist who was in charge of the Endangered Species Act for the area. I gave him a call. When you call a government office, you come to expect some degree of formality when they answer your phone call. Not so with this guy, who answered the phone with a very cheery, "Quack! Charlie Newlin, endangered species specialist."

Sometimes when you're under stress, the dumbest thing breaks the ice; Newlin's phone answering did it for me, and I couldn't help but laugh. I explained that I had gotten his number from Julie Carlson and was interested in a bird.

"Julie Carlson sent you? How is she doing? How are her kids? I love that school. I wish there had been something like that when I was a kid. Sure had fun working with them on their endangered species projects. Any chance they're going to do it again this school year? I sure hope so. You tell Julie that if she wants to, I'm her man. I got some great ideas for things we could do. I thought maybe we could include a plant identification unit along with the endangered species. Not to say that plants can't be endangered species, not to say that at all. Lots of plants are on the list, but Julie and the kids were mostly interested in the furry or feathered. Say, where did you say you were calling from?"

"I didn't, but I'm in the Spider Lake area."

"Spider Lake? Man, I really like that area. Have you seen any ducks or geese around? I love ducks and geese; they are so tasty. Anyway, Mr. ... ah Mr., what did you say your name was?"

"Cabrelli, John Cabrelli," I answered.

"Well, Mr. John Cabrelli, how can I help you?"

"I am interested in whether or not you have heard any reports of Kirtland's warblers in the Spider Lake area."

"Kirtland's you're interested in? Are you a birder? I am a bird watcher myself. They are fascinating creatures. I have several feeders out my back window. I could watch them for hours. Do you have feeders set up? The Fish and Wildlife Service has several sets of plans available for properly constructed feeders. I could send you some plans, if you give me your address."

"Maybe some other time, I am not quite settled here yet. Back to the Kirtland's warbler. Any reports?"

"Well nothing, nothing at all. The agency put out a bulletin to be on the lookout a few years ago. But nothing was reported. Now in Adams County, a couple hundred miles south of you, they have confirmed a handful of nesting pairs. But nothing here. Have you seen something of note? I haven't had much this year. There were a couple of reports of a Canadian lynx here or there, and, of course, wolves everywhere, but nothing as exciting as a Kirtland's. I can come out and take a look if you want. We would set up some observation spots and see what we could see. Do you know the general area of the sighting?"

"No, no idea. I am just interested in whether someone has seen any Kirtland's warblers and reported those sightings to you. Did anyone report any sightings?"

"Sorry to say no. But if you should see something, I would be happy to follow up. I can't be everywhere, so citizen observers like you are very important to our work. I can send you some information on the warbler if you like. Give me your address, and I'll get it right out."

"Mr. Newlin, thanks for the information. If I need anything more I will get back to you. But that's all I need for now."

"Mr. Cabrelli, call anytime. Glad to hear from you. And always remember the magic words: please, thank you, honk, honk and quack, quack, quack."

• • •

If Uncle Nick had found an endangered species, and no doubt he had, he had not reported it to the authorities responsible for wildlife's well being.

Bud showed up while we were sorting this out and joined us.

At this point a decision had to be made. The only way to keep a secret is to never tell anyone, nobody.

When you are launching an investigation like this one, it is damn tricky because your list of possible confidants and helpers are on the same list as your suspects. The only choice is to use your best judgment and forge ahead.

Julie and I brought Bud up to speed on what we found. He listened without comment. When we were done, the big gentle man across from us became a bigger and now very angry man.

"I'm helpin' you guys. When we find the guy, I am going to straighten him right out." As he talked, he flexed his massive hands.

This was a guy that would and could do serious damage to anyone that needed it. A good man to have on your side.

My old academy instructor taught us to gather, assess, and prioritize your resources. Use those resources that have the most potential gain and require the least amount of hands-on work by the investigative lead. Use your existing resources to their full potential before you run off chasing new untried possibilities.

With this in mind, I called my old partner J.J. Malone. Malone answered in his usual uplifting and cheery way:

"Malone," he growled.

"Bear, it's John."

"As I live and breathe, Nesmuck of the North has seen fit to call upon me, his long-lost partner. To what do I owe this pleasure?"

"Bear, I got something going on here, and I need a little help. I am convinced that my uncle Nick's death was a homicide. The local gendarmes have written it off as an accidental hit-and-run fatality. I have got some new information, and that theory no longer washes with me."

"No shit? Someone did your uncle in on purpose?"

"I am sure of it."

"What can I do to help?" Just like always, Bear is there, no screwin' around. You're my friend. You need me, I am there. They don't make them like him anymore.

"Do you still have that buddy with the feds that follows corporations, LLCs, and businesses figuring out who's who and who's laundering what money for what crook?"

"Sure do. I just talked to him the other day. He's helpin' us take down some drug dealers and the phony companies they are using. That guy is really good at what he does. He turns up solid stuff that no one else could ever find. What do you need from him?"

"I need to know who the principals are in two different companies: Northern Mining Corporation and ST Trust. Somehow one or the other, or maybe both, are involved in this. One guy, David Stone, is supposed to be a very bad man, and he employs heavily-armed security, pros by the looks of them, guys who don't come cheap anyway. There are two other guys, Derek Anderson, attorney-at-law, and Brian Lawler currently serving as one of Musky Falls's finest. I think these guys are both involved up to their ears in this thing."

"Anything else?"

"Not that I can think of."

"I will see what I can do under one condition. Set Tanya up with a first-class musky trip up there. She's nuts to go fishin', and her birthday is coming up."

"Consider it done. Thanks, Bear. I knew I could count on you."

"No problem, John. I'll get on it. Meantime, don't forget to keep your ass covered."

• • •

I told Julie and Bud about my conversation with Malone. "This guy is as good as gold," I told them. "We can count on him."

The question we needed to answer was who else was on our side? Who else could we trust?

"Your uncle knew a bunch of people, but I think his only real close friends were the chief and Ron Carver," said Julie.

"Which was the closest?" I asked.

"Ron, without a doubt," Julie and Bud answered together.

"They were really two of a kind but totally different, if that makes any sense," added Julie. "They shared the entrepreneurial spirit and are both super smart. Ron would come over all the time, and he and your uncle would talk about all sorts of things, but mostly they shared creative ideas. Have you ever seen that surveillance system in Ron's jewelry store?"

"Just the other day I saw it in action."

"That whole thing started out as a conversation one night here in front of the fire. I was helping Rose sort through a couple of boxes of old photos. We were having our own conversation when Nick and Ron got going. Ron was saying that practiced thieves were still hitting him and other merchants hard. Cameras in the corners of rooms were a great help in identifying them later, but by then, whatever they took was long gone. By the end of the night, those two had developed a plan to solve the problem. They came up with the idea of small cameras that produced clear images of the products. They coupled that with a discrete switch at each counter that could be activated by the sales staff, causing another camera to focus in on the counter. The backroom calls 911 and before the crook leaves the store, the police are there waiting. The best thing about it is they put this together using inexpensive components they bought online.

"Theft has dropped significantly. As a matter of fact, the professional shoplifters that drift in each summer have found easier pickings in the towns around Musky Falls and pretty much left us alone. These security systems worked so well it actually almost became another business venture. As a matter of fact, a few weeks later after they had installed a couple of the systems, the chief showed up one night for dinner with a whole marketing plan and partnership agreement for selling them. He was pretty disappointed when Ron and Nick told him they had already agreed to provide the systems to local businesses at cost, and had gone ahead and given out a list of the part suppliers and an easy 'how to' manual so business owners could install them in their own stores."

"What about the chief? He and Nick were close, right?"

"Yeah," Julie answered, "but not as close as Ron and Nick, but good friends. I kind of always got the feeling that the chief was, I don't know, a little jealous of those two."

"What do you mean?"

"Nothing really. It's just that Ron and Nick were pretty successful in their careers and financially very secure. Ron's jewelry business is a gold mine, and he is pretty well off. Although you wouldn't know it by looking at him, some folks around here say that he is one of the wealthiest people in town. I don't know if that's real or just talk, but he sure isn't hurting. Nick was more conservative. He wasn't wealthy, but he was comfortable and very secure in his place in the world. The chief was always kind of on the outside of their business dealings. He knew about them but was not part of their schemes.

"Later, after they left, I heard Nick and Rose talking. I wasn't eavesdropping. I was grading papers, and Rose was fixing Nick's old sweater again."

"Not his old gray wool army sweater?" I asked.

"Same one, I bet. Rose said he'd had that sweater forever, and he wouldn't let her get him a new one, even though it had repairs everywhere."

"When I was a kid, I fell in the lake when it was cold out. Uncle Nick put that old sweater on me while he got a fire going. It was so big, it went to my knees, but it sure was warm. Anyway, what did you hear?"

"Anyway, Nick was talking about how Don wanted to be the lead man in the camera security company. He figured he could sell these systems all over, and it would be a big boost to his retirement. When he found out that Ron and Nick were just about giving them away, he got angry and chastised them for not bringing him in."

Solving a crime requires that anything that ties one thing to another is recognized and duly noted. If later on it turns out to be nothing, you can always let it go. But in the meantime, you have to keep track of it. In this case, money may have been the motive that got Uncle Nick killed. Don Timmy is close to Uncle Nick and wants to beef up his retirement. Not so friendly Officer Lawler works for Don, and Lawler is connected with Attorney Anderson.

Probably just a small town coincidence, or maybe not. Best to keep track. For now, even though he was chief of police, Timmy would not be privy to what we had found. Not that I thought he was a real suspect, but you never knew.

I had a couple of ideas of how we could proceed, but I needed to think them through. We were not out to catch a shoplifter; we were looking for a killer. A premeditated murder conviction is a life sentence in Wisconsin. Most killers figured out that after the first murder, the next few didn't mean much, especially if they meant reducing your chances of getting caught and doing any time at all. I was thankful that Bud and Julie were willing to help, but there was no way I was going to put them in harm's way.

I needed to set a trap with the right bait. I think we had pretty well figured out what they wanted. The stuff on the Kirtland's warbler, the presence of the bird, and Uncle Nick's documentation of it were sure to sink their ship. They knew he had something. The search of the desk, and only the desk, led me to believe that someone thought that is where they would find what they were looking for. Why the desk? Some hired thief would go through that place like a tornado, probably counting on a bonus if he found what he'd been hired to find. It would also be against any thief's code of conduct to leave cash behind. Somebody who knows the lay of the land focuses their search on areas they know are likely hiding places, usually based on prior knowledge.

The fact that the thief had prior knowledge and knew about the bird made it crystal clear that they knew about the bird because Uncle Nick had told them.

The general rule is if you go to great lengths to hide something in a secret vault, whose location is known only to you, you don't go talking about what's hidden there with some guy on a bar stool next to you at the Moccasin Bar. You tell a trusted friend or someone who can help you with what you're trying to accomplish. Nick sure didn't trust his lawyer, Anderson, and there was nothing to indicate Anderson knew. No it would have to be someone real close, someone he trusted completely.

You start looking close to home. The chief and Ron were his best friends, and it was likely if he confided in anyone, it would have been one of them. The chief was a career cop. If Uncle Nick had confided in him he would have put two and two together and pushed the investigation. The chief just didn't fit.

This is how we arrived at the idea that Uncle Nick's old buddy Ron Carver might have something to do with this. Good friends are good friends, but throw a few million bucks into the mix, and well, things can change in a hurry. Carver was a guy who had been around, savvy to the ways of the world.

I sat down with Julie and Bud and told them what I thought. At first, they were convinced that I was completely off base, and then Bud remembered an incident that had occurred locally the year before.

"I don't think it's Ron, but remember Tom Porter and his mother, Julie?"

"I do. That was really strange. I went to school with Tom. He was always such a nice guy," she replied.

Bud continued, "Tom was a really nice guy and had lived with his mother all of his life. They went to church every Sunday and helped out in the community. Well, Tom's mom stopped showing up with him, and people naturally asked where she was. Tom told everyone that her sister had taken ill, and she had gone to help out. Turned out that what really happened is she figured out Tom had been secretly draining the money from her bank accounts. She confronted him, and Tom killed her and stuffed her in a freezer. Nobody ever would have expected something like that with those two."

We were all exhausted and gave it up for the night. I retired to my new residence, the cozy cabin behind the main house. I was tired, but sleep wouldn't come. Visions of sweet little Angelina Gonzalez visited me twice, blood on her face. She and I were joined forever by tragedy.

Morning came as only it can on a Northern Wisconsin lake. The air cooled overnight, and a light mist covered the lake as the sun rose, it burned the mist off and gave promise of a beautiful day. The little log cabin was small but cozy. There were only three rooms: a bathroom, bedroom and a combined living space that included a kitchenette area with a coffeemaker and—lo and behold—some coffee. I brewed up a pot and took a cup out to the dock. The sun was just coming up, and the morning light perfectly framed the shape of Julie sitting on the end of the pier.

"Mind if I join you?" I asked.

She just turned around, smiled, and moved over to make room.

"Are you really going to live up here, John? Walk away from your life down in the city and come here to live, where you get at least an extra month of winter each year, and usually the most exciting thing that happens is a bear or two shows up on Main Street?"

"Julie, I am staying. I need this place. I am not going back to the city. There is nothing for me there."

"You still have nightmares about what happened. I heard you through the window last night shouting. It must be terrible."

"It is what it is; wherever I land, I can be sure that Angelina Gonzalez will be there with me."

"Do you want to talk about it? I'm a good listener. I don't know if I can help, but I can listen."

"There's really nothing to tell that you probably don't already know. The whole thing happened so fast, and then I changed the Gonzalez family and me forever. Their hope and love died. I took it from them, and I am so sorry that words don't even come close. I didn't do my job, and the circumstance I set up got her killed. It was my fault, all my fault. I should have protected her. I didn't. I killed her, and as sure as I am sitting here, when I die, I am going straight to hell for what I did to them. I am so sorry. I wish I could do it over again—just turn back the clock. I know I can't, and I know that thinking that way is useless, but I can't help it. If I could only do it over."

My voice was shaking, and I just hung my head.

Julie reached over and put her arms around me and held me. She didn't say anything. She just held me. When she finally let me go, I saw that my tears had soaked the shoulder of her sweatshirt. We sat for a while longer and then went into the main house. There standing in front of the stove was Bud, wearing cutoff sweatpants, a ragged t-shirt, and a red and white Wisconsin Badgers apron. He had every burner occupied with scrambled eggs in one pan and sausage in another. A cast iron griddle stretched between two burners with pancakes bubbling away.

He announced, "Bud's kitchen is now open. Bring your plates and fill them up. There is plenty to go around."

Bud, for all his talents, was a very good breakfast cook, and Julie and I ate more than I thought possible. Bud ate the rest. It was delicious.

We were settled back, drinking coffee, when a car came flying up the driveway and slid to a halt by the front door. Attorney Derek Anderson exited the vehicle and stalked up to the door, pounding as hard as he could. I went to meet him. When I opened the door and saw him, it was clear that something was wrong. He looked like ten miles of bad road, rumpled clothes, uncombed hair and bloodshot eyes. He had a wild look of desperation.

My brain signaled possible danger. I blocked the door.

"What can I do for you, Derek?" I asked.

Unexpectedly, he bolted past me and into the house. He glared around. His eyes had a tic, and his movements were jerky. Then he began a screaming tirade.

"I'll tell you what you can do for me, Cabrelli. Get out of my life, sell this property, and go home. You're trying to ruin me. We don't need you living up here. We don't want another person from the city moving up here to discover themselves. I got you a two million dollar offer for a property that's worth half that. What is your problem?" he ranted.

No physical threat yet, so I just let him burn it off.

When he came up for air, I told him to settle down and offered him a cup of coffee. Caffeine was probably the last thing he needed, but it was what we had.

Derek took the cup and sat down only a minute before he got wound up again.

This time he made a mistake and turned his tirade toward Julie and began name calling that ended up with his barreling across the room at her. He was met halfway by a huge man still wearing an apron who lifted him off the ground, carried him with one hand across the room, and tossed him out the door like yesterday's trash.

I had underestimated Derek. He was up in a flash and came back at us with intent and malice. It was time to end this. Bud and I met him with like force, and Attorney Anderson found himself face buried in the dirt held firmly in place by one Arvid Treetall. I ran out and grabbed a stout piece of rope from the boat dock, and in a few minutes we had him tied hand and foot. I opted to leave him lying there in the yard screaming about suing me into financial ruin, having me arrested, and so on. I figured I would let him scream himself out and calm down some before he and I had a little visit.

When something big is going on and all hell breaks loose, it usually starts with something like this; the pressure gets to the weakest link, and the link breaks and does something—makes a move. It's that move that often starts the ball rolling. The weakest link was never the boss, the brains behind the whole thing. Guys like Anderson who think they are smart are used and abused by the real bad guys. They almost always get in over their heads. Then when things go bad, which they have a tendency to do, guys like Anderson always lash out, try to find someone else to blame. Whatever was going to happen had most likely already started. Now I needed answers, and I needed them fast. I was not the least bit concerned about how I got those answers.

I told Julie and Bud that I could take it from here, and that they should head to town. Bud didn't understand what I was really saying, but Julie did and gave me a sad look.

"John, you need to stop. I don't know what you're planning to do, but it can't be good," Julie pleaded.

"You're right, Julie," I said. "I should call 911 and let the police handle it."

I pulled out my cell phone and dialed 911, no service.

"I don't have any cell service. Try yours."

"John, you know there's no cell service here. You have to use the house phone."

"Watch him," I said. "I'll be right back."

I came back in a minute with the phone and dangling cord in my hand.

"Apparently during Attorney Anderson's rage, he ripped the phone out. I guess 911 is no longer an option."

"I don't remember him near that phone!"

"He was moving so fast I don't recall, but why would anyone else rip out the phone?" Again, Julie got it.

She and Bud made no move to leave.

"Julie, I am not going to hurt him or do anything crazy. I just need to ask him some questions. If it is just him and me, he will be more likely to talk. We need to know what he knows, and this is our best opportunity so far. Just give me a chance. If he doesn't cooperate, I will either let him go or haul him in to the sheriff."

"John, we'll go, but please promise you won't do anything crazy."

"Nothing crazy."

They both loaded up and left. I gave them a few minutes to make sure they didn't try and sneak back on me. ■

CHAPTER 20
Cabrelli

I crouched down by Attorney Anderson and rolled his head to the side. He looked up at me, still wild-eyed, but nothing like he had been.

Through dirt-caked lips, he spat, "Cabrelli, I am going to have you arrested and sue you into nonexistence."

With that, the devil in John Cabrelli came to the surface, and I nudged ol' Derek with my foot in the ribs, not so hard as to puncture a lung but a solid nudge nonetheless, enough for him to know I meant business. He moaned, and I gave him another for good measure. He was silent.

"Here is the deal, Derek. You are going to answer some questions and share some information with me. You have waived the right to remain silent. If I ask a question and you don't answer, I will move to the ugly part of this process. I know how to dispense ugly. Just how ugly depends on you. Understand your big mouthed threats only piss me off. They have no effect other than that. I don't care what happens to you. You had some part in killing my uncle. You will share what you know, starting now."

He had recovered enough to attempt more attitude. Threats only work if they are real. So I took Derek out on the boat dock and hoped to cool him off by holding him upside down with his head under water. It's funny how that affects a man when his hands and feet are tied. That water must have had a soothing, calming effect because Derek Anderson, attorney at law, began to sing like a bird. He couldn't get the words out fast enough. Every once in a while he faltered, and I again had to apply the healing powers of the lake, but soon I believed he had told me most of what he knew.

Derek Anderson was now mine. I had him. He was corrupt, and he had been caught in a compromising position that had allowed him to be manipulated and become part of the plan to steal Uncle Nick's land. He was naive enough to believe that the compromising situation, and David Stone finding out about it, were just happenstance.

David Stone had played him like a fiddle, and now Derek's life was flashing before his eyes. But Anderson wasn't a killer. He suspected that Stone had something to do with the murder but knew nothing concrete. He couldn't figure out the potential advantage to killing Uncle Nick. More importantly, he didn't mention the Kirtland's warbler. He didn't know about the bird. Stone had promised him a fortune if he got the property, ruination if he didn't.

I took out my pocket knife, cut him loose, and lifted him to his feet. We were face-to-face talking when a sheriff's car pulled in. It may be more accurate to say that I was explaining what I wanted him to do, and he was attentively listening.

I recognized Deputy Rawsom from the break-in. He got out of the car but stayed by the door eying up the situation before he made a move, his smarts and experience showing.

With my arm around Anderson, we walked toward the squad to meet the deputy. Anderson started slowly at first but then got my drift.

"Got a 911 call that there might be trouble here," the deputy said.

"Sorry to trouble you. My lawyer and I were having a discussion that got a little carried away. We're good now, though. Worked things out."

The deputy looked at me and then looked at Anderson. I was relatively unscathed, while Anderson, now soaking wet, appeared as if he had been dragged, as they say in the North, through a knothole backwards.

"How about you? You're Derek Anderson, the lawyer from town, aren't you? Any problems here?"

With little energy, but enough to convince Deputy Rawsom, Anderson agreed that everything was okay.

After a check of our IDs and a little info for his report, Rawsom got back in his car and drove out just as Bud and Julie, the 911 callers, pulled back in.

I truly believe that Julie was shocked to see the deputy leaving alone and even more shocked to see Anderson alive—if soaking wet.

Anderson and I had a seat at the picnic table, soon joined by Bud and Julie. They waited.

I filled them in. It seems that the brilliant Attorney Anderson had been offered a chance, through a client, to be on the ground floor of a new high-tech company. The client told him that without a doubt he would be able to double his money within a month. Everything was set. The company was ready to go. Why let Derek in? Well, this guy liked to take care of his friends, share the wealth. He would have to do some talking to the rest of the partners, but he knew that there was one share available. He would see what he could do.

Later that day, Derek's client calls him and invites him to dinner with some of the principals involved in the new company. The client tells Derek that they just want to meet him, but the client's recommendation would carry a lot of weight. The dinner was just a meet and greet. They have this dinner at a private home on the Namekagon River. They wine and dine Derek, and after dinner everyone is sitting around, and they get down to business. The dinner host, one David Stone, explains that it is highly unusual to bring someone in at this late date, but he often thought of having a lawyer on their team, and this may be an opportunity for all concerned. The shares are quite a bit of money, several hundred thousand bucks a piece.

Derek buys the whole thing hook, line, and sinker.

The problem is that our buddy here doesn't have enough cash or credit available to get the money. So he does what every red-blooded American officer of the court does, and he makes himself temporary loans out of several trust funds, mostly for elderly people, which he is supposed to be managing. In fact, he takes the whole amount plus a little extra. Then surprise, surprise, a month later, the new company opens and within a couple of weeks it is down the tubes, being examined by the SEC. Now Derek finds himself neck deep in loon poop. He just lost all of the clients' money he had stolen. He goes to Stone who says, "too bad." Oftentimes investments that have the greatest possible return will also have the greatest risk. Anderson pleads with him and spills his guts about where he got the money. That is when Stone sets the hook.

He knows Derek is handling Uncle Nick's affairs. He can help Derek out of the spot he's in if Derek can get Uncle Nick to sell him the property. Derek tries everything he can do to get Uncle Nick to sell, including bringing him an offer for a lot more than the market price. When that doesn't work, he tries several different cons, but Uncle Nick is too smart for that and fires his sorry butt. Nick demands all his records and files. But before he complies Nick gets run down, so Anderson remains the attorney of record. Stone gives him a choice: get the property or he will expose Anderson's embezzlement.

"That, my friends, is it in a nutshell. Our friend Derek here is a thief, a con man, and a liar. He thought he was smart enough to play with the big boys. Instead, he got played by the big boys. Now they own him. Right, Derek? They own your sorry ass, don't they?"

Anderson looked down but didn't answer. Often at this stage in an investigation, things will start to stall. The cooperative considers being less cooperative. Reminders are always good. I gave Derek a reminder, and after he picked himself up off the ground, he remembered our agreement and once again began to cooperate.

"Back to my question. They own you now, don't they?"

"I–I–I don't know how I got in this deep. I can't believe this. Yes, they own me. They own me and everything I have. These guys seemed so successful, and I thought this was my big chance. I am so sick of being a lawyer in a little town when some of my law school classmates are making huge salaries. I'm stuck here."

I dangled both a stick and a carrot. "Well, who knows, you worthless sonuvabitch. Maybe you help us, and there might be some light at the end of the tunnel for you. But let me be clear. You double-cross us and you're done, over. You'll be somebody's prison playmate, and I will make sure of it. Here is what I need to know. Who are the characters here? Who's involved front and center, and who is off in the wings?"

While I waited for his answer, I couldn't help but notice how he had changed since our first meeting. There was no polish left on this apple. He was dirty and soaking wet. He had a look of hollowness. His tanning booth color had faded, gray roots had started to show in his hair, and he had bags under his eyes. He looked like hell, which pleased me to no end.

"Now, Anderson. Start talking now."

• • •

He hesitated a second but gave in. "David Stone is the big guy. He is the one running the whole project. He's got some partners somewhere, because he has to check back with them on things sometimes. He is as mean as they come, but I got a feeling one of his partners is really dangerous. Stone might not be afraid of him, but he sure treats him with kid gloves. Once I asked him who his partners were. He laughed and told me that I should hope that I never meet them.

"All those guards he has, they shoot to kill. I think there may even be some bodies buried out there. I'm surprised they didn't shoot you when they caught you."

"Who is the client that hooked you up with Stone in the first place? Who brought you the investment idea?"

"A college classmate of mine. He bought a big second home on Twin Lake and started coming around. He had it all. He worked for a securities firm in the cities—big house, fancy car, beautiful wife, and money to spend. He convinced me that the difference between being wealthy or not was dependent on opportunity. Once the opportunity presents itself, you have got to be willing to jump quick. That's how money is made. He even let me in on a development partnership in the cities. I just gave him the money, and he doubled it in a month. It was so easy for him.

"It was right after that that he had me draw up papers for a limited liability company to hold a piece of property. I knew something was strange, but I just figured that was how big money guys went, so I went along with it and filed the paperwork on an LLC. I agreed to be the principal agent, but I don't have any idea who else was involved. Honest, I never met them or knew their names. They paid me to run things. I knew it was a conflict because the property was right next to your uncle's land in part of the mine acquisition area. I shouldn't have done it, but I did. They never told me why the secrecy, but I knew the new mine was potential big business, and if I wanted to cash in, I had to take the opportunity."

"You have no idea who the partners are in this LLC?"

"Not really, except that I know they buried that LLC in a couple of others. They were making an effort to keep things as secret as possible. I also think one of the guys is local. Stone said something to that effect once. He didn't mean to and didn't elaborate."

"Any idea who that might be?"

"No idea."

"Just so you understand, Derek, hold back one little piece of information from me, and I will make certain that the next many years of your already pathetic life become worse than you ever dreamed."

"Jesus, Cabrelli. I don't know. I really don't know. I thought I was a player in this, but I'm not. I am just a stupid small-town lawyer who threw his life and career down a rat hole. I do what they tell me, and they do not confide in me. They made it seem like I was on the inside at the beginning, but that was when they got me. Once they had me, they treated me like a gopher. You might as well know that I gave them copies of your uncle's files that Jonas had put together. They knew that he was not going to be able to fight the condemnation proceeding. After that, they didn't even take my calls. Then your uncle was run over, and died. He had sent me a formal letter firing me and telling me that he wanted me to turn over all his records and files within ten days. I just threw the letter away and held onto the files. I went to Stone and told him that I figured I had a pretty good chance of getting your uncle's property because you're from the city, and I didn't expect that you would have that much interest. I was wrong."

"You offered me two million for a property worth one. How much is it really worth to those guys?"

"I don't know for sure, but I did some research on my own. The property is the key to the whole mining operation. Without your uncle's land, no mine. The speculators think the mine will have profits in the billions, and from what I see, that would be accurate."

"What do you get out of this?"

"If I can get you to sell, they pay off my debts and give me a substantial amount of stock in the mine."

"How do you know they wouldn't just take advantage of you again?"

"I don't, but they were getting a little more anxious and trying to push things faster. I told them I would need something down to cover my efforts. I figured at that point I had nothing to lose. They gave me some cash up front."

"Enough to pay back those you stole from?"

"Not that much."

"They needed to keep their hooks in you."

"I guess so."

"When I was in your office the other day, you wanted me to sign some papers. When I wanted to see them, you dumped coffee all over them. What didn't you want me to see?"

He looked down before he answered, "Mineral rights... reassignment of mineral rights. It was an original form that your uncle had Jonas prepare. In case it became evident that he was going to lose in court, he planned to give the mineral rights away to an unspecified third party, probably one of the tribes. I figured if you signed it too then it would be difficult to dispute its legitimacy."

"That was your hole card. Once you had that, you could offer to fill in the mining company's name and sell the document to Stone and company. You are truly a slimy bastard, Derek. You even give bad lawyers a bad name. When you spilled coffee, didn't you ruin the original along with my uncle's signature?"

"I did. I panicked."

"Well, Derek, what was your next move?"

"I didn't have one. I just needed to get you to sell."

• • •

Bud and Julie sat quietly, listening to the exchange between Derek and me. To them, I am sure this was unlike anything they had ever experienced. A real-life crime drama unfolding before their eyes.

Julie was the first to speak. "John, we need to take this to Chief Timmy. He will know what to do and how to handle this. We're getting ourselves in a real situation, and I am afraid this is going to get more out of control than it already is."

"Can't do it," I replied. "Derek and I have a deal, and we're going to work things out my way. You and Bud need to step away from this. When I have the information I need to put Uncle Nick's killer away, then and only then will I go to the chief. Until then, I've got work to do, and unless I miss my guess, this thing is about to start to unravel itself. I am just going to help the process along."

I turned to Derek. "All right, Counselor. You remember what we talked about on the dock and what I want you to do, right?"

"I understand. If this works out, you promised to help me," he whined.

"I stick to my deal, you stick to yours. Now get your ass out of here."

As he started to get in his car to leave, I remembered one last question. "Hey, Derek, one thing more. What's the deal with Lawler? Is he one of Stone's guys?"

"He is a thug. He comes around to make sure I'm doing what they want me to do. He works for the chief, but he's got to be one of Stone's. He knows too much not to be. Anything else?"

"Nope. Have a nice rest of the day, Counselor. We'll be in touch. Get yourself a Leinies and an order of cheese curds. It'll make you feel better."

With that, Anderson left.

The silence was palpable as Julie, Bud, and I looked at each other. We were at the edge of the cliff. I was ready to jump. They were deciding whether to pull me back, hold my hand and jump with me, or just let me go. I told them that from here on out this was a one-man operation. I had to move fast, and too many people involved could put all of us in danger. I told them that in the unlikely event that something happened to me they should go to Lieutenant J.J. Malone in Madison and tell him all they knew; he would know what to do.

• • •

When Anderson got back to town, he was going to bait the hook for me. I was just going to watch the bobber. When it went under, I'd set the hook and see what I had on the other end. Julie and Bud protested, and I put that down. They needed to go about their business. Julie had plans with a bunch of students to visit an island and do some water quality monitoring and wildlife observations as part of a DNR study. Bud had promised to help a guy down the lake repair his dock. They needed to go on like normal for things to work.

A minute later, any potential for further discussion was interrupted when the beat-up old school van driven by Julie's aide pulled in and a dozen kids spilled out with exuberance that demanded immediate attention. Julie went quickly into teacher mode, gathering the kids around and getting them all facing her. She told the kids to say hello to Bud and me and then proceeded to outline the day's work.

Bud checked his tools, and when he was satisfied he had all that he needed, he got in his truck and headed out for the day.

I grabbed a cup of coffee for the road, got in the car, and drove to town. I would narrow the field of suspects immediately if they were as motivated as I thought they were. Too much at stake not to move, especially if they saw a chance to get what they wanted. No more muss, no more fuss. Cash deal and I go away, a lot of cash, but looking at the stakes, a fair price. I figured a businessman like Stone couldn't resist.

Musky Falls was hustling and bustling. Families were strolling on Main Street. Good thing I was still full from breakfast, because they were lined up out the door at the Musky Falls Bakery. I had to visit one person on my list of suspects and see if I could push him to make a move. I drove up and parked as close as I could to the jewelry store. I went in and saw that the place was packed. Ron was busy waiting on two large women who were considering buying a huge gaudy necklace, which I am sure was expensive as hell. He had them eating out of the palm of his hand. He excused himself and told me to go into the back room and wait for him. I did.

One of his staff was watching the monitors. I asked him if he had caught any bad guys today and he told me, "No."

A few minutes passed, and Ron came in telling his worker to take his place in the showroom.

"Hey, John. What have you been up to?" he asked.

"Just been busy trying to figure things out."

"Got any ideas on who killed Nick?"

"I've got some ideas. Nothing concrete yet."

"Well, how can I help you, John?"

"I just got one question that maybe you can answer."

"Go for it," Ron replied.

"When did Uncle Nick first see the bird? I don't need an exact time and date, just a general time frame."

"Huh?" Ron responded. "Bird?"

"The Kirtland's warbler, the endangered species Uncle Nick found."

"Nick found an endangered species? Good for him! He was always on the lookout. I bet that made his day. A little funny he didn't say anything, but who knows? I used to tell him that the real endangered species were men like him and me. Rose said just like the dinosaurs, maybe it was time for us to go extinct. What does this have to do with anything? Why do you care about a bird?"

I decided to push it. "Whomever he told about the bird had something to do with killing him."

At that Ron gave me a stone-cold look. He didn't move; he just stared into my eyes.

"You think I might have had something to do with Nick's death? Now, I'll tell you what. Get out of my store before you find out what it's like to get a real ass-kickin'. Don't you ever show up here again. Your uncle was the best friend I ever had. He and Rose were my family. You waltz in here with some dumb shit notion about a bird, a bird... Get the hell out of here."

Ron got up and went back to the showroom. He sent one of his crew back in.

Ron told the kid he sent to watch me and make sure I didn't steal anything on the way out.

Innocent? Or he who doth protest too much? I left. I didn't make it to my car before Ron came charging after me.

"John, hold up a minute. Just hold up."

I stopped and turned to face him head on, ready for whatever he was going to dish out.

He stomped up and got nose to nose. "I get it, Cabrelli. You're trying to poke the bear to get a reaction. Dangerous business doing that. You might be the second Cabrelli they find dead in Namekagon County if you keep it up."

"Is that a threat, Carver?"

"No, it's a warning. Getting yourself killed won't bring Nick back. I had nothing to do with Nick's death, but I don't expect you to trust anyone right now. That's probably good. But I got a bad feeling about this, real bad. Watch your backside, boy."

Ron Carver turned on his heel and walked away.

• • •

When I got back to my car, my cell phone message light was flashing. Unknown number. I checked messages and got one from Malone.

"I got some info back from the feds. You are up to your ass in alligators right now. Call me ASAP. Don't do anything until you talk to me. I mean it."

I called Bear. He answered on the first ring.

"John, what did you step into? You were right. Something up there is not kosher, but Jesus. These guys you asked me about, David Stone and Brian Lawler, are major bad actors."

"What have you got, Bear?"

"Let's start with Lawler. You say he's working as a cop?"

"Yeah, Musky Falls PD. "

"Well, Training and Standards has no record of him. He is not now, and has never been, a certified law enforcement officer in Wisconsin. Upon hiring, the department is supposed to file a set of prints with DOJ. Lawler's prints are not on file. I was, however, able to pull up two photos of him: one a newspaper picture and another from the Musky Falls PD roster. I gave those to the feds, who once they found out it involved David Stone, jumped to run them through the facial recognition database and bam, they got a hit.

"Lawler is actually a guy named Mark Lewis. Mark Lewis was a cop and was charged with three counts of misconduct in public office and one felony battery. He was never convicted. It seems that the key witness disappeared before the trial. Charges were dropped, and he agreed to leave the department. The gist of it was he was running an extortion racket in a part of his beat that had numerous businesses of questionable repute, as well as a thriving prostitution business. The prosecution claimed that Lawler, or Lewis, was shaking everyone down. They even suspected he was blackmailing some of those who had availed themselves of the local services. It looks like everything was based on the statements of one witness and some income and expenditures that didn't jibe with stated income. Anyway, the witness disappeared and so did the case.

"We got another hit on an AP wire photo. It's a captioned picture of a guy headed into federal court to be tried for income tax evasion. The guy on the left is listed as Mark Lewis, nephew of the guy on the right, David Stone."

"Lawler is Stone's nephew?"

"No Lewis is, but it appears as though they are the same person. There is more on him, but let's move on to Stone. I queried the federal database, and, much to my surprise, I got a phone call from a very demanding and assertive FBI special agent within ten minutes. It seems as though his current and only career goal is putting David Stone out of commission. As these high-powered crime fighting geniuses tend to do, this guy started off by treating me like Barney Fife. I hung up on him and called our local SAC Keith Dickson. I explained who I was checking on but not why. He was very quiet, but finally decided to speak. It seems that David Stone is front and center on every FBI radar screen. He would not confirm nor deny the fact that they are running a current op on Stone. Not abnormal federal agent behavior, but seeing how Tanya and I and he and his wife go out to dinner together once a week or so, I would have expected a little warmer reception. He told me he'd meet me at Ma's Diner in a half hour. He told me to forget whatever else I was doing and be there.

"We sat down at Ma's in the back booth. Excellent banana cream pie, by the way. He opened up a little but was heart attack serious about knowing why we were asking. I kept my cards close, or as close as I could anyway. What I am going to tell you is not for public consumption. I don't know if it will help you.

"David Stone is a hard ass. He has a huge net worth but exactly how much is difficult to estimate in that he has lots and lots of different corporations and LLCs shielding him, but it is fair to say the guy is worth a fortune. He is ruthless and has an almost pathological way of taking down those who get in his way. He is known as one of the most ruthless men big business has to offer. He has never been charged with anything other than the income tax beef, which he settled. He is known as anything but a nice guy. *Business Monthly* did a story on him; they called him a terrorist. They said he only knew how to play hardball.

"The feds are not just kind of interested in David Stone, they are interested to the point that they have several agents working on him.

Bottom line with Stone is that bad things happen when he is around and someone stands in his way. That includes a federal agent working undercover who went missing a year ago after getting close to Stone. The feds want him for that, and they will not rest until they get him. They didn't confirm a full-fledged op, but my guess is they got one going.

"Stone has made his fortune by laundering money from whoever needed it laundered. He sets up a series of different companies, corporations, LLCs and the like. He puts cash from one into another and keeps the ball rolling. The beauty is that the final big investments are all legitimate and profit making, real estate, mining, hell, even a professional hockey team. Big businesses with a lot of money coming and going, someplace where a million here or there won't be noticed. He does everything by the book, and with that one exception, always pays the taxes. The one exception occurred because somebody dropped a dime on him. He barely fought and settled with the IRS. He's been clean since then. They think he's working with the cartels. They are happy laundering a buck for every five they bring in, and Stone's schemes hook them up with legitimate investments that will allow them to rake in legal cash. He stays away from doing business where the cartels are operating and prefers more rural, less populated areas of the country. They think the Musky Falls area is his real base of operations, but he has stuff going all over the country.

"The key part of information to be gleaned from all of this is that they have nothing on him yet. They are trying, but they got nothing. Lewis/Lawler working as a cop in Musky Falls is new information and is very interesting to them. They also let me know that they want any other information that comes our way, and if we withhold anything, they are going to make our life as miserable as possible. Understandable because of the missing agent.

"John, this guy is a heavy hitter, and you need to be careful. I want you to listen to this and please consider actually doing what I ask. I have the contact number for the agent closest to the case. You need to talk to him, work with him. What you are into is not a one-man job. Call him now. Stop whatever it is I know you must be doing and call him. You get yourself killed, you accomplish nothing. Work with them and maybe you get the whole thing: Uncle Nick's killer, find the missing agent, and put Stone down. John, I can't help you with this anymore. Please call this guy."

Before I spoke, I considered my good friend's request, for about a second anyway.

"No worries, Bear. Thanks for your help. I will think this through and do the right thing."

"Fuck, that's what I was afraid of."

"Thanks, Bear."

"See ya around, Johnny. Good luck. Oh, wait one second. I've got something else you wanted. Yeah, here it is. The ST Trust you asked me about is a subsidiary company of what sounds like a legitimate investment group out of the Twin Cities. Doesn't look like they are involved. The only thing I really found was what the ST initials stand for."

He told me and it took my breath away. Things came together. I had already played my hand, and now I was sure as I could be that I had pushed the right button.

I drove back to the lake, and I was deep in thought when I parked and got out of the car. I was so deep in thought I did not see the attack coming, but come it did, fast and hard. Punches to my head, several to the back of my legs, and a leg sweep put me face down on the ground; a knee in the back kept me there. A Glock pistol put up to the side of my head assured my compliance.

A voice I recognized told me what was to come next. Lawler/ Lewis told me that was nothing compared to what would happen if I got any ideas.

He stood up and with a brutal push of his knee backed a few feet out of my reach and holstered the Glock.

A vicious bastard and a bully, he was in his element. "Cabrelli, I haven't got time to waste. I need the stuff your uncle put together on the damn bird. I'll get what I came for. You decide how much trouble I have to cause you before you give it up."

He took a collapsible police baton, extended it to its full length, and used it to hit my hamstrings a half dozen good licks. Practiced blows from someone used to giving them out, someone who liked it.

"Tell me where the stuff is. Once I have it I'm gone," he said.

Then he gave me a crack across the lower back, just to make sure I was listening. My head was not yet clear from the initial assault, but my legs and back now screamed in pain. My ability to do anything to protect myself diminished with every blow.

"Enough," I told him. "I'll get what you need. But stop, I have had enough."

He sat over at the picnic table and waited for me to get up. It was three tries and ten minutes before I was on my feet. My head was clearing and, except for the blood leaking out of my face, everything was intact, hurt but in original condition. I maybe could have gotten up in one try, but I wanted him to think I was hurt worse than I was. Once I was standing, he pointed the Glock at me. There was no way this guy was going to leave me alive. I don't know how all this figured into a successful plan, but there was also no way I could see me as part of his future.

I walked toward the house, slowly giving my head as much time as I could for it to clear.

He kept his distance, following behind me. "Where is it?" he asked.

"In the desk, the desk in the front room."

"Bullshit," he snarled. "We went through that desk. Nothing in there."

"We" went through the desk, we is people, plural. It let me know that he or his partner had been the burglars that had ransacked the desk earlier.

It also let me know that they were principals in the murder of Uncle Nick. I was pretty sure I knew who his partner was, but I wanted to make sure. All the pieces were coming together.

I told him that I had just recently put it in the drawer, that's why it wasn't there when they searched. When we got into the cabin, I turned toward the desk. I reached to open the double large file drawer when Lawler/Lewis stopped me.

"Back away from the drawer, Cabrelli. I'll open it. I don't need you pulling a gun out of there and making this more complicated. Go stand by the fireplace," he told me.

I did as directed. He bent down to open the drawer, his right leg to me. I remembered the surgical scar. I grabbed the trappers ax leaning against the fireplace, and with all my strength, I swung it at his exposed leg at the side of the knee, hitting him full force with the blunt edge. My aim was perfect. The blow landed with a crack that sounded like split wood. Lawler/Lewis was down. The Glock went skidding across the floor, out of his reach.

Adrenaline pumping through me, I moved fast toward the door where I stopped and picked up the old LC Smith shotgun Julie had used to get my attention in a previous incident. Tables had turned. He was down and his knee was done for, and I now had a gun and he didn't. He snarled and spit in rage as he tried to pull himself up using the desk as support, but his knee would not hold him. His gun was across the room, and he would have to crawl to get it. If he did, there was no way I would miss with a 12-gauge scattergun at this range.

His screaming stopped even though he seethed with blood anger. I could see that his leg from the knee down was at an unnatural angle, and that it was about all he could do to sit up with his back against the desk. The truth is, I just wanted to shoot him and get this over with. I was hurt. He was still dangerous. Then he settled down and just sat there looking at his leg. Finally, he spoke, pain still evident in his voice, but under control.

"Cabrelli, we are going to make a deal. I didn't kill your uncle, but I know who did, and I can give you proof, hard evidence. I was just supposed to scare you off. I didn't kill anyone, and I didn't even know about it at the time. You let me go, let me get out of here, and I'll give you what you need," he said.

Suddenly, an explosion filled the room, and Lawler/Lewis's head came apart. In the doorway, gun in hand, was the guy I had been looking for, my uncle Nick's killer ... and one of his best friends, the "T" in ST Trust—Chief Don Timmy. Of course, who else would my uncle trust with the information about the bird? His friend and career law enforcement officer.

He walked a few steps, bent down, and picked up Lawler/Lewis's gun. He didn't say a word. He didn't have to, as what he was thinking was clear. He had the way out and could get everything he wanted in the process. The chief comes out to see me, a friendly visit. He walks in just as Lawler/Lewis shoots me, and he shoots him.

Thirty-year law man, doing his duty. Dead men tell no tales.

He holstered his own gun and pointed Lawler's at my head. ■

CHAPTER 21
Hospital

"John, we need to call it a night. You're fading, and so am I. Let me call the nurse for you to give you a dose of pain medication so you can sleep through the night. You need to rest up, and we can continue tomorrow," Bill Presser said.

The truth is, I was struggling to keep going on. I was tired, in pain, and fuzzy-headed, and the thought of rest and sleep seemed like a wonderful idea. I don't even remember Presser leaving. The night nurse came in, along with a lab tech to draw some more blood, continuing with the series of tests, making sure the antibiotics were having the desired effect. I asked the nurse what the schedule for tomorrow was, and she pulled up my chart.

"It looks like everything is set for surgery. All of your other signs are good. So barring anything unforeseen, you should be good to go. But right now, what you really need is some rest. The doctor left some medication to help you sleep if you want it, although the dose of pain meds I am giving you through the IV may take care of that. It is safe for you to have both, and sleep is going to be critical to your future, but whatever you think."

I wanted to keep a clear head in my conversations with Presser, but when the medication hit me, the sensation was like a warm wave, and it felt so good to have the pain go away.

Nurse Holterman had returned to her battle station and woke me up at exactly 6:00 a.m. I was groggy but actually kind of glad to see her. Somehow I figured that if Nurse Holterman showed up, the world would continue.

"Mr. Cabrelli, how are you feeling this morning?"

"A little out of it, but I'm okay."

"I am going to look at your wounds and change the dressing. When the old dressings are removed, the doctor will come in. Let's check your vitals and get to it. You can get another dose of pain medication now if you would like to help with the pain associated with the wound inspection and dressing removal and replacement. I would recommend it. The doctor may need to probe a little into the wounds to check for evidence of a secondary infection. The results of your lab tests are due at any moment, and once we have received those, there will be a visit from the surgical team and a consultation to determine the course of action."

"I'm good right now, Nurse Holterman. I can wait on the pain meds."

"As you wish, Mr. Cabrelli," Nurse Holterman said as she peeled back the edge of one of the dressings. The doctor came in and began to press, prod, and probe. He asked me to roll up on my side a little, and when I did, I was struck with the most incredible, excruciating pain I have ever felt. It was like someone had just stabbed me in the spine with a hot knife.

It was too much for me, and I howled in pain.

The doctor was immediately concerned, "Mr. Cabrelli, where does it hurt? What is your pain level from one to ten?"

I could barely spit out, "Doc, my back, pain level solid 12."

The world became fuzzy. Something was going on, but I could not grab hold of it. I could hear Nurse Holterman's voice and others. They seemed like they were talking louder than usual. Then I went to sleep, peaceful, wonderful sleep.

• • •

I came to in my room with new devices hooked up to me. I couldn't really move. I could see, but my focus was off. Someone held my hand and spoke to me.

"Mr. Cabrelli, welcome back," a new nurse said.

I wanted to ask where I had been but couldn't get the words out. I could only look around and blink.

The nurse offered me some ice chips. My lips felt like they were as cracked as dry mud. The chips were good, really good.

I was so tired I just went back to sleep.

After what could have been days or just hours, things started to clear up. Speaking was incredibly difficult due to an ass-kicker of a sore throat. I just croaked answers to questions.

"Mr. Cabrelli, how are you today?" Dr. Jónsdottir asked. "Do you feel well enough to talk with me about what you have just gone through?'

"I think so. Just go slow."

"Dr. Árnason will be here in a minute, but we might as well get started. You are in the intensive care unit. During the course of your wound inspection and dressing changes, the bullet in your back shifted, causing you extreme discomfort. Your respirations became strained, and at that point it became clear that you were in distress. We immediately moved to maintain your airway by intubating you. You may have a mild sore throat from the tube having been inserted. We were able to stabilize you in the room, and then we rushed you off to emergency surgery. The surgery took over four hours. You had the best possible team. We removed the bullet lodged next to your spine, along with several bone fragments. There was a small pocket of infection in the damaged bone. That piece of bone and the infection were surgically removed. The infection was isolated and should be of no further concern. You are a very lucky man. The bullet was in the bone and did not damage the spinal sheath. We removed some bone from your hip and transplanted that to your back."

"Doc?"

"Yes, Mr. Cabrelli?"

"I feel like hell. Am I going to make it?"

The doctor just stared and looked over as Dr. Árnason entered the room. "Well, let me take that one," he said.

"Mr. Cabrelli, you are going to make it. You will have a long and challenging recovery, but you are going to make it. You have been through it all. There were many points of real concern on our part, but I never underestimate the power of the human spirit. Your spirit rose to the occasion and helped us save your life. There was no doubt from anyone who met you that you would in fact survive. You will be here in intensive care for a few more days, then moved to the floor. As far as when you will get released, no predictions. We will have to see how you progress. For now, though, no visitors, even though I think I speak for the whole staff when I say we would love to meet Julie. She must be quite a girl."

"Huh, what, huh, what are you talking about? What about Julie? How do you know about Julie? I don't even know about Julie. What the hell?"

"I am sorry, Mr. Cabrelli," Dr. Árnason chuckled. "When you were coming out from under the anesthesia, you just rambled on about Julie. I believe the term you used was 'the goddess of the lake.' You told us you must see her right now; you had things to say. It is amazing some of the things we hear. It is further amazing how many of those things turn out to be the unbridled truth. Whether you choose to say these things to Julie or not will be all up to you. I am just the repairman."

After three days, they moved me back into a regular room, announcing that the following day I would begin some physical therapy. Visitors could come, but would be limited. I was anxious to see someone who would not want to poke, prod, or otherwise assault my dignity. Honestly, after all that had gone on, I was pretty much immune to embarrassment. They gave me a sheet with people who had made contact with the desk about visiting. I was surprised to see several different news entities, along with some familiar names, Laura, Bear and Tanya, my old chief and assorted others, including Julie and Bud as well as Bill Presser. Like any good reporter, he needed to hear the end of the story, almost as much as I needed to tell it.

The nurse came in. "Is it okay if I have a visitor?" I asked.

"You may, but only during the hours of 11:00 a.m. and 2:00 p.m.," she answered. "By the way, Nurse Holterman stopped by earlier today to check on you. She said I should tell you thanks for not letting her down."

• • •

I called Presser from my bedside phone; he answered first ring. "John, jeez. I am glad to hear from you. I was afraid you weren't going to pull through. It sounds like you did great. I won't bother you about the story. Take your time and get better. I'm going to go back home for a few days, then when you feel up to it, give me a call."

"I feel up to it. You can visit between eleven and two. Where are you?"

"It happens that I am in the hospital lobby. Just in case you wanted a visitor."

"Get up here, and let's finish the story. I need to get rid of the past so I can start on the future."

• • •

Bill settled in next to my bed. I began to tell the rest of the story. This time it was different. Before, I needed to tell the story because something inside was telling me I might not make it. It was on my bucket list, and while I had not yet kicked the bucket, my foot was sure as hell on the rim. Now something told me my life was just beginning. Telling the story was part of my past.

"John, we left off at what I think we could call a real cliffhanger."

"Yeah, right. The chief and me. Lawler/Lewis's brains, hair, and skull fragments were splattered on the wall, blood spray on my shirt. The chief had the unmistakable look of deadly intent. He had me where he needed me to be. The only thing was, he couldn't pull the trigger. He needed what I had on the damn bird; without that he was no better off." ■

CHAPTER 22
Cabrelli

"Cabrelli, lay that scattergun down on the ground. If you don't, we'll see who is faster. I won't miss at this distance, and I got your head in my sights."

I laid the shotgun down.

"John Cabrelli, you are a pain in the ass. You come up here and butt in and cause me all sorts of trouble. You're a real smart guy just like your uncle, got all the answers. Well, you screwed yourself this time. I want the information you have, and I may let you live. Otherwise, I am going to do just what Lawler would have done. Shoot out your knees first and see whether or not that makes you more cooperative. The way I see it, I've got a free pass: Lawler's gun. He's dead and maybe no one will ever find that information.

"What I am saying here, Cabrelli, is you got no cards to play. Give me what I want and who knows? But one thing is for sure, I will get what I want."

I had no plan, and there was no way the chief was going to leave me alive. If I gave him what he wanted, I was dead. If I didn't, I was dead. That is when the shit really hit the fan.

Outside the air rang with children's voices. Julie and the kids had returned from their island trip. They jumped off the boat and headed toward the house, Julie asking, "Who wants ice cream?" The heavenly sound of children's voices entering the hell of Don Timmy.

I told him, "Chief, put your gun away and leave. I won't do anything, just go. Those kids, they don't need to be part of this." I begged him, "Please, Chief, don't get these kids involved. You can have all the documentation. I will give it to you right now."

The kids were getting closer to the door. I yelled at the top of my lungs, "Julie! Stop! Go away! Take the kids now! Don't come in here!" The kids' voices were quiet. I could see sweat beading up on Timmy's forehead. Pressure building.

In what seemed like a distant dream, I heard the roar of a Harley and the wail of a siren. I didn't know who called them, but someone had called the troops, and they had just arrived.

The chief had become a desperate man; he had it all figured out until he didn't. His time had run out. Julie knew I was still alive when I called out to her and the kids. He was a few minutes late on killing me and getting away with it. He was looking for a way out of a locked room, any thread, any chance.

The throb of the Harley stopped; squad car doors slammed; Julie was yelling at her students to come by her. The kids were oblivious to anything but the promise of ice cream, not one of them knowing what was going on inside the house. Through the window, I could see the sheriff's deputy and Ron Carver approaching. Timmy was twitching. He looked right and left; he needed to make a move, any move.

He glared at me and said, "You're a dead man, Cabrelli," and he pulled the trigger.

I jumped, and he missed. At the same moment, the back door burst open, and five happy, smiling wide-eyed kids blew into the room headed for the freezer. Timmy, in a blind panic, turned to fire toward the door and the kids. Akinetopsia: the world slowed as it had before. The students were led by a smiling beautiful brown-eyed young girl, not a care in the world, intent only on ice cream. She was a girl much like the one who lived in my dreams.

I could not let another child die, I did the only thing I could. I jumped in front of Timmy as he fired; my hands grabbed the gun. I covered the muzzle with my body. I felt nothing as the bullets tore into me. I was able to turn the gun with a strength I didn't know I had as it went off one last time. We both fell to the floor, his limp body on top of me. ■

EPILOGUE

After his discussion with Cabrelli, Ron Carver realized that John was right. Nick would have shared the information with someone he could trust, someone in a position who could do something. Ron put two and two together, and the proverbial light went on in his head when he saw Lawler leaving town with Timmy not far behind. Nick had trusted the chief of police and his good friend. Carver called 911, told them to get rolling out to Spider Lake, and then he gave his Harley a kick and roared off in pursuit, a willing man.

Chief Don Timmy died of a close range gunshot wound to his heart in the struggle. No children suffered physical wounds, although they will most certainly live with these events for the rest of their lives.

David Stone was interviewed and investigated. However, other than a perfectly legitimate business arrangement, he was said to have known nothing of Timmy's activities. As far as Lawler/Lewis went, Stone did ask Timmy to hire his nephew to give him another chance at having a productive life in his chosen career in law enforcement. It is with great sadness he learned of his continued involvement in illegal activities. No charges were brought against David Stone. The FBI undercover agent remains unaccounted for. In a news report, Stone said, "I am always saddened when those we trust betray that trust. If I would have realized what type of men Derek Anderson and Don Timmy were, I would not have had anything to do with them. I am embarrassed to say I was fooled like everyone else." Candace has been replaced by Brandy. Stone is now busy planning a new addition to his home.

Derek Anderson was charged with fraud and theft by fraud. While out on his own recognizance awaiting trial, he allegedly took his own life, although circumstances were somewhat suspicious.

That fall a musky fisherman hooked the catch of a lifetime. Casting a Bulldog musky lure, he snagged what turned out to be a white Ford Expedition that had been impounded by the Musky Falls PD and was listed as having never been returned to the owner. The real owner thought his truck was stolen and turned it in to his insurance. They were unable to recover any trace evidence to help determine who the driver may have been.

The formerly proposed mine site was declared an area of special concern. A combined team of wildlife biologists from the state DNR and U.S. Fish and Wildlife Service, headed up by Charlie Newlin, determined that this location may be one of the last strongholds of the Kirtland's warbler. The area supports a previously unknown breeding population significant enough that may very well lead to the Kirtland's being removed from the endangered species list.

···

On a warm sunny day, John Cabrelli was released from the hospital. There was much fanfare and lots of hand shaking and pats on the back. The hospital folks had become family, and as glad as he was to get out, he would miss them. The last person he saw as he left was Nurse Holterman.

"Mr. Cabrelli, your chariot awaits you. Although I know you were expecting a ride from Lieutenant Malone, I believe he was delayed, and they have found a reasonable substitute driver. On a personal note, I do hope things work out for you. If I may, let me give you one piece of advice. If you're so inclined, Mr. Cabrelli, take a chance on living life and finding love. It will heal you much better than any medicine. Also tell this Julie, whoever she is, that she is very lucky that I am not 25 years younger, or I would give her a run for her money." With that, Nurse B. Holterman turned and walked briskly away.

The attendant pushed John up to the car in a wheelchair, locked the wheels, and opened the passenger side door. There sitting in the driver's seat was the girl with blonde hair and laughing eyes. Julie Carlson looked over at John with that beautiful smile and said, "Hi, John Cabrelli. My name is Julie Carlson. I am here to take you home. Are you ready to go?"

"I am. I definitely am."

They left the hospital heading north to the land of lakes and forests, north to a small cabin full of memories and future promises. North to a new beginning, sunrises and sunsets, and adventures yet to be had. ∎

"Even a blind sow finds an acorn now and again."
–Warden John Holmes, 1939-2017.

ABOUT THE AUTHOR

Credit: Victoria Rydberg-Nania

Jeff Nania was born and raised in Wisconsin. His family settled in Madison's storied Greenbush neighborhood. His father often loaded Jeff, his brothers, and a couple of dogs into an old jeep station wagon and set out for outdoor adventures. These experiences were foundational for developing a sense of community, a passion for outdoor traditions, and a love of our natural resources.

Jeff's first career was in law enforcement where he found great satisfaction in serving the community. He was a decorated officer who served in many roles, including as a member of the canine unit patrolling with his dog, Rosi.

Things changed and circumstances dictated he take a new direction. The lifelong outdoorsman found a path to serve a different type of community. Over half of Wisconsin's wetlands had been lost, and more were disappearing each year. Jeff began working with willing landowners to develop successful strategies to restore some of these wetlands. This journey led to creating a field team of strong conservation partners who restored thousands of acres of wetlands and uplands in Wisconsin.

During that time, Jeff realized that the greatest challenge to our environment was the loss of connection between our kids and the outdoors. He donated his energy to restore that connection through Outdoor Adventure Days, an interactive experience giving school children a wet and muddy day in the field. Building on this foundation, Jeff co-founded one of the first environmentally focused charter schools with teacher Victoria Rydberg, and together, they brought the "hands on, feet wet" philosophy to teachers and students across the state.

A pioneer in the ecosystem-based approach to restoration and a tireless advocate for conservation education, Jeff has been widely recognized for his work. *Outdoor Life Magazine* named him as one of the nation's 25 most influential conservationists and he received the National Wetlands Award. The Wisconsin Senate commended Jeff with a Joint Resolution for his work with wetlands, education, and as a non-partisan advisor on natural resources.

Jeff is semi-retired and writes for *Wisconsin Outdoor News* and other publications. Whether he's cutting wood, sitting in a wetland, fishing muskies, or snorkeling Spider Lake for treasure, Jeff spends as much time as possible outdoors. ∎

Visit www.feetwetwriting.com to get a free short story, updates, and read more from Jeff Nania.

 @jeffnaniaauthor
@jeffnania

DID YOU LIKE *FIGURE EIGHT*?

Share this book with a friend.
Leave a rating and review on:

goodreads.com

amazon.com

JOIN JOHN CABRELLI
ON HIS NEXT ADVENTURE:

Spider Lake
A Northern Lakes Mystery
by Jeff Nania

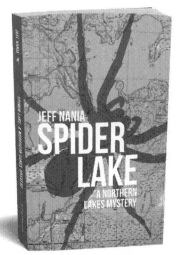

A missing federal agent, suitcases full of cash, a secluded cabin in the woods. Spider Lake is no longer the peaceful retreat John Cabrelli needs to recover from his gunshot wounds and start a new life. Knowing Cabrelli is a former law enforcement officer, the new chief of police recruits him to help untangle a string of strange events in the little town of Musky Falls. Cabrelli and a colorful team of local residents land in the center of a fast-paced action thriller with a surprise ending that's sure to make your head spin.

Made in the USA
Middletown, DE
21 November 2021